OTHER WORKS BY BHARTI KIRCHNER

FICTION

Murder at Andaman: A Maya Mallick Mystery

Season of Sacrifice: A Maya Mallick Mystery

Goddess of Fire

Tulip Season: A Mitra Basu Mystery

Pastries: A Novel of Desserts and Discoveries

Darjeeling

Sharmila's Book

Shiva Dancing

NONFICTION

Vegetarian Burgers

The Bold Vegetarian

Indian Inspired

The Healthy Cuisine of India

MURDER AT JAIPUR

MURDER AT
JAIPUR

BHARTI KIRCHNER

**CAMEL
PRESS**

Kenmore, WA

CAMEL
PRESS

A Camel Press book published by Epicenter Press

Epicenter Press
6524 NE 181st St.
Suite 2
Kenmore, WA 98028

For more information go to:
www.Camelpress.com
www.Coffeetownpress.com
www.Epicenterpress.com
www.bhartikirchner.com

This is a work of fiction. Names, characters, places, brands, media, and incidents are either the product of the author's imagination or are used fictitiously.

Design by Scott Book and Melissa Vail Coffman

Murder at Jaipur
Copyright © 2023 by Bharti Kirchner

Library of Congress Control Number: 2022946236

ISBN: 978-1-68492-085-3 (Trade Paper)
ISBN: 978-1-68492-086-0 (eBook)

Printed in the United States of America

Lovingly dedicated to:

Didi, Rinku, Tinni and Tom

For holding the light as I take another step

"Men honor property above all else;
it has the greatest power in human life."
—*Euripides*

"Loss is nothing but change and change is Nature's delight."
—*Marcus Aurelius*

"Generosity is the flower of justice."
—*Nathaniel Hawthorne*

ACKNOWLEDGMENTS

Wʀɪᴛɪɴɢ ɪꜱ ᴀ ꜱᴏʟɪᴛᴀʀʏ ᴊᴏᴜʀɴᴇʏ and trying to finish a book during the pandemic has introduced a new set of challenges. It is my good fortune to have been able to stay in touch with a small group of writers throughout this period, which resulted in a mutually supportive environment. I thank Judy, Jan, Roxanne, and Cherie, talented writers all. You deserve my sincerest thanks and very best wishes.

I consider myself fortunate to be working, once again, with my editor Jennifer McCord. I can never thank you enough, Jennifer. Your interest in this project, your many contributions, and our interactions have been a source of inspiration for me. My thanks also go to the Phil Garrett, President, Epicenter Press, for his many considerations as well as to others in his publishing team.

I am indebted to a number of friends and well-wishers, who are not connected with the book, but whose presence mean much to me. What follows are their names, in no particular order: Rekha Sood, Santosh Wahi, Dr. Lakhsmi Gaur, Nalini Iyer, Alan Lau, Shau Lee Chau, and Wendy Kendall.

I want to acknowledge the members of our Bookworm book group—Jan, Lyn, Teresa, Karla, Ginny, Karen, Judy, and Judyth. Thank you for your book suggestions and long convivial lunches.

And, last but not least, my deep gratitude flows to my husband

Tom. Your love and caring enriches my writing. Ultimately, it is your steadfast support that makes it all possible.

ONE

SMARTPHONE IN HAND, STANDING BY THE window of her friend Lee's flat in Kolkata, Maya reviewed the email, then read it for a third time, shock rippling through her. Neel behind bars? *Good grief.* Maya's jaw dropped; her surroundings had gone dark. She trusted Inspector Mohan Dev, affectionately called the "top cop" by his subordinates, to provide her with accurate information.

She pictured the well-groomed, dignified officer, whose graying mustache spoke to his high rank in the Indian Police Service. Dressed in a khaki uniform and polished brown shoes, he wore the insignia of his rank on his shoulders with an impressive, straight posture. A matching beret couldn't obscure his penetrating eyes. Last year, she'd worked with him on a homicide case in the Andaman Islands. He'd said he owed her for its successful conclusion. They had become professional friends of sorts. This was the first Maya had heard from him since leaving Andaman.

How could Neel be implicated in a robbery case? A deep sense of apprehension grew within Maya. For a heartbeat she listened to the horn of an autorickshaw and the silken voice of a cake-peddler calling out to the neighborhood children, the sound not so comforting now. She checked her cell phone, only to find a terse text message from Uma Mallick, her widowed mother, asking how she was doing. Well, she'd been out late with Lee and a few other chums last evening—after all, she had spent her youth in this town—and as a result had failed to respond to that message. Guilt gnawed at her.

Only a couple of days earlier, Maya had flown here from Seattle, her home base, on a well-deserved vacation, to be spent with her close friend, Lee. Last year, taking an assignment in the Andaman Islands, Maya had caught the culprit who murdered Rory Thompson, Lee's husband. Widowed, with a child born since Rory's death, Lee hadn't yet gotten over that trauma. Maya had planned to hang around with her a few more days, then go to see Uma for a week in Jaipur before flying back to Seattle. She'd been growing excited about her Jaipur trip.

Maya suppressed a yawn, still not used to the Indian Standard Time. Given that she'd lived in the U.S. for over fifteen years—going to college and then joining the workforce—it had taken a bit of adjustment to the twelve-hour time difference and to get over jet lag. Anxiousness coloring her voice, she placed a call to Uma and, after being bumped to a voice mail, left a brief message. How she wished she could dash out and drop in on her mom in person right now, to get a full report from her, to experience her nurturing presence, and to assist her in any way she could. That would be impossible. Jaipur, capital of the state of Rajasthan, situated in the western part of India, bordered the Thar Desert, and shared a boundary with Pakistan. Its distance from Kolkata, located in the east, was 1500 kms, the flying time being two hours. That is, if you could manage to purchase an air ticket for this popular route on short notice

Cars zoomed by on the street below, even this early in a megalopolis that never slept. Maya loved Kolkata, her birthplace—the city that had produced Poet Laureate Rabindranath Tagore, high quality literature, the ceremony of Durga Puja, music, films, and a world class cuisine. Standing by the window, she watched the rising sun cast a warm yellowish glow on the red-brick mansion across the street, a historic edifice designed in the Mughal tradition. She read the time on the clock tower situated next to it: eight a.m. Lee and her three-month-old son were asleep in the adjoining bedroom.

With Uma's chiseled face popping into her head, Maya's worry deepened. In her role as a private eye, she managed the satellite Seattle office of Detectives Unlimited. Daily, she received urgent telephone calls, emails, and visits from victims or their relatives in need of her services. But this involved her mom. The very thought of her brought warm feelings to Maya's heart. Uma, an honest, sincere woman who never lost her cool, who always communicated the "I care" message, and who lived to help others, but who, according to Inspector Dev, might now be seeking help for herself. Maya could almost see Uma's squinting eyes, furrowed forehead, and an expression of disbelief that had stolen over her kind face.

Once again Maya wondered: What did materialize for Neel, Uma's partner, a gemological expert, distinguished scholar of history, and raconteur?

The noise of a garbage truck outside the window punctured her thoughts. Although Lee had planned a jam-packed day for her to shop, picnic, take in a show and sightsee, Maya could already tell it wouldn't go as planned. She decided then and there: at the very least she would hold off her morning run until after she'd spoken with her mom, even though the smog would worsen as the day wore on. She was about to rise and wander out to the kitchen to make a cup of chai—Lee had insisted that she should help herself in the morning—when her cell phone trilled from a side table. Maya snatched it.

"You read my message?" Uma's voice was laced with a dark undertone. "You called me back right away?"

Those words reminded Maya that she didn't always do so quickly. She bit her lip. If only Uma understood how full Maya's days could be. In Seattle, she'd be looking into serious crimes: rapes, kidnapping, and murder. She loved Uma and would do anything for her. However, this point of contention—of failing to respond to Uma in time—clouded the air between them. Even at the age of thirty-five, Maya couldn't claim to have a smooth relationship with her mom.

She swallowed and squared her shoulders. "Got an email from Inspector Dev. What's going on, Ma?"

"Oh, dear child. I'm so worried I can't eat or sleep." Uma's voice was sharpened with anxiety. "My Neel has been nabbed without a warrant. He's in jail, where he's on a hunger strike. I'm a mess."

Hunger strike. The two words jolted Maya. Yes, she could envision Neel, an outspoken man, refusing food, doing so in protest. The more she pictured an emaciated Neel, the more her heart cried out, and the more she felt desperate to get him discharged from the prison. And the thought of Uma suffering, Uma who loved Neel so much.

Maya's heart skipped a beat. "Is he at least taking water?"

"No, not even water. To the jail authorities it's only a pressure tactic." Uma's voice sounded strangled. "Can you imagine how that makes me feel? He's not a young man. What if he died in police custody because of prolonged fasting?"

"What has he done?" Maya asked, charged with curiosity mixed with dread.

"Nothing, absolutely nothing. They're blaming an innocent man, of all things, for stealing a ruby. Can you believe it? Apparently, Section 41 of the Indian Criminal Procedure Code allows the police to arrest whomever they want, provided there's 'reasonable suspicion.'"

Phone to her ear, with the jumpiness she experienced, Maya paced up and down. She'd detected a vacillation in Uma's voice, as though she wasn't revealing the full story. "So, what kind of a ruby is it?"

"A star ruby, a huge purplish-red one, what they call a pigeon's blood ruby. Neel feels terrible about its loss. Do you remember how Indian astrologers revere that gem, call it the 'glorious sun?'"

It came to Maya's consciousness in a sudden jolt, the tremendous importance of a ruby and other precious gems in Indian households. "Oh, yes, ruby stands for royalty. Doesn't it? Ruby has cachet. Losing one is equivalent to a death sentence, astrologers say. So . . . did the police glimpse any evidence of this precious pirated property either in Neel's possession or in your place?"

"Nope, not a trace anywhere. Neel thinks a mad collector has appropriated it. Gem hunters consider a ruby to be one of the most coveted. Its value skyrockets over time."

"Who do the gem belong to?"

"Who else but one of the richest businessmen in Jaipur, the dashing, young, 'cool stuff' Rana Adani? Your age. He calls it Meree Ruby, or my ruby. We're distantly related. Long ago, a cousin of mine, was adopted by an Adani." Uma paused. "Soon after we moved here, Rana heard about Neel's reputation as a gemstone guru. He wasted no time in hiring Neel to consult about his private gemstone collection handed down through four generations of his family."

Six months ago, Maya now recalled, Neel had accepted a distinguished visiting lecturer position at a Jaipur college and he and Uma relocated from Kolkata. Maya couldn't have been more pleased. Jaipur—a smaller and more livable town that boasted visual art, museums, forts, fine cuisine, and formal gardens, was also rich in culture, tradition, and jewelry-making. Neel had grown up there. His elderly father, Kavi Saha, lived there, although his name never came up.

"Neel couldn't stop smiling when he told me how this high-profile assignment would put him on a level with the top gem appraisers in India," Uma continued. "A valuation certificate from a respected professional like him guaranteed that a gem was natural and untreated, not enhanced in any manner. For a gem buyer, that's a dream come true. Neel's consultation with Rana was going superbly. They were tight—they would have long talks over endless cups of chai, running late into the night at his mansion."

Maya's mind raced. "Did you ever go with Neel?"

"You bet, often, until the ruby vanished from a display drawer inside a safe box in Rana's bedroom. Vanished. Out of the blue. It was late in the evening when Rana called and filled us in on the mishap. He said he'd made a statement to the police but had no suspects in mind. We were stunned and speechless. Didn't get a wink that night. At dawn, the police—their faces were so grim—came marching to our door. They picked up Neel under false charges, took him into their custody, shoved him into a police van against his protests and drove away. What a sight that was. I shake as I recall it." The sound of a long sigh, thick with dread and disappointment, poured down the phone.

Maya peered out the window, churning the details in her mind and trying to make sense of them. The branches of a stout mahogany tree with dark green leaves shook violently from a gust of wind. "I'm told that collectors guard a gem with their lives. Tell me then, if you know, if Rana had a security system installed."

"He did. Maybe the system wasn't turned on or it was bypassed. The battery could have been dead. The police have done a thorough inspection for physical evidence, or so they say, and have no clue." Uma's voice shook. "Guess what my suspicion is? Rana has been careless. Forgot to lock the combination safe, busy executive that he is. He has at least a dozen servants running his mansion, not to mention the delivery men and construction crew who often lurk about. One of them could have swiped the darn stone."

Maya took a stab in the dark. "How is Rana handling it?"

"Not too well. Rana believes that piece of rock is his talisman, his 'third eye.' It keeps him physically safe, gives him warning when needed, makes him who he is. Now that it's a no-show, he's beside himself. He's homebound, says he came down with influenza, refuses to welcome visitors, including me."

"Has the incident been reported in the news?"

"Not yet," Uma said, relief evident in her voice. "Rana has suppressed it, with the clout he has in the media, and that's quite all right. It'll be a hot topic. Neel's name will be all over in the papers. He'll die of shame and humiliation, and I won't be able to bear it. I'll be under the magnifying glass as well."

"I feel a need for hearing more about this Rana."

"A most interesting young man, who went to college in America, then came back home to take care of his family fortune. A good-hearted business tycoon, he's married to a Malaysian beauty."

"Has Rana retained a private detective to look into the matter?"

"No. Wish I could fill you in more, but . . . my dear . . . for all I know this line is bugged and the authorities are listening."

Such paranoia. Had she been a client, Maya would have tried to calm her down. With Uma, she found herself at a loss for words.

"You told me," Uma said, voice rising in hope, "before leaving Seattle that you'd be here next week. Are you still planning on it?"

"Looks that way, Ma." No doubt she'd pop in on Uma, renew their bond in person; Jaipur had other attractions for her as well. That included a garden cottage Uma had bought on the outskirts of the town. She often reminisced about relaxing in that tranquil, rural atmosphere, sitting in the garden, sipping lemonade, and listening to the birds. After a few days in noisy, busy Kolkata, Maya would welcome the change, which would also help her renew the bond with Uma. "And with this email from Inspector Dev—"

"Could you . . . make it a tad sooner? Both Neel and I would very much like you to . . . Having you close by would soothe me. Look at it this way. You'll help free an innocent man, bring back the light of my life. That's all I expect you to do. It goes without saying you'll disrupt your time with your friends in Kolkata, which upsets me a whole lot, but . . ."

Maya gulped, cognizant of the disappointment she'd bring to Lee, her close buddy and gracious host. Yet she was so very aware of the distressed note in Uma's voice.

Returning to the window, Maya watched a cat jump from a neighbor's window ledge—a sturdy, muscular, long-tailed, gray-spotted Billi çat, a common specimen around here. It dawned on her now that she was in India where precious stones were important in the cultural context, referred to in the mythology, and mandatory in the attire that social events dictated, especially weddings. Families attached enormous meaning to these treasures, with the result that a huge jewelry industry had been built. Maya preferred to dress simply. She'd never paid much attention to gems and jewelry. A faint feeling of resistance rose in her; she suppressed it.

"I'll try my best to help you, Ma." Saying so, biting her lower lip, Maya realized that she must consider the legal system in India, its reputation for being slow in delivering justice. Even though she'd handled a homicide case in the Indian territory of Andaman Islands last year, she didn't consider herself fully familiar with the intricacies of the system. Pacing the room again, she gave herself a mental: *You'll have to manage it somehow, Maya. It's your mom.* "Like how soon?"

"Like later today or tomorrow morning, at the latest? Kolkata to Jaipur is a popular flying route, but you should be able to book a direct flight. Or you can fly to Mumbai and rent a car. Jaipur is only a short hop from there by automobile. I realize how much you want to spend a few more days in Kolkata with Lee. Do you need time to think it over?"

Neel is family. He's on hunger strike. A delay could cause him to lose weight, might introduce medical complications, perhaps could even kill him. The next millisecond, a glimmer of hesitancy inside Maya's head asserted itself. '*What are you getting mixed up in? Even if you've worked as a P.I. for about five years, how will you find your footing?*'

"I'll look for a flight right away."

"You're so very considerate, my dear daughter," Uma said. "I'll breathe much easier when you reach here. I'll pay your standard fee, air fare and living expenses. If you want to call your assistant in Seattle and invite him to join you here, that'll be all right. I'll take care of those expenses, too."

An attractive offer, no doubt, but it'd not be easy. Usually, when Maya listened to a crime report, she preserved her calmness and tried to think things through. But this was family. Her shoulders slumped and her thinking muddled. Decades ago, at the age of nine, she'd lost her father, right here in Kolkata. A legendary detective with the Kolkata Police Department, he'd been assassinated by a perp he'd apprehended, a perp who had escaped. The Subir Mallick Murder Case had remained unresolved. The criminal-turned-fugitive had never been captured. The loss of her father, a man who lived to help others, had provided Maya with motivation to be of assistance to those in need—she'd discovered her calling. Didn't it follow that her father would have liked her to dedicate herself this way? However, she preferred not to be compared with him. His were big shoes to fill.

Maya mulled over the details, agreed, then digressed. "What are you having for breakfast?"

"Oh, haven't even thought about it. Whatever is in the fridge. If there's anything, that is."

"What did you have for dinner last night?"

"Dinner? Didn't have any."

An alarm bell went on in Maya's mind. Uma's evening ritual consisted of donning a fresh tunic-and-pants ensemble. Then, under soft overhead light, she would sit down with Neel to a leisurely multi-course dinner. And what a meal that would be, a symphony of tastes and textures, accompanied by ivory linen, candlelight, sparkling china, and fresh flowers. Sam, her expert cook, a heavy-duty white apron covering his upper body, would hover over them. "More rice? he'd ask. "No? How about a helping of labra?" Spicy mixed vegetables. "Or a serving of cardamom rice pudding?"

No doubt, with the catastrophe of Neel being locked up, Uma wouldn't consider such an elaborate ritual. But she'd at least take a seat at the dinner table. Sam would ensure that. Maya saw more complications.

"Where's your cook?" Maya asked.

Uma sighed from the other end. "Talk about things bunching up. Can't get my head around it. It makes me miserable to say this—another misfortune has kicked in." Her voice faded, then returned. "Our Sam is missing."

How can that be? Uma's somber voice gave Maya a chill. The domestic helper, who had worked for Uma for a decade in Kolkata and who didn't think twice about moving with her to Jaipur, had dropped out of sight? Maya had met Sam, a reliable employee, her age. A slight man with curious eyes, he had a calm, gentle disposition. She'd chatted with him, had a tender spot for him. Best of all, he'd become a part of the Mallick family. "Since when?"

"Earlier this week, he asked for a day off to call in on his relatives in another town. It was well-deserved, as you can imagine. He's housebound, except when he goes kite-flying. You might remember that he's a kite competitor and a regional champion. I gave him my okay. I've read the newspaper story of a kite match being planned in Jodhpur, a five-hour drive from here. Kite-makers, fly-ers, and fans were already congregating there. A day later when he wasn't back, I called and found Sam's cell has been disconnected. Shocked, unable to process it for a few minutes, I finally contacted his relatives, who lived in a village near Jodhpur. The festival had come and gone. His relatives never saw him or heard from him. It shattered my heart to hear it."

Maya took a choking breath: Uma, all alone at night in a city new to her, with her partner in captivity and her cook's status unknown. "Any idea where Sam might have gone?"

"None. Oh, I look back and think about my job interview with him. It happened more than a decade ago, after you left for the States. Sam didn't come through a placement agency. Rather, he was a referral from an acquaintance. I was so impressed by his respectful manners and friendly conversation that I never did any police verification like you're supposed to do. I didn't even ask to see his identity card. I hired him on the spot. Over time, he became like a son to me. He tended to every need of mine."

"Have you reported to the authorities?"

"Naturally, except that they don't have a clue. Nor did they pursue the matter in a thorough manner, typical police behavior, you might say. I should have known. Sam's only a domestic, not a rich celebrity whose vanishing would make a headline. 'He's a runaway,' they told me. 'Or he's faking it. Are any valuables gone from your house, Madam?' I shook my head. When I insisted that they do a thorough inspection, they said, 'Those boys come back sooner or later. When they run out of cash. When they've done enough mischief and need a place to hide. When they need a shower, a hot meal, and a bed. You wait.'"

"That's not like Sam, not at all," Maya said, disbelief tightening her throat. "From what I could see he was a different breed, a reliable individual. Did he chauffeur you and Neel to Rana Adani's house?"

"Yes, often. His usual routine was to drive us there, go back home and wait, then bring us back an hour or two later." After a momentary pause and a long sigh, Uma added, "I didn't mean to stress you, dear. Sam could show up any time now, with a supply of new kites and a big smile on his face."

That assurance didn't help. A dismal mood had descended on Maya. She heard Uma saying, "Got to run. To have tea and a talk with Kavi Saha, Neel's father. Neel doesn't stay in touch with him. I do. See what he has to say. He's a reputable astrologer, you know."

An astrologer, a stargazer, a fortuneteller? How unfortunate that Uma would be grasping at straws. Maya had never met Kavi Saha. She recalled an incident from her youth, in which she'd accompanied an aunt to the studio of another popular astrologer for a consultation on her challenging financial status. Although astrology is dubbed a "Science of light," Maya didn't see so in action. In that studio, a vest-clad "fate corrector," a red dot on his forehead, sat at a desk, a laptop in front of him. He smiled, cast his eyes at the ceiling, and said to her aunt, *"I have 100% solutions for all your problems. 100% guaranteed results."* Nonsense. He talked about mercury retrograde, whatever that meant, and asked her aunt to fast, meditate, and give alms; he didn't otherwise deliver. What if this quack steered Uma in the wrong direction in a similar fashion? Rather than dispense practical advice, what if this Kavi Saha asked her to bow before this-and-such deity in the corner temple and tithe a vast sum, none of which would produce any result and leave her feeling even more frustrated? Such a conjecture added to Maya's discomfort, and she again walked back and forth in the room. Much as she tried, she couldn't fault her mother for barking up the wrong tree, trying to seek answers from wherever she could.

"Talk soon?" Uma interrupted her thoughts.

Maya said yes and disconnected the call. She wondered, not for the first time, who had ripped off the ruby and what the motive might have been. This wasn't an ordinary theft—the kind where someone robbed to meet their basic expenses—that much was clear. A common query from an investigator's perspective, as far as it related to a residential burglary, arose in her mind: Who would most benefit from stealing the ruby?

Then and there, she made a preliminary plan as to how she'd proceed. Once she reached Jaipur, she'd have to interrogate the victim—Rana Adani, the owner of the ruby, the central figure in this intrigue. How had the swindler gained access to the valuable? She would gather the proof of the heist and scour the crime scene for any physical evidence that might have been overlooked. She'd also identify any suspect, probe for any pattern in their behavior, ultimately reaching a solution and rescuing the pirated gem. Given that this investigation involved her family, and she had a weak spot there, these weren't routine procedures. A higher sense of urgency prodded her.

It stood out the mention of Kavi Saha, Neel's father, the stargazer, and Uma's impending consultation with him. In due time, Maya would speak with him.

Another set of questions plagued her: Did the police nail Neel by mistake? Or for another cause unrelated to the ruby? And Sam—was his disappearance linked in any way to Neel's confinement and, therefore, the ruby? Most of all, had Uma disclosed to her all that had happened? Or had she tried to shape the story to her liking?

TWO

D ISTURBED BY THE JAW-DROPPING turn of events and mull-
ing over the fact that her boss, Simi Sen, was a friend, Maya
sat at the desk and punched her number. She must update Simi
on her change of plans. A fifty-something woman, estranged
from her husband, Simi headed Detectives Unlimited, a company head-quartered in Kolkata. Her office, located a fair distance from where Maya resided, made a face-to-face briefing on
short notice a tad difficult. Maya figured that buzzing Simi would
be the best.

Simi answered in a cheerful, professional voice and yet had to
put Maya on hold. While waiting, Maya looked back at how she got
into this profession and her first conversation with Simi. Five years
ago in Seattle, she'd received a call from Uma in Kolkata. Uma,
who could always discern what her daughter needed even before
she opened her mouth: such as her need for a higher income, to
pay the mortgage, to deposit money in her savings account, or to
be able to afford a vacation. Also, as the sole proprietor of a nutrition consultation business, Maya had run out of challenges. Uma,
through her network back home, had made the initial connection
with the Kolkata-based detective agency.

"What if you took a shot at it?" she'd asked Maya.

"Let me do a think," Maya had replied.

In the days to come, against Maya's protests, Uma had even scheduled a job interview with Simi. "Although you make good money in Seattle, you're tired of whining clients and playing the Food Nazi," Uma had informed her. "You have energy, intelligence, toughness, and level-headedness. Why not fly back here and have a chat with this company? They'll pay a decent wage. A gut feel— you'd like the high-adrenaline occupation of a P.I. You'll help to bring justice to your society."

Typical Uma, always thinking of her daughter and trying to help. Maya, feeling appreciative and a bit overwhelmed, said, "But, Ma, about this firm. Isn't it a little unusual for an Indian outfit to branch out into other countries?"

"Not so unusual anymore, my dear child. In fact, it's becoming increasingly common. India is growing at an astonishing rate and many Indian conglomerates are trying to get a foothold abroad, in what is known as 'Overseas Market Growth Strategy.' Look, holding a position in a transnational firm, while still living in the States, you'll have opportunities, such as exotic travel, which you currently don't have."

"Okay, nice idea, and we do have a large Indian population here in Seattle," Maya mused. "But crimes? Not that many incidents happen in our community or for that matter in other Asian neighborhoods."

"Give it time, dear. Crimes involving Asians could become a growth industry." Uma's voice assumed a joking, light touch. "And yes, they'll want to see you in person."

In the end, Maya had flown to Kolkata for an interview with the detective agency. Sitting behind her high-gloss desk, Simi opened the meeting. "We're the first all-women boutique agency in India, discreet, confidential, and private." A determined face and a strong presence lifted her to beyond-pretty level.

"When we first started this outfit," Simi plowed in, "a few pompous male detectives made fun of us for upsetting the traditional order of the society. 'Those ladies in sari want to beat the streets and chase gun-wielding gangsters? Won't they faint at the sight of a drop of honest blood? And where will they hide their cell phones?' Look at us now. We have the finest set of agents, recently celebrated our tenth anniversary, and expanded to nine cities. Women are better at it. We're discreet and reliable, have intuition and people skills, and we don't divulge sensitive information. Our employees are vetted.

"For many families, approaching the cops is a matter of shame, so they contact our agency. Nobody can beat us when it comes to pre-and post-matrimonial investigations and cheating-spouse cases, 'Wedding Detectives,' as they call us.

"Now I want to branch out to Indian communities in the U.S. You know better than I do that Asian Indians are one of the most successful minority groups there. They must also have piles of pre-dicaments. My guess is our Indian people will seek another *desi* for help if one is available, people of the Indian subcontinent, and if they're able to afford it.

"What interested me about your resume, Maya, is you live in Seattle, which is supposed to have a few high-crime neighbor-hoods. You'll find plenty of cases. And oh, in the assumption that you're wondering about having to carry a gun, that's optional for our detectives, although all of us take self-defense training. You might want to investigate that. My guess is detecting is in your genes. Your late father, the heroic Subir Mallick—a top detective with the Kolkata Police Department—who hasn't heard of him?"

Maya lowered her gaze. Simi had reminded her of her dad's brutal murder decades ago, which had remained unconcluded and left an open wound in her heart.

"I'm sorry." Simi paused as a bearer served them each a glass of steaming chai and a plate of chire bhaja, salty-sweet rice snack, a local favorite. After taking a sip from her glass, she concentrated on Maya's resume in front of her. "I see that you paid for your col-lege tuition in the U.S. by taking on a part-time gig as an office assistant to a private detective. Not hard to see why that might have worked. You studied criminology in college. Even earlier, you helped your mom when a burglar broke into your flat in Kolkata in your absence, ransacked the place and made off with all your possessions. Only twelve then, you, Maya Mallick, gave quite a testimony to the police and helped indict the perp. That made the front page of the *Statesman*?"

At her nod, Simi said, "Your eyes are sharp and searching. You want to contribute more, can't wait to get bigger opportunities, you're an independent soul. Our company will be ideal for you. The bottom line is you'll have autonomy as far as the cases you wish to investigate."

"How will I do it all by myself?" Maya asked. *You don't exactly inherit those qualities from your dad, do you?*

"We were on our own when we first started. You'd laugh if I told you whom we designated as operatives to help us canvass an area, to serve as our eyes, ears, and sixth sense: Cabbies, servants, street vendors, neighborhood busybodies and bored grandmothers. The point is, Maya, we study people, talk with them, or elicit information about them, however old-school that might seem. Research and surveillance are our other tools."

Maya held her back straight. She'd always considered herself a thorough researcher. She tuned in to people. She could listen between the lines. Her clients in the nutrition business, however distressed they were, opened to her. To understand their concerns and what they wished to accomplish was on top of her list. She had good analytical skills, as well as intuition. She jumped into action when necessary. But could it be that easy? "What's your success rate?"

"We're hitting sixty to seventy percent. Our competitors think they're doing well if they come close to the fifty percent mark." Simi beamed. "You're interviewing me? Cool. Interviewing skills are crucial in our field."

After a long dialogue, she offered Maya a position as a private investigator based in Seattle. "We'll give you as much support from here as we can. You're wondering how? Well, we have a worldwide network of informers and plenty of secure apps, databases, and online research tools at our fingertips. I'm available on the phone whenever you need me. We offer competitive salary."

Seated in the visitor's chair, Maya hesitated. To labor long distance for a foreign outfit in a line of business would be new to her. She could be trapped, stabbed, kicked, or shot at, without her colleagues knowing about it. Yet, she could also see herself on the street, excited to be chasing a lead and identifying a culprit. One good break and you're made, as they say. And from what little she could remember of her father—a tall, slender man, with a light of mischief in his eyes—he enjoyed his chases. Once, coming home late, he bent over her and said, "What do I do all day, my darling? I give bad guys a run for their lives."

How fortunate also that she'd gathered several investigative tips from her part-time job during her college years: Do your legwork. See, hear, smell, and intuit. Read the client, evaluate the evidence, and lie, if you must, to get to the truth. She looked up at Simi.

"When can you start?"

A sudden burst of happiness coursed through Maya. Silently, she thanked her mother, and replied to Simi, "It'll take a couple of months to complete the background screening requirements and meet the criteria for an investigative license from the Washington State Business Licensing Services. Will need a few more weeks to obtain a liability insurance policy. Adding it all up, I should be able to join within the next few months."

"Rent an office space and hire a smart assistant." Simi offered Maya a joining bonus to help cover both expenses.

In the months that followed, with the official papers in her hand, Maya had opened the Seattle branch of Detectives Unlimited. She'd leased an office space of her own and recruited an assistant to help her. She'd continued her independent study to gain expertise in investigative and forensic techniques.

Now Simi's voice came down the line from a nearby neighborhood in Kolkata. "How's your vacation so far? Can you swing by later so we can have tea together?"

"I'm enjoying the vibes of Kolkata again. Depending on my flight schedule, I might be able to come over this afternoon. But ... something—rather serious—has come up. Let me bring you up to date." Maya spoke about her family situation: how rapidly it had developed, the new assignment as given by Uma, her plan to halt her vacation, and make a beeline for Jaipur. "My mom is fretful about Neel's physical and mental state, which upsets me."

"I don't blame her." Simi's voice was laden with dread. "It's a tight spot to be in, to say the least. Yes, I admit this'll be a tough case, Maya, hazardous, too. Jewelry heists can remain unsolved for generations. Do you know why? Thieves often go across national boundaries. Laws being different in a different land, they can dodge prosecution. They can be ruthless. But I can tell that you're close to your mom. You'll do what it takes to track down the ruby."

"One more thing. I've never hung out much in Jaipur. You know how much I depend on the location for clues, especially in the event of a theft."

"Let me fill you in. Jaipur is called the 'Pink City' or the 'Pink Elegance.' That's the old part of the city. Pink is a royal color and a symbol of warmth, etcetera, etcetera." Even though Simi's voice was matter of fact, it carried a trace of warning in it. "Once a calm, peaceful town, Jaipur is no longer in the pink of condition. The crime rate has risen and is now one of the highest in India. There are bad actors out there. Several gangs are fighting turf wars. One hears of drive-by shootings, contract killings, and honey-trapping."

"Honey-trapping?"

"A female gang member will start an affair with a rich, powerful man, videotape him in a compromised position, then blackmail him. A male gangster will do the same with a privileged woman and demand ransom from her family. Abductors are also active. A man could abduct a woman who doesn't want to marry him in what is called bridenapping. Then there are 'death by kites.'"

A faint chill, a trembling sensation, swept over Maya. "Jaipur is famous for kite-fighting competitions, known the world over, but accidental deaths?"

"Yes, kite-mares, as they're called. Kiting is a risky sport, to say the least. People like to be out on their rooftops for hours, maneuvering their kites. Accidents happen. Kids can fall off the roof. A glass-coated kite string can come down from the sky and strangle a person's throat—it could be a pedestrian strolling on the sidewalk or a teenager riding a motorcycle. Both happened in Jaipur not so long ago. The pedestrian died. The teenager is in intensive care in the hospital. That's not all. Last year, a kite string got tangled with power lines and caused blackouts. Only a month ago, a six-year-old boy's throat got slit by a fallen string and he bled out a miserable death, as you can well imagine. A procession of thousands mourned the death. And listen to this. A week after that, a multi-vehicle traffic accident occurred when a pedestrian chased a kite on a bustling road. I could go on and on." Simi went silent for an instant. "You'll find many cool things there, too. Puppet shows, elephant rides, being able to live like a royal on a shoe-string budget, spying a tiger in the forest, not to forget the delicious local cuisine you'll be able to taste. As they say, 'Perfectly imperfect.' That's Jaipur. But look out for yourself, Maya."

THREE

H ER EXCHANGE WITH SIMI PLAYING IN HER HEAD, Maya booted her laptop and launched herself into making a travel reservation. Given the short notice, it wouldn't be an easy task. At first, she couldn't book an airline flight that didn't involve a lay-over. After a half hour, she located a direct flight from Kolkata to Jaipur early the next morning and purchased a ticket. That done, scratching her head over the unfortunate new developments in the life of Uma and Neel, Maya opened her wallet and gazed at a 2"x3" photograph.

Neel, aged 60, stood in front of the lush backdrop of raised flower beds in her yard in Seattle during a trip last year. He had accompanied Uma. His lined face, a mustache, and a mass of wild, shaggy Einstein hair peered out at Maya. Neat and well-groomed in other respects, the aging academic had both a querulous and a charming, lighter side. "He had a temper on him," Uma would say, and indeed he was prone to have blowups. Then, at the dinner table, he'd forget the incident and regale those present with one or more amusing historical anecdotes, accomplished raconteur that he was.

Neel often talked about gemology, his hobby. He'd inherited that passion from his father, Kavi Saha, a craftsman who had excelled in gem cutting until he lost much of his vision due to a job-related accident. Neel spent hours peering through a microscope, identifying, and examining natural precious stones such as diamonds, rubies, opals, sapphires, and amethysts for defects. His cronies affectionately called him a "rock-hound." In a high, cheerful voice, he'd hold forth on the four c's—color, cut, clarity, and carat weight—as well as how to spot imitations. He'd devote an entire tea session to a discussion about faceting—the small flat surfaces and angles that allowed light to travel through a gem. Although he held no degree in geosciences, he'd studied all available ancient Indian texts on gemstones, as well as scientific literature on the subject. He insisted he could identify the real thing, that he could "read" them. His clients called him a "gem therapist." He could match a gem to a person, such a practice, in his consideration, being of high importance in terms of health, longevity and wealth accumulation. Never a collector himself, he nonetheless always carried a small snap-top case, which contained a magnifying glass, a pair of tweezers, a gem cloth, and a few other necessary tools. It was as though he wished to be ready to size up a gem, his "rock star" anywhere at an eyeblink.

Next to Neel in that glossy photo stood Uma. Time had been kind to Maya's mother. Now in her late fifties, she'd managed to remain a stunning beauty, perfect of face and figure, with clear alert eyes, a smooth complexion, and lustrous long hair pinned on top of her head. Maya lamented that although she'd inherited her mother's big dark eyes, lush black hair, and slender petite frame, she lacked her head-turning beauty. But then, she reminded herself, she was at least attractive, which gave her a certain air of perky self-confidence. In that photo, Uma nestled close to Neel, whom she preferred to call her manfriend, rather than a partner. "That sounds too business-y." They'd been happy together; their affectionate smiles provided ample proof. Indeed, Neel had proved to be a perfect match for the long-widowed Uma, who had met him only a couple of years ago in Kolkata.

Although Maya couldn't quite see it in the image, she could visualize the custom-made gold ring on Uma's finger. Neel had presented the oval blue sapphire from Kashmir, in a claw setting, to Uma on her last birthday, an extravagant purchase. That was no wonder since Neel liked to spend money. He'd devote hours shopping for expensive items. A sapphire from Kashmir was believed to be a rare specimen; the mines there had been depleted over the years. Hence it was attractive to Neel. Yet another fact: His name Neel came from the word Neelam, which stood for a sapphire.

Uma's cheeks flushed a soft pink when Neel slipped the lustrous, glittering ring on the long, delicate, middle finger of her left hand. He stated that wearing the ring on the left would bring her maximum benefit. How Uma held her hand over her chest to give Maya a closer look. The sapphire sparkled in contrast to the soft velvety glow of the gold—the stone that, in Uma's opinion, would show the best in daylight. It was blue as a peacock's neck, bluer than the bluest sky on the clearest day. Tradition said it'd strengthen the bond between her and Neel. "The stone touches my skin," she would say with pride. "As a bonus, its chemical compounds give a lift to my spirits."

As a schoolteacher and single parent, Uma had never been given to luxury of any sort. She lived a quiet, honest, and frugal life. Of late she'd come to believe—which perhaps had been due to Neel's sway—that a sapphire brought happiness, that it spelled fortuity, that luck was on her side—this from a woman who had never been superstitious by nature. The irony now struck Maya.

Somewhere, a motorcycle revved its engine, a common sound in Kolkata. Maya scooped up her cell phone and called Hank, her administrative assistant in Seattle. With the twelve-hour time difference, which would make it evening in Seattle, Hank would be lounging in his flat in the Capitol Hill neighborhood. A bookish guy, he stayed up late, reading a novel or listening to music.

Almost three years ago, she'd selected the MFA student—earnest and non-intimidating—from a pool of a half-dozen candidates, and they'd clicked. When not busy with his thesis—a set of linked short stories centered on dating—Hank acted as the first line of communication for her. Although he had no previous experience in the field of criminology, Hank, a short story maven, fast learner, and cyber geek, fit in his part-time role rather well. He familiarized himself with news archives, investigative databases, and court procedures. He secured and safeguarded sensitive data that Maya collected from criminal cases and excelled in preparing reports.

Hank answered the phone, concern etched into his tone. "Is everything okay? You've been gone only a few days. I mean . . . I didn't expect a call so soon." He always noticed the slightest change in her voice.

"My mom's alone in Jaipur and she's in trouble." She gave him an outline, explained the quandary she'd found herself in, and laid out her itinerary, making it clear she might have to stay longer in India.

"My heart goes out to her," Hank said. "Anything I can do for you?"

"Positive." Maya tasked him an assignment: gather facts about the plundered ruby as well as the Adani family.

"I know diddly-squat about precious rocks," Hank replied, "but I'll get instantly on it."

"Call me when you have enough data."

"Perf, boss."

That was Hank's way of saying perfect. A small sense of relief fluttered in Maya now that Hank, solid and dependable, was up-to-date and on board.

"And, oh, got a call from a Ms. Bradford," Hank said. "She's looking to hire a private investigator to examine her family assets. An acquaintance of hers whom you met at a meeting of the Association of Licensed Investigators recommended you. I told her you're traveling abroad. Be back in a couple of weeks. She's willing to wait. Meantime, I've sent her the fee structure."

"Appreciate you're handling it."

After ringing off, Maya sat at the desk and worked through a set of emails. Minutes later, she heard noise from the adjoining bedroom. Time to get dressed. She'd have to bring Lee up to date. It saddened her to contemplate she'd have to leave her friend sooner than expected.

Drifting to the closet, Maya opened her suitcase, where she

selected a pair of twill pants, a flower-printed top, and an ivory jacket. She flipped open a small brass jewelry box embossed with a leafy design. The velvet-lined interior compartment held the few pieces of jewelry she'd traveled with. In India, women dressed up when they went out and that included ample application of jewelry. It delighted Maya to run her fingers over a pair of silver chandelier earrings studded with amethyst. When had she last worn them? Or the layered pearl necklace snaking around the earrings? And what about the gold-mounted blue lapis ring nestled in the center of it all? A warm feeling washed over Maya. Wordlessly, she thanked her aunts, who had gifted these pieces on her birthdays when she was growing up.

Auntie Vimla crossed her mind, the chubby matron, who adored all precious stones, but especially rubies. Face radiating a healthy glow, she would show off a full-red stone bulging from its rose gold mount on her finger, radiating a halo.

"Not a mere pretty bauble, mind you," she would say in an emphatic voice to the children of the extended family. "Do you know what we call a ruby? Ratna-Raj, the king of gemstones. My ruby warms my heart, it's my guardian. I wear it all the time, but it never gets a scratch. You ask why? Allow me to explain. Next to diamond in hardness, but rarer than the diamond, mind you, Ratna-Raj can stand up to any pressure. You kids should meditate on that quality and mold yourselves that way."

Maya and her cousins would exchange glances and smile behind auntie's back.

After scanning the collection one more time, Maya slipped the lapis ring onto her finger, admired its blue halo, and closed the jewelry case. If she were in Seattle and it was morning, she'd rush out the door, keys in hand. Heading south under an overcast sky, she'd weave through a series of streets and make it to a low-rise modern office building, Future Space, situated in the Green Lake district. She'd take the elevator to the second floor, where her office in #206 was tucked next to a row of other small firms. She'd pause at the door and examine her nameplate.

Inscribed in bold black letters, the brass plaque would read:
Detectives Unlimited of Kolkata
And the legend below in a smaller script:
Maya Mallick, Private Investigator and Manager, Seattle Branch
Usually, she got a charge when she viewed the inscription even in her imagination. Not today. A question haunted her. Would she make it as a P.I. in India? That is, given the limited number of cases she'd handled here thus far. The Indian judicial system, she lamented, bore the influence of the old colonial edict. It was slow and pricey. On top of that, the police often lacked professional standards and resorted to abuse. Short of manpower, they could be ineffective against criminal elements. What if she didn't succeed? Picturing Uma suffering all alone in Jaipur and receiving no help from anyone, she experienced a ripple of anxiety passing along her spine.

Her cell phone rang and broke her reverie: Hank calling her back from Seattle. So soon? Maya could picture the 24-year-old: Clothed in a T-shirt and chinos he sat in a chair in his living room, his blond hair sleek and combed back, expressive blue eyes dominating a pale narrow face. They would be shadowed with empathy.

"How're you doing?" Hank asked.

"Trying to cope." Her voice was off, she could tell.

"When you told me that Neel is behind bars, I was like . . . I was agit." That was Millennial-speak—which showed up in Hank's speech every so often—his way of conveying his agitation. "Your mom—she has people?"

"Not that many in Jaipur."

"Makes it tough."

"My mom's tough." Maya swallowed her discomfort. To Hank she extended Uma's offer to finance his trip to Jaipur. "It all happened so suddenly. And it's a long way to travel. Are you up to flying here? You could help me with ongoing research. I could use an extra pair of eyes in gathering information. But give it some thought. Be aware of the dangers involved—unfamiliar territory, different languages, different customs, and who can tell what you might run into."

"But its Jaipur, right?" Hank replied, his voice edged with excitement. "Why, sure, it'll be fun and adventurous, will it not? Never been to mainland India. Can't wait to spend time there. And I'd love to meet your mom. Sophie would, too."

Maya could picture Hank leaning, blushing, and fiddling with a silver-framed photograph placed on an occasional table. It was that of Sophie, his girlfriend, a gutsy young woman. Part Aussie, part Thai, and a college student in Seattle, Sophie wore a mischievous smile. Spruced up in skimpy ripped shorts, a décolleté top with jeweled borders, and chic black polish on her fingernails, she appeared to be animated. She had it made, in the look department.

"Sophie knows a bit about gems and jewelry," Hank said. "In Sydney, she runs with what they call a 'silk-stocking' crowd. Plus, her late mother left her a pearl set. My girl's a genius. She can run a finger across a pearl and tell from the feel if it's real or fake. Sophie's been talking about taking a spring break, a breather. Do you mind if she comes along?"

Oh, no. At twenty-one Sophie, a senior in college, wasn't a child, but she did as she pleased and, lovable as she was, often managed to get herself in a pickle. She could also put both Hank and Maya in a predicament. She'd done so in the past. Given that Maya had enough problems on her plate, she didn't need the extra complication, even if the woman could distinguish between faux and genuine pearls. "Well . . ." She let the sentence dangle.

"Sophie's adulting, you know. She'll behave. Will even try to help. She's fascinated by India."

That's what I'm uneasy about. That Sophie will go wild here. Then the realization dawned on Maya: how much Sophie meant to Hank. She'd seen it in his expectant eyes, the forward lean of his body, the way he held his breath when speaking about Sophie. The young woman, as maintained by Hank, majored in Good Times. She brought light to his life. Also, as the daughter of a wealthy industrialist in Australia, Sophie could pony up her share of expenses related to the trip. Maya thought for another instant, then caved in with a sigh and offered her consent.

Hank thanked her, a smile in his voice. "Yolo. You only live once."

"So, what do you have for me?" Maya asked.

"Rana Adani's track record, which took no time to put together. Exposés I've dug into says he got his MBA at Cornell, migrated back to Jaipur, and shouldered his family's textile business as the CEO, an upper-cruster, you might say. Sounds like he'd be a snore. Well, no, he's a hip jetsetter who has been everywhere, done everything, seen action. Was briefly posted with the Indian military in Kashmir. And the dude's only thirty-five. A cool dresser and a charmer to boot, considered 'model material,' he lives in a mansion which has 'heritage status,' and where he throws glittering parties. He's also involved with charity work. How can anyone be so lucky?"

"I get the picture. Let's wait and see if he's as lucky as we think he is." Maya heard the clicking of the keyboard. "What have you found out about his precious rock?"

"Lots from news reports. Not long ago, Rana showcased his 'natural wonder' for a limited time in a small museum in Jaipur, the exhibit being a part of a 'public education' effort. The media drooled over his ruby, which was displayed in the museum's Grand Gallery in a secure desktop-style case, which had a temperature control feature. An introductory label placed near the display case explained the geological formation of rocks, cultural status of rubies, brief history of the Adani family et cetera, et cetera. School children, public, gem traders and the press flocked to view the private collection. It'd have stayed there much longer, like a month, except for an attempted break-in that took place after the show had been inaugurated for a few days. That evening, after hours, a witness saw three masked burglars, who were equipped with hammers, trying to smash a window. He called the cops. As soon as they blew in, the thieves, believed to be amateurs, cleared out. The very next day, the curator of the exhibit, who was devastated, returned the treasure to Rana, saying he couldn't guarantee its safekeeping." Hank waited a few seconds. "Why would Rana consent to having such an open showing in the first place?"

"You mean given the gem's heritage as well as its emotional value to his family?" Maya said. "To gather more prestige, I guess. Not to mention to raise the stone's market price, so he could get top dollar if he sold it. Or he could try to make it easy to steal so he can get insurance. I'm positive the price of that piece has sky-rocketed since then."

"The next screen. It says his advisor had okayed the showing."

Maya let the latest fact sink in. It must have been Neel who had advised Rana to put the gem on display. "Did Rana make any public statement after the safe return of his ruby?"

"None. He was reported to have been out of town. His wife, who received the 'eternal beauty', expressed her regret to the media for the 'premature closure of an important exhibit.'"

"Which means there's a chance of a scam here. Someone could have swiped the real thing and slipped in a fake to Rana's wife." Maya allowed a few seconds to elapse. "What can you tell me about the real rock?"

"It's beyond my imagination," Hank said in a professorial voice. "The rock originated in a mine in upper Burma—I should say Myanmar—which, I gather, produces top quality rubies for the international market. You already know that rubies come from the corundum mineral. Hard and durable, they're in short supply. This irreplaceable ruby, one of the largest in the world, weighs 8,000 carats—which I can't even picture. A lustrous, unmounted natural gem, it's a stunner, has no visible flaws or evidence of heat treatment, which are among its many attractive qualities. If you look closely, you're supposed to be able to see a six-pointed star."

"Ah, that star might be a way you can tell the real from a fake."

"You got it."

"I've heard it explained," Maya said, "that color alone can determine the price of rubies."

"Right, got you. Rubies come in pink, orange, purple, dark red, and other shades. This one is pigeon-blood red, the eye of a cuckoo, considered the most precious."

"I also remember Neel saying, 'Clarity comes next, followed by luster and symmetry.'"

"I'm with you on all three."

"How much will it go for?" Maya asked.

"It's worth megabucks. Many dealers would kill to have it, foreign dealers as well as international gem societies." Hank's voice bespoke the factual nature of the material. "Thirty million would be my guess. By the way, rubies are rarer and more pricey than similar-sized diamonds."

"Any picture?"

"Not so far. That 'glow-in-dark' rock has a light of its own, an inner fire, experts say, so bright you can't hide it anywhere. That's freaking cool." Hank paused. "One day, okay, maybe not too far in the future, I'll come up with an exotic fact like that to make my short stories come alive on the page."

Maya held a small smile. "So, where's our 'fire-hearted' rock?"

"Dunno. Like you suggested it could already be in a fraudster's hand."

"You might want to keep tabs on the web. See if it's being sold anywhere online."

"I will," Hank said. "My exploration led me to another fascinating fact. Buying and selling gemstones is one of India's oldest trades, tricky as it gets. You grew up there. Is that really so?"

"Yes, the gem sector—that's a biggie in India's economy. The city of Jaipur—I'll be there tomorrow—is not only a grand place to snap up gems and jewelry, but it's also the hub of the country's jewelry design business. A global center, it employs a huge labor force. Buyers descend from all over the world to browse, to buy, to 'flip,' to dream. Everywhere you look, you see showrooms where wholesalers and retailers deal in first-rate rings, bangles, necklace, belly belts, and ornament for any part of the body you wish to decorate. If you want to avoid scam and acquire the real thing, however, you'll need to familiarize yourself with the tricks of the trade. You'll need to go to a certified shop. You'll get it appraised. And you'll ask for lab reports."

"Sophie would flip," Hank said. "Bling is her thing."

"As it is for a lot of Indian ladies. Pearl and rubies are their BFFs. They're not for decoration alone, mind you. When you wear a gemstone, you get the beneficial effect of the planet connected to it, or so they say. The quality counts. Any cracks on the gemstone would prevent light passing through it, I'm told, and so you might not get the desired benefit wearing it. Indeed, you could be harmed."

"What about Indian gents?" Hank asked. "Do they go for jewelry, too?"

"Very much so," Maya replied. "More and more gents wear jewelry as accessories, as creative expressions of themselves. Some say jewelry makes them stand up taller. Others count on a stone's supernatural powers. They could get rich overnight—imagine that—be cured of a disease, win the lottery, or win the love of someone they dream about."

"I'm not much for jewelry. As I mentioned, my Sophie loves retail therapy."

"Uh-oh. Always, as a buyer, you must be vigilant," Maya said. "A stone could be dyed, reconstructed, or damaged, or it could prove to be an imitation. You hear stories about how tricksters lurk around, dupe you into buying fake pearl, synthetic diamond, or glass ruby. Word on the boulevard is: Seek the opinion of a gem police, an expert that is, before buying."

"I can see why Neel's work was so important," Hank said.

"Quite. Neel has a high reputation, which means a lot in that trade, given the amount of fakery that goes on. Pity that his passion led him to trouble with the police, and possibly with his good friend, Rana Adani. I suppose you've come across more gossip about Rana?"

"You better believe it. A snob columnist reports that our hot dude is estranged from his wife. So, what's the big deal? It happens every day. But his cronies are shocked beyond belief that the power couple have separated. Well, well, aren't they're supposed to be 'blessedly happy?' Less than two years ago, they had what is known as a love marriage which, as I understand it, wasn't arranged by the parents. She'd made a trip to Jaipur on a holiday. They'd met at an auto repair shop, of all places. He got all moony over her and married her after only a few dates, a whirlwind courtship, you might say. Called the wedding of the decade in Jaipur, it was attended by more than five thousand guests."

"Any proof that all is not well in his marital department?" Maya asked.

"The word is out, as anonymously confirmed by a domestic helper. They'd been fighting a lot lately. She finally walked out after a 'physical altercation,' a fist fight, which she supposedly won. Left late at night with a small suitcase in a taxi, sobbing, screaming, and cursing. Hasn't been seen in the mansion since."

"I smell something here," Maya said, gratified that she now had a way to kick-start the case. "What's her name and who's she?"

"Beatrice Adani, Bea to her friends, birth name is Bonita Nagarajan. Stylish and dramatic—those are a columnist's words— she's believed to be both meek and feisty. A stage actress in Malaysia—that's not her only 'qualification'—she has done time, been a dissident, hails from a dirt-poor family, and considered an oddball."

"An actress, a dissident, and a fist fighter who married up?"

"She's also supposed to be hot."

"Any idea how to get hold of her?"

"None. I've probed, but so far have run into a wall. No trace of her anywhere. She's lying low."

"That's not surprising. The Adanis are luminaries in Jaipur. She might have brought shame to them. My first order of business when I get there will be to track her down. She's the underdog, who also has a good bit of inside intelligence about the ruby, which could put her under threat. In fact, she could wind up being tortured for information."

"Omigod," Hank said. "To risk your life over a piece of rock? Glad I'm a starving grad student."

Maya pondered: Poor Neel, embroiled in what could be a heist. In the commercial corridors of gemstones, the walkway of the privileged, that could mean more: high stakes, glamour, mystique, deceit, secrecy and even murder. Maya trembled. She saw bigger complications in her mind's eye.

"Hope Bea Adani doesn't try to flee India." Maya felt a pang of apprehension, considering the implications. "If she does so before I have a chance to question her, that could stymie our investigation."

"You don't imagine she ran off with the ruby, do you?"

"Can't say. Everyone's under suspicion at this point. And there's a bigger question than the ruby, an existential one, which I'm trying to formulate in my mind."

"One other stray fact that made me smile," Hank said. "That ruby is supposed to be an aphrodisiac."

Maya laughed. "And so, the absence of it . . .?" She reviewed the debacle in her mind, paused, and turned serious. "I must call my boss, Simi, again. Her office is about fifteen kilometers away from where I am. We'll meet for tea."

"The lady who knows everything?"

Maya assented. Simi, who had informants all over the place, might be able to give Maya the lowdown on the elusive Beatrice Adani.

"That'll free you up. You and Sophie can get busy with your travel plans. How would that be?"

"Perf, boss. Next week, Jaipur."

FOUR

"FOLLOW THAT MARUTI SUZUKI, PLEASE." MAYA shouted to the taxi driver above the road noise the next day, her first morning in Jaipur, slightly out of breath in anticipation. She was tailing Bea, the estranged wife of Rana Adani and a suspect in the ruby heist case, based on a tip from her boss, Simi. After pointing to the fire-engine red car, she settled back into her seat, eyes fixed straight ahead. As said by Simi, Bea went shopping early in the morning, one of the few times she emerged from her hiding place. Maya didn't want to miss this opportunity. She must speak with Bea. From this distance, perched on the backseat of the taxi, she could see the silhouette of Bea in the driver's seat of the car ahead. She could imagine how Bea's super straight black hair must be glimmering.

Maya's watch displayed: nine a.m. Only yesterday she'd heard of the absent ruby and news of Neel's imprisonment from an email sent by Inspector Mohan Dev. Following that, she'd had a long talk with her mom about Neel and his predicament. As a result, she hadn't slept well during the night, had taken an early flight to reach here, landing about an hour ago. She'd checked into a hotel, had a quick word with Uma on the phone, and scheduled a visit with her later in the day. She had messaged Lee about her safe arrival.

She heard the voice of the taxi driver, battling the morning rush-hour. "We're approaching our loudest traffic junction, Madam."

Oh, perfect.

"First trip to Jaipur? Well, Jaipur isn't as classy as New Delhi or as beautiful as Agra," the cabbie continued in a cheerful manner. "But we're historical, energetic, and welcoming, a cultural giant."

Maya wasn't amused. On this morning, hot and dry save for an occasional gentle breeze, typical of Jaipur's desert climate, she suffered from exhaustion. Accosted by the traffic noise, suffering from jetlag, experiencing the bumps on the road, she now felt irritable, and disoriented. After taking a deep breath, she shrugged her shoulders, and resolved to make the best of the situation. She'd get right on the case and put her full attention to it. Best of all, she'd be able to lounge around with Uma this afternoon and comfort her.

"Why do foreigners chase people, if I may ask?" The taxi driver, a slender man of middle years, turned to look at Maya. Dignified in a crisp checked cotton shirt and a turban, he seemed unfazed by the fast traffic. "Yesterday, this Aussie gentleman hired me to snoop on a diplomat from his own country, one who turned out to be his uncle."

Maya laughed, her mood improving. "Well, I'm not a foreigner. I was born and raised here, a *pukka* Indian, you might say."

"No offence, Madam, it's your accent. I'd call it British or international, although your loafers are American."

"Never mind my accent or my shoes. Please keep your eyes on the road."

"For certain, Madam." The driver swung back, faced the steering wheel. "I'm not a cabbie who says things like: We're the 'Masters of the Road,' or that we 'Optimize Fleet Utilization.' Nor do I ask for 'compulsory' tipping. I take my passengers where they wish to go, safe and sound, in record time. You can also hail us online."

As he wove in and out of cars, lorries, three-wheelers, hand-drawn carts, and camels, Jaipur stretched before Maya: sandstone-façade palaces, brick edifices, latticed windows, shady banyan

trees, strutting peacocks, as well as classic columns and porticos, all
bathed in a mustard-hued light. Rugged hills surrounded the city.
Maya called her own attention to the fact that the town was built in
1727 by Maharaja Sawai Jai Singh, the Great King. He established
the city. He laid it out in compliance with the principles of ancient
India, known as Vastu Shastra or "Science of Architecture," a guide
for channeling healthful, positive energy through a space.

Such energy would not be hard to find, not on this late spring
day. Late spring, what was known here as "short summer," due to
rising temperatures. A long-tailed, cinnamon-bodied rufous tree
pie, settled on a tree branch, made a musical call, as though rejoic-
ing the arrival of hot weather. Women, draped in flashy saris or
voluminous, ankle-length, *ghagra* skirts embellished with crystals
and sequins, crowded the sidewalks. They shared the space with
teenage girls in tights, tapping on their cell phones, as well as food
hawkers. The air held a fragrance of roasted peanuts and spices
such as chili and cumin. The sights, sounds and hues enchanted
her, even though Maya didn't feel as reassured by them as she'd
have liked. Not with her gaze fixed on Bea's car, wondering if she'd
have a chance to meet Bea and how crucial that was.

"What do you do for a living, if I may ask?" the driver asked.

"I'm employed as a private investigator."

"So, you're a cop. Might have known. You have intense eyes."

"I'm not a cop. I operate privately."

"I can understand why you might not want to be mistaken for
a cop. In our town, people hate the khakis. That's what we call our
cops because they wear khaki uniforms. We also call them police
raj or police king. They act like kings. They break any traffic regula-
tion they like. See that building over there?" He pointed to the left.
"Believe it or not, it used to be a popular temple, a shrine, always
teeming with devotees. It was falling apart and sinking into the
ground, so they converted it into a police station. Now nobody
wants to set foot there." He laughed. "We're heading toward
Ramganj. Are you familiar with that neighborhood, Madam
Investigator?"

"No, but it interests me to hear about it."

"I'll tell you as we go. It's a mix." Soon they plodded past a series of dusty shopfronts housed in tin-roofed, brick-walled buildings located on a back street. "You're seeing the production centers of our artisans."

She drank in the sight of potters, marble carvers, and sculptors bending over their work and shoemakers sitting cross-legged in fierce concentration. Under dim lights, with their doors open, as was the custom, they toiled in their workrooms.

"We're proud of our artisans and their cottage industries," the driver said. "Jaipur is called a 'Craft Destination.' You see, we consider making things by hand honorable even to this day. Let me warn you, however. Despite the creative mess you see all around, this district is considered 'sensitive.' Last year a woman strolling on the sidewalk up ahead was harassed by the police on false charges. Which led to much public uproar, street demonstrations, and rioting. Then there are pickpockets and robbers who wander about, and you even can run the risk of being stabbed. And you can encounter loonies, who will verbally abuse you. This area also has, what they call 'poverty with dignity.' Are you familiar with that term, Madam? Most run-down homes you can imagine that are kept spotlessly clean inside and organized. Since you're an investigator, you must be acclimated to rough-and-tumble far worse than this. Still, I must ask you. You want me to head in that direction?"

"Yes, I'm positive." She thanked the driver for many pieces of pertinent information.

"Only a native like me can figure out Jaipur. Where to go and what to avoid?"

Up ahead, a motorcyclist jumped a red light. Horns blared all around, engines whined, the sounds seeming to rip the sky apart, and she lost sight of the Maruti Suzuki. *Drat!* Any delay and Bea could disappear from this locale and with her would vanish a possible source of information regarding the ruby.

The driver must have read her mind. "Please don't fret. This traffic mess is our everyday headache, but I'll get you there in one piece. I'll figure out where that car is daring to go. In the meantime, relax and allow the city to win you over—be immersed, as they say, in the 'Jaipur Dream.' Do you hear what I'm saying?"

Maya felt far from restful and dreamy. "I hear you."

"I ask because our noise level is very high in this traffic," the cabbie said. "As high as a rock band."

Maya didn't doubt that. As the cabbie drove through a maze of streets, she found her vision assaulted by dilapidated buildings, shuttered store fronts, squatters' tents, and broken fences. Before long, the traffic thinned out a fraction, the sound lessened. Then, much to her relief, the Maruti Suzuki again flashed before her eyes. It pulled up into a dusty narrow lane, Maya's taxi zipping after it, and stopped near a tin-roofed teashop, whose door was wide open. Two men huddling inside gawked at Maya, as though inquiring: *What are you doing here?*

At the end of the block stood a three-story, weather-beaten, dingy apartment house. As Maya watched, Bea parked her car in front and slid out, her eyes shaded by Dior Shield sunglasses. After giving her surroundings a quick glance, she floated up the weed-choked path to the entrance and marched up the front stoops, only then removing her sunglasses. A plastic shopping bag packed with her purchases hung from her arm.

Maya asked her driver to halt. She paid him, arranged for a pick-up, and exited the taxi. A vine tickled her arm as she brushed past a tree with lacy leaves, side-stepping a pile of rubbish. She crinkled her nose from the odor and jogged up behind Bea, slightly disoriented from this trip.

Standing with poise at the entrance, Bea fiddled with a set of keys. The trim, attractive woman, about 5'6" in height, had perfect posture, buttery-smooth complexion, an expressive body, manicured nails, and a sleek haircut. Her glimmering, shoulder-length black hair pushed behind her ears displayed a pair of jade earrings. Indeed, she matched the pictures Maya had seen of her on the web. On a closer inspection, the corners of her mouth were creased, which reflected the trepidation she must feel. Her squinting eyes, puffy and reddish from crying, revealed she concealed a lot inside.

She turned, threw one look at the departing taxi, spotted Maya, and froze, a terrified expression on her face.

Maya started off strong and clear, but pleasant. "May I come inside and have a word with you, Mrs. Adani?"

Bea shrank. "Why? No. Who are you?"

Maya pressed a calling card into Bea's hand. "Maya Mallick, Private Investigator. I work for Detectives Unlimited. Have you heard of them?"

Bea glanced at the card, her diamond ring winking in the sunlight, "Yes, they provide detective service for women and families, don't they? Strange—I haven't contacted them. A friend of mine hired them and was pleased with the result." She pushed the door open. It made a squeaking sound. She stepped into the room, turned half-way, and inspected the card again. She looked Maya up and down.

"Are you really based in Seattle, U.S.A, Ms. Mallick?"

"Yes, flew to India a few days ago. Landed in Jaipur this morning." Standing outside the front door, Maya kept her voice warm and inclusive. "You can call me Maya."

Bea's eyes were large and beautiful, but tired. "What brings you here, Maya? Why are you stalking me? How do you even know who I am?"

"I have in mind to speak with you in private."

"Why . . . Why?" Bea asked in a raised voice. Although her frumpy flowered dress acted like a camouflage, an elaborate jade necklace gave away her status as a moneyed woman. "What if I told you I don't wish to . . ."

"Listen, your life is in danger." At these words, Maya noticed a shudder coursing through Bea.

"What are you talking about?"

"You know what I'm talking about. It's the ruby, but that's not the end of it, there's much more." Aware that Bea might have more faith in a woman P.I. than a male detective, she added, "I'm a woman trying to help another woman, my mom, in this case. May I . . .?"

"Alright, alright, come in." She let Maya in through the front entrance and gestured toward an apartment situated across the hallway. "Damn. I rented this flat under a different identity and you found me?"

"That's not enough security, if you were to ask my opinion."

Saying so, Maya inventoried the studio apartment, which was hot and stuffy from a lack of air-conditioning and had the odor of not being regularly cleaned. Cobwebs hung in the corners of the aging walls in need of a fresh coat of paint. A smudged window, facing the street, appeared as though it could be easily broken. Dust had settled on the windowsill and the floor. A twin bed, a desk, a dresser, a chair, and a stained old carpet, all functional, but all of which had seen better days, made up the furnishings. There was no radio or television. The south wall accommodated a sliding closet with rickety, bi-fold doors. Although Bea, a stage actress, electrified the environment with her presence, this was hardly a pad for a multi-millionaire's wife.

She motioned Maya to the chair and blurted, "You're thinking, how can she live in this dump?

"That's the least of my worries about you."

"I grew up in Kuala Lumpur, then migrated to Singapore." Bea pushed a strand of hair away from her forehead. "If you think all Singaporeans are filthy rich, you're wrong, wrong, wrong. My family was the poorest of the poor. I'm used to much worse than this."

"You're making a lot of assumptions about what I think, Mrs. Adani."

"You can call me Bea. I'm sorry, I'm not quite myself these days. Let's see . . . oh, would you like a drink? A cup of tea?" In response to Maya's shaking head, she said, "Oh, you must have tea. Do you like it strong or weak?"

"Strong." Maya noted Bea's hospitality instinct and liked her for it. Given how things stand, Bea would calm down if she kept busy. Drinking a cup would also help Maya make it through this encounter. Not to mention, she would gain Bea's goodwill by sticking around her.

Bea drifted toward a mini kitchen located on the left, equipped with a stove, a counter, a refrigerator, and a sink that held a few soiled dishes. Keeping quiet as she prepared the tea, her back toward her visitor, she seemed to pay attention to the noise in the hallway of a child shrieking. Maya heard tea being poured.

Bea reappeared with two steaming cups—full-leaf black tea swirled with rich milk—and handed one to her guest. Cup in hand, she plunked down on the edge of the bed. "Have you any idea why I let you in, Maya?"

Maya raised her curious eyes. "No, why?"

"Has to do with your straight-forward manner." Bea fluffed a pillow with one hand. She took a swallow of the tea, closing her eyes for a short time, as though the warmth helped her cope. "You've come up the hard way, haven't you?"

Maya sampled the strong brew, which burned her tongue. The rich man's wife hadn't had to prepare her own tea in the last few years. "Yes." She sighed. "My single mother spent her last penny to raise me, her only child. We had to struggle. Not enough resources and few relatives around us. We had to do without much. Made the most of what little we had. Had to be creative. Looking back, remembering all the good times, I must say: I had a childhood I wouldn't dream of switching. You know what I mean? I appreciated the role my mom played in my life, the support she gave me. We were aligned. That felt so secure. When time came for me to go to the States for study, she didn't try to stop me. She wanted my best, even though eventually I'd leave the nest and it'd be a loss for her. To this day, I appreciate her unselfishness."

"Same here," Bea said. "You get a ton of love, even if you don't have enough toys to play with. You get strong, you get motivated, which keeps you going as an adult. People from my background don't dare to go into the acting profession. I did, even though it was considered frivolous. Relatives tried to talk me out of it."

Maya looked Bea straight in the eye, appreciating her frankness. The questions, however, remained: Why was she hiding out in this place? What was her connection to the ruby, if any? Why did she leave her powerful husband? And how would she, a woman alone, protect herself in this street-level apartment in a crime-ridden part of the town?

Her tone, low, quiet, and comforting, Maya said, "I'm not trying to scare you. But don't admit someone in your apartment because you *like* them."

"What do you do as a private detective?"

"Save people from harm," Maya said, her tone darker, "provided it's not too late."

A ripple of fear passed across Bea's face. She gathered herself, put the cup down on the floor, and stood. "I'm trained as a stage actress. My body is my vehicle, and I'm strong, physically. I can protect myself." One slender arm tore through the air and made a circular movement, as though twirling a knife. She sparkled from that little act, if for a second, before regaining her seat. "Are you on my side, Ms. Detective?"

"I don't take sides. That is, until I've gathered all the facts. What can you tell me about the burgled ruby?"

Bea averted her gaze and drew in a shallow breath, her voice hardening as she said, "That rock. Why do you think I was privy to any knowledge about it?"

A lie, Maya could tell from her voice and body language, but decided it would be best to play along. "It was solely Rana's affair?"

Bea slouched a bit, as though weakening at the mention of Rana's name, and nodded. Their relationship consisted of love, hate, and tons of frustration if Maya were to make a guess. That fact was also evident from the melancholy that had settled in the atmosphere.

Maya put down the half-full cup on the floor, spilling a little on the carpet, apologized and added, "I'd like to speak with your husband, if I could."

"Yes—well—you and a hundred other people. Good luck with that."

"Why should it be so difficult?"

Bea sighed. "They line up every morning to pay *darshan* to the town's most charismatic tycoon." An audience. "You follow, no? To be in his calendar, to schmooze with him, to listen to him is worth much in Jaipur's social and economic circles, even when his advice is shit. And women, they line up, or should I say, they deliver themselves to him in a conveyor belt, as it were. All of that to get their hearts shattered. If you go through regular channels, you'll get nowhere."

"You know his whereabouts better than anybody," Maya said. "Where can I 'accidentally' run into him?"

Seeing Bea hesitate, Maya said, "Please, as I mentioned, I'm here also for my mom's sake. Her life is turned upside down because of that mislaid, priceless object. Her partner Neel has been put behind the bars. I suppose you know Neel."

"Yes, but I can't fathom him. His father, Kavi Saha, is a big-named astrologer and has a reputation of being down-to-earth You might remember how in India we book a chat with an astrologer when times are tough. Right now, I could see myself doing a face-to-face with Mr. Saha. But he doesn't take in too many new clients."

Once again, Maya's curiosity was aroused in connection to Kavi Saha. It'd have to wait. For now, she focused her attention on Bea. "Times are tough, indeed. A lot more people could get hurt, including yourself. I have an urge for stopping that before it's too late."

"To be frank, I've had the feeling of being chased. Not positive by whom or why, but a rogue is after me and I'm all alone here. Why would anybody want to hurt me?"

"The ruby, naturally, the ruby. Someone would like to find out what you know about its whereabouts."

"That cursed stone. I know zilch about it."

Maya pictured Neel behind bars. A shiver rippled along her spine. "So, you're saying only Rana . . . ?"

Bea sighed, her poise faltering, voice thinning. "That'd be his style. Our town's 'superstar' seems forward, but he holds a lot inside."

A complex man. Maya's curiosity was aroused. "Once again, please, how can I meet him?"

"Since you insist, I'll tell you. Are you familiar with the lush green area in the center of the town, the popular Central Park? It has a four-kilometer running track. Every Wednesday and Friday mornings at about eight, Rana runs there."

Watching Bea closely, Maya said, "Are you in touch with him?"

"No way. I've severed all connections." Bea peered down into her cup, her face pale in remorse, her tone confessional. "The last fight was enough. Started out with a silly argument, ended up in a fist fight. I consider myself damn lucky to be alive."

"How did you learn to fist fight?"

"That was easy." Bea wore a wild-eyed look. "I was raised in a tough neighborhood where from the age of five you bone up on how to curl your hand into a fist and focus on something or somebody with intention. I aimed mine at his eyes."

"What did he do?"

Eyes averted, Bea said, "Hit me on the forehead, slipped, cursed . . ."

"What time was it?"

"I don't remember."

Was Bea speaking the truth? Maya couldn't be sure. "Where in the house?"

"Can't remember that either. He hurt me but it got my blood flowing, got my intention revved up, and so . . . Afterwards, I . . ."

"Yes?"

"Saw him wobbling. He looked like he didn't believe I could be so strong. Next, I saw him lying on the floor, with a black eye. I'd hurt him badly, yes, but I'd won. At that point, I took off with what I had on me and didn't go back. He'd have killed me if I'd made an appearance at the mansion."

"What happened then?"

"For the next few days, he pretended to have caught the flu—that's what a friend told me. He stopped going to his office or receiving callers."

"What on earth was the fight about?"

Bea gripped the handle of her cup. "Aren't we getting rather personal here, Detective Lady?"

A rock-hard silence followed. Bea's nervous gaze demonstrated her apprehensiveness and regret, a desire to blot out past actions, and to be domiciled in a safer habitat.

"Did the fistfight happen before or after the ruby's disappearance?" Maya asked.

"Before."

"What was your reaction when you heard the red beauty had disappeared?"

"The ruby, any knowledge about the ruby, why should I tell you anything?"

"Why shouldn't you?" Maya said. "As it stands, you're not safe in this town. What if your husband comes after you? Or someone who assumes you have the ruby? No one will help you, no one except me."

Bea paled, took a gulp of her tea, hands shaky. "Without a doubt. That fellow trailing me . . . I'm not sure who has recruited him. I spot him in shops, whenever I stop to get gas, anytime I go to Radha Produce to shop for groceries, and anytime I'm out of this dump."

"What does he look like?"

"Can't tell you. I freeze when he's around. He has a black mask on. That's all I can remember. Next time, I'll give him a closer look."

"I'm afraid you need police protection," Maya said.

"No, no, I don't want the khaki to be able to track me. Do you understand why? They're cruel. They can be influenced. They can be bribed." She blew out a sigh. "Sorry to get carried away. What are you up to?"

"My goal is to get to the bottom of all that's going on, beginning with the disappearance of the ruby. For that I need your help." Maya put a plea in her voice. "Could you please throw me a bone? A launching point of sorts? At least for contacting people who might help shed a ray of light on this matter?"

"To meet Rana's relatives—that'd be my first step," Bea replied. "As you very well know, Indian families are a complicated emotional network. I had to learn all about the intricacies of the relationships, the hierarchies, the hidden connections. So many established ways, such as how to show respect to your elders. You address your maternal aunts differently from your paternal aunts. Same for uncles. I got them all mixed up. They made fun of me. 'The girl is a little too green.'

"And the varieties of customs you must follow each day. You even prepare special dishes for the deities and feed them first." Bea frowned, giving the impression she didn't get along well with the Adani family, nor did she appreciate their formalities, and was thankful to be out of touch with them. "As a member of the Adani family, I had to dress up every time I went out. Rana told me I didn't have to, but his relatives . . ."

"Any particular relative I should speak with?"

Bea lowered her head. She wouldn't reveal any more, not at this session. Maya would have to arrange to meet with her at another time.

"How would I contact you?" Confronted with silence, feeling exasperated, Maya said, "If you want to stay alive . . . you'll do well to share your mobile number with me. You have my card. Call me whenever you feel it's necessary, if someone is following you and you're getting panicky, okay?"

She must have hit a nerve. Bea recited her number, indicating she was into the game.

Maya jotted it down on her cell phone, leapt to her feet. She'd made a start. "Thanks for the tea. Allow me to suggest a few tips on how to stay hidden. Change your habit. Don't go out the same time every day. Vary your route; vary your destination. Have your groceries delivered."

"You mean I shouldn't venture out at all?"

"If you can help it. Otherwise, alter your appearance. Put on a wig. Leave the jade out. Go scarf-less if you usually throw one on. I mean get comfortable wearing a disguise." Maya assumed a lighter tone of voice. "That shouldn't be hard for an actress, should it?"

Bea nodded, flashed a smile, a rueful one. "You know I've always wanted to play a damsel-in-distress on stage. And now . . . and now . . . I'm playing it in my own life."

FIVE

FIVE

DAY 1

AROUND NOON, MAYA DID A TREK from her hotel in Jaipur to Uma's flat, a two-kilometer distance. She could hardly wait. Nothing like a good talk with Mom to fill Maya's heart. Although she'd spoken on the phone with Uma twice in the last three hours, this was going to be an in-person rap, even more significant due to Neel's return. Big news: Uma had reported that Neel had been released from the jail early this morning after what she called a "blessedly brief" time. *Such a relief.*

The question remained: How had this incident affected Neel, physically and mentally? And Uma? Who, as a loving partner, had been so anxious, seeming to expect a negative outcome? Maya wanted to protect her mom at all costs. By spending time with her, she would be able to offer some solace.

Imbued with uneasiness and curiosity, Maya took brisk, purposeful steps as she strolled past a milk market. She diverted her attention by surveying the area. Stalls displayed tin cans of farm fresh milk. *The cow is earth, the cow is heaven, the cow is God Vishnu. Drink milk. Feel great.* So declared a sign placed in front of a stall, reminding her of Hindu mythology, the sacred nature of milk, and the popularity of milk products in this town. Maya watched as shoppers and vendors haggled over prices, in a city that was considered price conscious.

Further on, she strode past a pillared temple, which sported a marble floor. Against a trellis in front of the temple, a cheery, purple, heat-loving bougainvillea shrub bloomed in a gesture of welcome. Maya heard the chanting of noon prayers, which reminded her that Jaipur was often called the "City of Temples." Invigorated by the town's daily rhythm of life, the golden sunshine, gentle breeze, and the vibrancy of the flowers, she reached Uma's apartment complex. She got into the elevator, buzzed the doorbell, and waited, if breathlessly.

A beat later, Uma opened the door. Draped in a creamy chiffon sari, a shadow clouding her chiseled face, she gave Maya a hug. "Come in, my dear," she said in a low voice.

Something was amiss, Maya could tell, as she stepped into the spacious two-bedroom flat. Uma, usually composed, never wore such a bleak expression. Also, no food aroma emanated from the kitchen, which alarmed Maya. Uma always whipped up snacks for her, went over the top, as a matter of fact. She served Maya's adolescent choices—samosas and laddoos—all home-made, accompanied by frothy, milky chai. A big talk was in order. And there would be ample time for that.

The ruby hadn't been recovered yet, but Neel had passed the polygraphy test, indicating he hadn't run off with it. Uma had informed her so in a brief phone chat earlier this morning immediately upon her arrival in Jaipur. Although not considered conclusive, the police didn't have enough evidence to detain Neel. However, Uma believed that the police would continue to have a tail on him. "They could cart him away again tomorrow," was how Uma had put it.

Which would make this a perfect opportunity for Maya to see Neel, the gemologist, one with the insider knowledge about the missing ruby. Had his hunger strike in jail weakened him? Or was he good spirits from being freed? Once Maya ascertained his psychological condition then, armed with relevant details, she'd be able to make her next move in the pursuit of the ruby. She'd make sure that the rare gem had been restored and repossessed by the owner. Then and only then would the police leave Neel alone.

With that prospect firing her up further, Maya settled herself on the satin-covered sofa in the living room. She smoothed the folds of her embroidered, parrot green georgette sari. She'd worn this dressier outfit to cheer her mother, to make this occasion special. She had also curled the edges of her hair and put on a layered pearl necklace.

Uma expressed her appreciation for Maya's arrival, asked her how the flight was, then slipped a tumbler of chilled mango juice into her hand. It was then Maya noticed. Uma wasn't wearing the sapphire on her finger, a most unusual phenomenon.

Her heart leaping, she squeaked out, "Where's your ring?"

"You look lovely," Uma said. "*Amar sonar maye.*" My golden girl.

Maya savored a small sip of the fruity drink. Noting the undertone of distress in Uma's voice and her evasion, she decided not to pursue the ring issue any further.

Putting it mildly, she said, "Everything all right?"

"No, no, I feel terrible," Uma said. "I got panicky and made you cut your vacation short to get here. Now that Neel's back and I'm relieved, you can go back to Kolkata. Yes, dear, you can book a flight."

"Oh, no, Ma, I'm happy to be here. Now I'd be able to spend a week or so with you and Neel." Noticing Uma staring at the door, Maya wondered what had changed. Why wasn't Uma as welcoming as she usually was? Could it be a conversation with that astrologer? "What was your talk like with Kavi Saha?"

"It was pleasant. Will you please excuse me? I have to run a few errands now that I don't have Sam around."

Something told Maya that was a cover-up. She gave Uma a closer look. Uma appeared harried and distressed; her voice sounded higher than usual. That impression of her lodged in Maya's chest like a piece of stone. "Do you need my help?"

"No, no, don't trouble yourself, my dear."

"Any word from Sam?" At Uma's headshake, she added, "Facebook, Twitter—"

"That boy was never into the social media. Last night I put in a call to his uncle, Meher, again. He said Sam had acted kind of odd before his disappearance. When I pressed him for specifics, Meher replied he had a previous engagement and couldn't speak for too long." Uma laughed derisively. "'Previous engagement,' in that God-forsaken little village, with no electricity after hours?"

"It does sound fishy."

Uma raised a hand toward Maya in a gesture of blessing. After making a show of inspecting her watch, she said, "Dear me," turned and swept to the door. "Neel will be with you shortly."

"Do you have a minute, Ma, before you go?" Maya asked Uma's back.

By then Uma had hustled off toward the corridor, her low-heeled sandals flapping on the floor at a rate faster than usual, leaving Maya a bit mystified. Uma asking her to return to Kolkata? Uma seemingly closed off from her. Even as an adult daughter, she needed her mom. Losing her would devastate Maya. She wanted to bring the darkness between them to light.

For now, all she could do was wait. She sat back against a mirrorwork throw pillow in upbeat red and orange, two popular Jaipur shades. Admired the décor Uma had chosen to liven the room, which had created an effect of comfort, elegance, fine taste, and spaciousness. Her gaze landed on a pair of marble-top side tables, works of art, that stood on either side of the sofa. Neel had paid for these, that much was clear. Uma couldn't afford such luxury on her schoolteacher's pension.

From a vase on top of the mahogany coffee table, another expensive acquisition of Neel, a medley of sunny yellow marigolds and wildflowers spilled out, infusing the air with their subdued scent. Next, Maya's attention strayed to a dreamy pink-and-blue mandala tapestry hanging on the opposite wall. The rest of the wall was lined with a pair of bookcases stocked with antique, leather-bound history volumes, collector's items. They gave off a smell of old books; reading history was Neel's pastime of choice.

It dawned on Maya how Neel would bring a historical anecdote alive for his listeners as though it was a movie in his mind. One such, much loved by Maya, dealt with the status of women courtesans in the 17th century, during the reign of Mughal Emperor Shah Jahan. "Pitiful, rather pitiful, how those women were treated," Neel said, an impish light in his eyes, a glass of whiskey in front of him. "Except for a mischievous girl—a court dancer, a cocktail waitress in today's terms, who might have been a spy for a rival kingdom—and who managed to make it fun for herself. The cute young thing got her drinks mixed up, got the wrong people drunk, paired up the rivals, and initiated the most vicious fight. Then she smiled and danced the evening away—her revenge for having been subjugated."

Sitting alone, Maya wondered: What kind of an anecdote might Neel tell her next, if he was indeed in a mood to do so? She peered around the room. Neel and Uma were such good companions, they pampered her so much, and this was a tastefully decorated apartment situated in a high rental district. She loved this place and would have stayed here. Uma had, indeed, invited her to do so, prior to Maya's leaving Seattle. Uma had dangled additional perks: The security of the building, the presence of a 24-hour doorman and an efficient concierge to cater to the residents' every single need, such as delivering a pizza at midnight.

Because of the change in circumstance, Maya had booked herself into a nearby hotel, cozy as it gets, named Hotel Nivas, or Hotel "Home." Reasoning? Given the hazards of her job, she needed privacy to carry out her duties, coming and going as she pleased. She didn't want to get Uma worked up or render her sleepless at night if she came home late. Under no condition, did she want to expose Uma to danger. Nor did she want her mother to question her every move. This morning in a phone call, Maya had informed Uma of her decision to park in a hotel and the impetus behind it. Oddly enough, Uma didn't offer any resistance—but why so?

A small light brown package resting on the side table next to the sofa—an innocuous padded envelope ready to be mailed—riveted Maya's attention. Destined for a Mrs. Anita Adani, it had Neel's return address scribbled on top left. Who was Anita Adani? Maya reached out to pick up the mailer, pulled out her cell phone and took a picture of the address label. A small sound caused her to place the mailer back in its place. She dropped down on the couch and shot a glance toward the door.

Neel shuffled into the room, put-together in a blue khadi cotton shirt and blue-gray striped trousers, a gloomy silence about him. Maya smiled warmly at him. In the last couple of years, he'd become a father figure to her. She respected him, a college professor, her late father's age. He always asked about her life in Seattle, her job, and any issues she wished to share. Affectionate and caring for the most part, except when he flew into a temper, he'd lend her an ear. She would open to him, discuss all sorts of personal matters, and seek out his advice. Over the years, they'd developed a certain kinship, a strong loyalty. And so, the more Maya watched him now, the more it hurt her to do so.

His face glum, shoulders rounded, and gaze low to the ground, Neel perched on an armchair across from her. His salt-and-pepper hair had turned snowy white almost overnight. It sent a knife through Maya's heart that he didn't seem pleased by her presence. Nor did he, a garrulous man, offer her any words of welcome.

She asked him how he was, although the answer was obvious. In a subdued manner, he said, "Not so well."

She leaned closer. "Well, after the ordeal you've gone through . . ."

"Damn." He waved for her to stop. "I don't care to talk about it."

A letdown, but one she'd live with. He hadn't gotten over the trauma of being accused of a theft and locked up, so evident from his raw voice. Starving himself while in police custody didn't help, either. He looked as though he'd lost weight and that concerned her.

"Should we wait till tomorrow?" she said. "I'll come back, give you a chance to recuperate in the meantime."

"No, Maya. I don't wish to speak with you about this matter, now or later." Perhaps noticing her astonished face, he added, "Your mom and I love you very much. We appreciate it that you flew from Kolkata on such a short notice, disrupting your vacation with your buddies. But allow me to express my genuine feelings, the way I see it now. You shouldn't get involved in this matter. Understand? Gems are my territory—I'll handle all complications myself."

Another blow. At first too dumbfounded to reply, Maya shrugged it off and allowed herself time to gather her thoughts. As a P.I., she faced challenges and fought as well as anybody, but this was family. The rules of the game, if there were any, didn't apply here. Further, it was Uma who had asked her to make a trip to Jaipur, supposedly to benefit Neel—and now this?

She got a grip on herself, rolled back her shoulders. "Could you clarify?"

"I never believed I'd throw you out of the house, but it has come to that. It's not safe for you to be in Jaipur. In fact, it's dangerous. You get the point? Go back to your hotel, pack up, and catch the next flight back to Seattle. Take your assistant with you."

Her cheeks burning, she tore her eyes away. She was unwilling to buy his story. On top of that, he, a patriarchal figure, had undermined her ability. She fixed him with a level gaze. "Why might I not be safe here?"

"The ruby is still missing."

She kept her voice steady. "And so?"

He fell into a cruel silence, eyes downcast, and sat heavy in his chair.

"Not clear what you're trying to tell me, Neel, but I'm here also for my mom. She begged me to get here as quickly as I could. And you can be certain I'm habituated to all sorts of threats and intimidation. Comes with the territory."

"This is between you and me, Maya. Either you vacate this premise right now . . . or . . ."

The room froze before her. "Or what?"

"Your mom—might get hurt."

"What?" There didn't seem to be enough air in the room to breathe. From the sharp look he threw at her, Maya could tell he meant it. "You're threatening to hurt my mom? Have you lost all your senses? Get real, Neel, I'll bring the cops into this if necessary."

"Cops?" he tossed out, face purplish in rage. "You don't have any police pals here. Why would they listen to you?"

Well, if truth be known, she did have a police pal here. Neel hadn't heard about Mohan Dev's transfer to Jaipur as the Inspector General. As soon as he returned from his vacation, she'd update him. Right now, stunned by Neel's behavior, Maya was left to wonder. Had she ever known this man, her mother's partner for the last two years, who now acted less like a victim and more like an aggressor?

She sank deeper into the sofa and adopted a forceful manner. "I'll sit and wait till my mom comes back."

"I've instructed Uma to stay out for a while." A dismissive smile parted Neel's lips; his eyes flared. "Won't do you any good to wait around. She won't be back till I call to say that the coast is clear."

By what right would he do that? Maya's face flushed in anger; her voice choked. "This is bizarre, Neel. What's going on?"

"We have a saying here, 'Ignorance is peace of mind.'"

Maya was about to say, *I disagree*, when he rose from his chair and motioned her toward the door. Eyes clouded with obstinacy, he spat out, "I'd leave if I were you."

Was he bluffing? Regardless, she concluded, there was no point enduring this bullying behavior. She scrambled to her feet. Although he was a good six inches taller than her and bulkier, she stood firm and shot him a piercing look. "You better not hurt my mom. Do you fathom? If anything happens to her, you might find yourself back in that other slammer."

"You better not be back here," he said.

At the last minute as she left, she gave him a severe look, listening to the door slam behind her, and overheard him mumbling, "What the fuck . . . these young people, if they had any sense . . ."

He could, just as well, had stabbed a knife in her back. Outside in the radiant sunlight, her breath caught in her throat, mouth dry, she wiped the perspiration from her hot forehead with a tissue. Her thoughts raced at hundred miles per minute. She pondered how this incident had thrown a different light on the whole crisis, on Neel's character and his state of mind.

Who was he, really? What kind of stress might he be undergoing? What had provoked him? Most importantly: Had he been abusive to Uma? The very thought made Maya feel like her heart would explode. She made her way along the footpath a few more steps. Unable to take it any longer, she left a text message on Uma's cellphone. "Love you, Ma. Need to talk. Call ASAP."

She kept on walking, aching for Uma to call, legs wobbly in anticipation, but no such luck. How could that be? She'd never known her mother not to respond to an urgent message in a prompt manner. Sadness tugged at her, chilled her hands. She watched a young couple passing by. They were holding hands and smiling, which made her more miserable.

She wanted to leave another message for Uma, but her voice couldn't form the words. What was going on in Uma's environment? Had Neel concocted a scheme to keep Uma under his control? If so, for what purpose? What was the status of their relationship? Maya could have kicked herself for allowing Uma to leave the flat. But then how would she have known what Neel had planned? With the wave of fury that crashed on her, her first impulse was to contact the authorities and ask them to at least implement a surveillance on Uma to protect her from any harm inflicted by Neel.

On second thought, realizing that Uma wasn't in any obvious danger, she decided to calm herself and allow the events to play out. As she wandered over another block, breathing in as much air as she could, another possibility hit her. Contrary to what Neel believed, and however new she was in Jaipur, she could seek the help of Inspector Mohan Dev. His email had been instrumental in bringing her here. He'd respond to her.

Except he was on vacation, off the radar.

Yet another thought, as she took another step, her legs steadier now: Why did Neel mention the ruby out of the blue? This was not clear, but worth taking note of. Then and there she made a decision: Even though neither Uma nor Neel appreciated her presence, Maya would continue to stay in Jaipur. As long as necessary. Keeping Uma's safety in mind, she'd remain involved in the missing ruby affair.

SIX

HALF-AN-HOUR LATER, MAYA SAT ON A BENCH at a long table in a yogurt stand on M.I. Road. After her run-in with Neel, trying to figure out her next step, she needed to be in a place with a cheerful vibe and this hip joint promised it. She nursed a glass of lassi, a frothy white yogurt concoction, garnished with mint leaves and other spices. The drink, sweet, creamy, cool, and silky on her palate, with a pleasing herbal undertone, was a specialty of this hotspot. The secret spices were said to cure traveler's tummy. Even a few sips had taken the edge off that bruhaha and reignited her with a sense of purpose. To determine what might be going on with Neel. What, if anything, his mood had to do with the loss of the ruby? She'd like to speak with Uma and be a co-conspirator in this matter. That is, if Uma ever returned her call. With each passing moment, Maya doubted the call would come. Was she being rejected? Her eyes misted.

Next to the building stood a silk cotton tree blooming with red flowers, visible from where she was positioned. Through the open door, she watched the busy street teeming with automobiles, motor scooters, pedestrians, and camel-drawn carts. The shrill honking of impatient drivers punctuated the atmosphere. Then came the thrill of viewing a decorated elephant. Decked out in a red-and-yellow saddle cloth, layers of jeweled chains hanging around its neck, it was being led down the street. Maya could almost hear the thumping sound it made. Perhaps an elephant dance would take place at a local venue. Perhaps the elephant would be a part of a family celebration. Maya had to admit that Jaipur had grabbed her attention, distracted her from an ordeal, even if it hadn't won her over yet.

With her habit of surveying her surroundings, Maya observed a few details. The server bustled around the benches. They were crammed with chattery office personnel, a tourist bent over his mobile phone, and a mother trying to soothe a sobbing young daughter. A lone blind man, with large ears and an acned complexion, who wore huge sunglasses, hunched over a corner table. A cane by his side, he lifted his face from time to time and looked toward her. She couldn't figure out why.

Hank and Sophie, her two favorite people, had walked in a few moments ago and taken a pair of seats across from her. She'd suggested this hangout to them, away from tourist attractions and patronized by locals, where they could enjoy each other's company and have a dialogue. They'd gotten in yesterday and were staying at her hotel, both on their first trip to India. The well-matched couple sat close to each other, their shoulders touching. Hank flaunted a timeworn *Can I Live Without a Like?* T-shirt and slim-fit jeans. His laptop rested on the table before him.

"How do you like your drink?" Maya asked.

Hank looked cheerful and gulped from his glass, saying, "It's a kickass drink, punchy, too. It could become a habit after sight-seeing."

"Speaking of sight-seeing," Maya said. "Don't miss the Jantar Mantar observatory, which has the world's largest stone sundial."

"It'll be on top of my list. I'd like to be able to read time. Will send my mom a postcard and oh, she'll get green-eyed. My mom and I don't get along too well. She thinks I'm a pain in the butt. I think she's a pain the butt, too. She controls me. So, I'm overjoyed to be here, to have space for myself, and I can be my true self." Hank paused. "How's your mom? Did you get a chance to see her?"

"Well, yes, I did," Maya replied. "Can't explain it—she didn't seem happy to see me. In fact, she wanted me to leave—to go back to Kolkata. Can you believe it? Why did she cut me off? This has never happened before. It kills me, just kills me. Growing up the only child, I was close to her. We understood each other, we were best friends. Now I live far away, but we talk on the phone often, and every time I come back here for a visit, we hang out and have a great time. Except this time. We seem to have drifted apart, far apart, really. What changed?"

She stopped speaking when she saw the waiter bringing in a refill for her.

She took a sip and diverted her attention to Sophie. Sophie sat in a posture of eager alertness, ready to join the conversation. She was swathed in a white, plunging-neck cotton sheath, a beat-up denim cap, a vintage silver choker necklace, and a white gold bracelet. A green bindi affixed on her forehead completed her look. Her "sunnies" rested next to her.

"I don't have a mom, so no mommy issues for me." Sophie swirled the lassi in her glass, sampled, and mumbled, "This beverage—it's like, like, what should I say, crazy light. I could get used to this."

"What's going on, as far as this robbery case is concerned?" Hank asked Maya.

Maya took the plunge to bring them up to speed on her meeting with Bea earlier this morning and later with her mother and Neel. Once again, she experienced how hurt she'd been by her mother's attitude and Neel's inexplicable behavior toward her. Only when she put down her glass of lassi on the table with a thud, did she come in touch with that pain again.

Hank's voice brought her back to the present. "You jump-started with Bea Adani and have question marks in your mind about her?"

"Yes. For my next step, I'm planning an accidental meeting with her husband, Rana Adani." Maya paused. "Also, not sure why, I remain curious about Kavi Saha, Neel's father, the astrologer."

"But it's Neel who's turning out to be a bigger asshole, a nut job, a trigger for more suspicion?" Hank said. "And he might provide an explanation as to why your mother cut you off?"

Maya sighed. "Correct. Will you please do a background screening on Neel? Although he's become part of our family and the very thought of prying into his history abhors me . . ."

"I'll get on the Net and chase him down," Hank replied. "Will nose around the college campus where he teaches and see if I can catch sight of him anywhere. Later in the day, I'll check the pawnshops in this area, in the event the ruby's being peddled. That'll be something, won't it? From what I gather, most burglars operate in their own town."

Pleased by the initiative shown by Hank, Maya smiled. "Try the secondhand jewelers as well." Noticing the frown on his forehead, she asked, "Anything bothering you?"

"Well, this place is all hunky-dory," Hank replied, "but I don't get it all. Like that loiterer in front of our hotel. What the hell . . . I see him from our window, camping out on the sidewalk and he's there whenever I exit the building. The guy hangs around, watches all comings and goings, even grins at me."

"What does he look like?" Maya asked, apprehensive.

"A Caucasian like myself, a little older. About 5'9", ginger hair, wears sunglasses, jeans, logo-less T-shirt, and a nose ring. I can't even—"

"Why don't you talk with him?" Sophie's face glowed peachy and youthful. "Or maybe I should, even if he looks like he can be an icky?"

"No, Soph." Hank leaned toward Sophie. "You don't want to get involved. I'll chat him up."

Maya's gaze rested on Hank. "Jot down his timings, if you would."

Hank pulled up his cell phone. "Makes sense, boss."

Maya turned toward Sophie. She clicked with people easily and Maya wouldn't mind a second opinion about the loiterer from her, without asking a direct question.

"What about you, Sophie?" Maya asked. "What have you seen so far?"

"This place is so alive, Maya-di, I'm hooked." Sophie's expression brightened. "You told me about the 'Palace of the Wind,' which I went to visit yesterday. Can't get over the pink-and-red sandstone building. Gorgeous. The guide told us the windows were designed for women to see through them, but no one could see them from outside, which gave them full privacy. How clever.

"That's not all, Maya-di. A bazaar I came across sells all sorts of brass animals, like my cherished goats. Isn't that a hoot? Then too, I'm discovering all sorts of cool customs. The hotel clerk told me that you zap a respectful 'di' to the name of an older sister or a cousin, even someone you've just met. I was like . . . how lit is that? Never had a sis. Now I can have a houseful."

"Tell her about your bindi," Hank said, "your 'life-altering' experience."

"Yes, bindi, lovely, lovely. At first, it felt weird to fix that little dot on my forehead. Even more so when the store clerk called it a 'painted-on third eye' An extra eye? I'm so hype, I'm positive I see more with it, and it's become a 'can't-do-without.'" Sophie paused. "And Maya-di, people are so friendly here. A limousine driver passing by asked if I needed a ride. I was several blocks away from the hotel, would have hitch-hiked and almost said yes, but—"

"No." Maya kept a firm voice. "Never bum a ride from a stranger."

"Totally, Maya-di. Please don't be cringey. By the way, that loiterer Hank mentioned, he's a red flag."

"How can you tell?"

Sophie shifted. "Just like that."

She'd already happened upon an expression that the locals deployed when they didn't want to answer your question. "You're making a guess about the guy?" Maya asked.

"Right, right, Maya-di. My third eye might be helping. For your sake, I'll check him out more."

"Not your job," Hank went. "You stay out of it."

Sophie remained silent for a twinkling. Then, as though wishing to change the topic, she said, "When do we get to meet Uma-ma?" As she hunched forward in eagerness, a single black curl fell over her eyes. "May I call her Uma-ma? From all I've heard she's the best mom in the world. Despite her coolness toward you. I'm sure you'll be able to figure out the reason and do what's necessary to fix things. You know I flipped out when I discovered the sidewalk flower stall next to our hotel. Oh, the colors, scents, and designs. They sew fresh marigold heads into bright orange garlands and put them a pile for selling. It's a scream. I'll buy a garland for Uma-ma, drape it around her neck, then bow to her, another lovely ritual the hotel clerk dished out."

"Well, I have a fancy for arranging a get-together with my mom." Maya heaved a sigh. "But first, I want to be convinced she's alright, and she wants to see me."

"How're you going to accomplish that if she's not answering your calls or texts?" Hank asked. "And if Neel won't let you in?"

"Well, that's where my boss Simi comes in. I'll buzz her and ask her to recruit a spy to trail both my mom and Neel. To find out what they're up to. I'll ask her also to contact the building superintendent to ensure Mom's safety. Simi has her ways. I'll be on alert myself."

"I totally follow," Sophie said. "It's not going to be, like, easy."

Maya stood and made a thumbs down gesture. "Never in my wildest dreams did I think that I'd have to shadow my own family."

SEVEN

DAY 2

MAYA GLIMPSED HIM ON THE CENTRAL PARK'S running track. Past the sanctuary of a flower garden, through the morning's vivid yellow sunlight, with a pigeon swooping through the air, he approached her from the opposite direction. Looking handsome, if a tad distracted, he ran at an even pace. His forehead shone with sweat.

She'd struck it lucky, this being only her second day in Jaipur. Picked the right day and time to meet with the ruby owner and the town's "heartthrob." Her goal was to get acquainted with Rana Adani and form an alliance with him, even more crucial now that she'd lost touch with Uma and Neel. The very thought of her family gave her the blues.

Compact and well-built, of average height, appareled in dark green shorts, a pale green T-shirt, and black racing flats, Rana was recognizable from his pictures on the internet. Maya, clothed in black running capri pants, a matching T-shirt, and lightweight trainers, had come prepared for this encounter. She churned her legs, reached a speed faster than his, turned a bend and sped up even further.

Then came the perfect moment to exploit an element of shock. She flew at him, crashing into his muscular chest and, for a brief second, as they stood face-to-face, there existed hardly any space between their bodies. As though they were dancing together. She could smell the salt in his sweat, hear his breath, and read his mind. Her thoughts froze.

He caught his breath and appeared to come to terms with the intensity of this encounter, his face brightening into a picture of joy and wonder. She paced back, tried to look apologetic, grabbed a tissue from her pants pocket and dabbed her arm, while trading glances with him. Up close, his features—oval face, thick eyebrows, small dark eyes, a prominent nose, and wavy black hair—didn't add up to perfection. Yet this suave enabler, confident in how he presented himself, influenced women. She concluded so from the current that had run through her, the slight disorientation she felt.

Ruddy-cheeked, he laughed from the shock, then said in a voice rich and resonant, "Pardon me. I wasn't paying attention."

"It is I who should apologize. My fault."

He smiled, a well-bred smile, focused fully on her. "I suppose we're sweat buddies now?"

How approachable he must appear to women with his easy manner; his was a shoulder to cry on. She returned the smile. "I was going too fast."

"Like they say, speed gets you to the future faster." He paused and caught another breath then, appearing not to waste any time, "Well, it's not every day you speed into a beautiful woman. What's your name?"

"Maya. I'm visiting here."

"A pleasure. Rana."

"By the way, I like the name Maya. From what I grasp of the Hindu cosmology, Maya is the goddess of illusion and creation, the source of energy and light."

She hid her inner amusement. "Flattering, I should say."

"Suppose as part of my apology, I take you out for afternoon tea, no illusion, Maya?"

He was hitting on her and that was quick, but fortunate. In this town, afternoon tea was considered a leisurely affair, which would allow her to engage him in a more intimate exchange. In the next instant, a small rebellion from inside struck back. He might be playing a game of his own. *Let's wait and see what happens*, she argued with herself.

"That'd be lovely."

"How about this afternoon at four?"

Her gaze veered toward the bamboo grove. She could feel a flush of color thumping on her cheeks. "Where?"

"At Delia's."

She'd heard about the place, but never been there, the most fancy-schmancy, the most romantic tea establishment in the city, with the motto "It begins at Delia's." Some customers said they infused their chai with an aphrodisiac. Others insisted it was their cozy, quiet, semi-dark environment that did it. It even had a dress code of "Smart, casual, comfortable." Why there?

He must have noticed the question mark in her eyes, for his voice went down a notch. "Are you wondering if I'm a married guy? Yes, I am, I mean I still am, but my marriage is over."

"Sorry to hear that."

"Have you ever been married?"

"Nope."

"For us, it started out with wine, roses, and moonlight. Went on like that, like being in paradise, for a while. We were so giddy, so blissful. She was an actress. Even though she never made it on the stage in Jaipur, I was starstruck. But acting is a fickle profession. She became bitter, a crybaby, called me blue-nosed, goody-two-shoes. Even so, I never would have considered abandoning the ship, our marriage. Then, the day-to-day reality of life intervened. We fought. We made up. We wanted to kill each other." He paused. "Apologies, I got carried away."

"Not at all. Honesty helps."

"Would you—would you care to get together?"

Maya went quiet for two beats. "I'm supposed to ask why me?"

"You're attractive, intriguing, someone I want to get to know."

"Why do you want to meet at Delia's?"

"It's a popular hangout," Rana said. "Most women would ask how soon? But you're different. Does the place interest you at all?"

Maya summoned a smile. "You don't miss an opportunity."

"My chauffeur will pick you up—the directions are rather complicated. You must have noticed how easy it is to get lost here. Okay?"

"Yeah, thanks for your consideration."

"Very well, then." He dug a hand in his pocket and extracted his cell phone, his expression one of triumph. "Where are you staying?"

A pigeon swooped through the air. For a fleeting second, following the instinct of a private investigator, Maya wondered if she should offer such personal details. Then again, to accept this invitation, which might prove to be a shining opportunity, she'd have to do so. Putting the wavering in her mind aside, she shared the name and address of her hotel.

He keyed the information down on his cell phone, pocketed it, and exchanged a glance with her. In that blink, with the tranquility that pervaded the space, she sensed that they were forming an alliance, now only in its initial stage of development.

Rana fixed his gaze on her, diverting her back to the present. "Do you know you look fresh and rosy after a run?" He began a slow jog, turned, and waved. "Later."

Fresh and rosy after a run? Good line that made her smile. She became motionless, gazed at his vanishing figure, and admitted to herself she was excited, curious, and keyed up about this upcoming tête-à-tête. With none other than Rana Adani, the keeper of the ruby, who could be a victim as well, which would be another puzzle for her to bring together. Like they say: "In India, it starts early and moves quickly."

The Park came alive for her, leaves of trees sparkling, voices louder, the path more inviting, and the sun shining on her back. Feeling the need of a tough workout, she curved around and broke into a run.

EIGHT

DAY 2

A T FOUR P.M., MAYA FOUND HERSELF settled on a plush couch in Delia's, a fancy tearoom. First task: She checked out the interior, her habit as a P.I. The same door was employed for both entry and exit, not convenient in her book. The tables, covered with copper-colored, block-printed cloths and lace runners, created a formal ambience. Gold-and-amber tiles on the ceiling added elegance from another era, as did an indoor tabletop water fountain. The light pink wall facing her, decked in a red-and-tan floral tapestry, provided an expensive treat for the eyes. Through a wall-sized window on her left, she could view a well-cared-for bed overflowing with white and yellow flowers. Overall, the dimly lit place reeked of riches, status, and materialism, which added to her discomfort.

She'd taken the time and effort to dress for the occasion by donning a maxi silk skirt in black and a satin crop top in light pink. Both, she believed, were currently in fashion with young Indian women. Her hair fell in loose curls over her shoulders, another popular style.

Rana, positioned across from her, sported a white, mandarin-collar shirt and faded charcoal jeans. He appeared to be in a cheery mood, eyes shining with interest. They traded a few polite sentences. She'd go slow, be friends with him, and only at an appropriate moment quiz him about the family legacy that had gone missing. How much was the police helping him? Why hadn't he hired a private detective on his own?

Her eyes resting on his face, she couldn't control the rapid increase in her heartbeat, accompanied by a subtle sensation in her lower abdomen.

That sensation had to do with Alain, her live-in partner of the past. They hadn't broken up formally. But, for all practical purposes, she'd been single ever since he whizzed out of her Seattle apartment one evening on the pretext of making a business trip to Borneo. That was six months ago. At first, she'd taken it as a routine business affair for a man who bounced from one humanitarian project assignment to another, oftentimes in short notice. But this time, he didn't call or return her phone messages. Only a month later did she find out that he'd been mistakenly captured by a troop of radicals in Borneo, held in captivity for a week, then released. Maya had passed her days in agony and tried her best to get any news of him. Worried sick, she'd also gathered with Simi's help that he'd been injured during his captivity and had spent time in a hospital, that he'd been freed, that he'd returned to the States—but not to her. He had undergone changes in his personality. Needing to build a "new life," whatever that might mean, he'd cut connections with his old cronies—even with Maya, despite months of professing love for her, sharing a household and convincing her it was forever. What a fool she'd been, Maya had thought upon hearing the update from Simi. How could she have fallen hard for someone so unreliable? Sidekicks would ask: *When is he coming back? When will you two get hitched?* She had no answer. To this day, she continued to suffer. Now she imagined strolling through the lonely rooms of her Seattle house, musing about him, and hoping he was safe. She could smell his cologne, experience the texture of his hair as she ran her fingers through it, feel his warm lips on hers. She could see his softly lit eyes. How he'd put his glasses on so he could get a close-up of her face. After his departure, the stuff he'd left behind in her house—a handkerchief, hardbacks they'd read together, a partially filled box of chocolates—all smelled of him, all made the place seem lonelier.

Rana, as though aware of her discomfort and trying to put her at ease, said, "So what else do you do in your spare time? I mean other than running and bumping into strangers on the track?"

Maya gave a short laugh. "My interests are tame. I read, garden, cook, get together with friends and travel." She kept it cursory, unwilling to spill too many details about herself too soon. "What about you?"

His eyes sparkled. "I'm a hunter. Big game hunting is my hobby." He hastened to add, "I do it safely, ethically, and support our government's conservation initiatives."

It might have had to do with his tone of voice, the warning in it or the subdued lighting up above, but Maya shivered. At the same time, she admitted that a certain sense of recklessness about him added to his charm.

The waitstaff, a man in his 30's, stiff and formal but pleasant, appeared with the tea service. With utmost care he placed a silver tray on the table, bending from the waist, making almost no sound. The tray held cups and saucers edged in gold, a rose porcelain pot brimming with chai, as well as platters of accompaniments: triangular vegetable-stuffed samosas, luscious tea cakes, and dainty finger sandwiches. A spicy sweet smell danced in the air and made Maya aware of her hunger. When he vanished from view, she followed Rana's lead, sampled the chai, and dug into the feast, finishing a samosa in no time.

Rana caught Maya's eye. "Hobbies are what we live for. Would you agree?"

"You got it." She took another sip of her chai infused with clove and rose petals, grateful to have the relief of this fragrant beverage. "How did you get into this hobby?"

"It was a gift from my late grandpa, a famous hunter and a formidable person." Rana's voice relayed genuine interest. "At the dinner table, he talked about nothing but hunting, *shikar*, even though—you'd never guess it—he was a strict vegetarian. Nana taught me how to bond with nature. I'd bow before the trees, kiss the earth beneath my feet, throw my arms open to the stars, and breathe all the air I could. He took me to target practice. Told me you couldn't be a real man, couldn't experience real thrill until you've hunted." Rana paused. "I got more than enough shooting drills by practicing on clay targets. Now it's in my blood."

Hunting? For pure joy, while considering it to be ethical? She shook out of the flashing feeling of dread, delighted he had let his guard down. "Isn't hunting banned in this country? I mean haven't wildlife advocates helped pass strict conservation laws to preserve the endangered species?"

"Right on, but you see I work around it. I go on hunting expeditions to rich, forested areas where our indigenous brothers and sisters live. They have permission to hunt and kill."

Agreed, that's a clever way to get around it, but then . . . Maya lifted a tiny sandwich from her plate to keep her hand busy. "What do you kill, if I may ask?"

"Big game—tigers, they're the 'the king of the jungle.' But other animals as well if they're predators, if they terrorize rural communities, which they often do. We need to protect these communities." A smile of satisfaction played on his face. "I get a special permit for that."

"I suppose you have personal safety issues to deal with."

"True enough, but the sheer joy of tracking the beasts makes you forget them. The more dangerous and bad-tempered the beast, the greater the risk, the bigger is your trophy. Last year I was involved in a military-style hunt to capture a tiger called T-X, which had killed a dozen people in a village. We had forensic evidence—footprints, but it wasn't going to be a picnic."

"I happen to remember reading about that in the newspaper," Maya said. "You tranquilized T-X, as I remember. Later, the tigress was moved to the regional zoo."

"Right. I didn't kill her. She was five or so years old, but she meant business. She lunged at me, scared the daylight out of me. It's only an animal, but in that instant, it became bigger, something to conquer. I baited her with buffalo meat, then tranquilized her with a dart gun. What a supreme thrill that was. My blood was up, my eyes were filled with tears. I shook, I was thankful. To imagine that it'd be safer for the villagers to go out at night was a thrill. It was so until such time that a gang of activists wanted to prosecute me." He stared at her. "Am I making you uncomfortable? I'm quite tender if you—"

"No, no, I appreciate having this insight into your sport."

"Let's talk about something else. I'd like you to have a pleasant time. What do you do to make a living?"

She smiled. "Believe it or not, I'm also a big game hunter of sorts, a private investigator."

His face changed color; his lips tightened. "A detective? Are you based in Jaipur?"

"No, I'm from the U.S., Seattle to be exact. Made it here a few days ago."

"I did my schooling in the States. I return to the West Coast at least twice every year on business. My company has an office in Portland, Oregon. I'm also well familiar with Seattle, a city I enjoy. So, what brings you to our fair city?" His eyes scrutinized her face. "Who are you chasing, if I may ask?"

"No one in particular at this point."

"What branch of investigation do you specialize in?"

"Homicides are my ball game, although I'm not limited to that."

"Homicide? You must lead an exciting life."

"I love my job," Maya said.

"I bet you do. I can keep secrets, should you wish to share any intelligence about your current chase."

"If you really want to know . . . I flew here on behalf of a man named Neel Saha, my mom's partner and—"

He cut her off, elation evident in his expression. "You're Uma Mallick's daughter? I see the resemblance. And you already seem to know who I am? So, that collision—"

"Wasn't an accident. I must apologize. I wanted to meet you and figured that'd be the best way—"

He interrupted her with a laugh. "Hey, cool. Shows you're clever and resourceful. You'll go to whatever length is necessary."

She allowed herself an instant to appreciate his compliment, how easily he gave it to her, and formulate a direct question. "I'm interested in figuring out Neel's status. Why did the police throw him in jail?"

"That was a mistake on their part, as far as I can tell—he's off the hook now." Sorrow stole into Rana's voice. "He's a close buddy. I've never been so miserable in my life. He'll get a monetary compensation from me, which should close the incident."

Neel's face flashed in Maya's mind, how upset and bitter he'd appeared, how angrily he'd behaved. "Do you believe that'll suffice for a person like Neel?"

"You're a detective. I can see that."

"I wonder if there isn't more to this than a mere arrest. The police seemed to be interested in him."

He met her eyes. "That has occurred to me, too."

From his open, direct gaze and steady posture, she could tell he was speaking the truth. "Shall we compare notes at some point?"

"Get to know me, Maya. I'll tell you what I see so far."

The waitstaff came around, moving as precisely as before, hoisted the teapot, refilled their cups, and gathered the soiled plates, then marched to the other end of the room.

Maya leaned back in her chair. "Can I ask you something else?"

"What's that?"

"How's the loss of the ruby getting to you? It hasn't come back, which is perhaps as important, if not more important to you, astrologically speaking, if I were to make a guess."

He sighed, looked toward a stone statue on his left. "I agonize over the loss of that gem, our family icon. The astrology angle that you mention is a crucial one. If you wear a gem or own a gem, then you're under the influence of a corresponding planet, which could affect you positively or negatively."

"Tell me more," Maya said.

"Okay, fine, if you want to know. The sun, our sovereign planet, influences the ruby. Not only does its warm waves cure cold and flu, but they also heal other behavioral issues. And believe it or not, they can push a person up the ladder of success in the corporate world. Happened with my dad." Rana snapped a tiny raisin scone in pieces with his fingers. "He became one of the most influential business professionals of his time in Jaipur."

From the heightened expectation on his face, she could tell how much societal status meant to him. "And the loss of a ruby?"

"You can foretell something terrible will happen."

She stared at his stricken face. "That being the dilemma, have you recruited a professional to probe into the theft?"

He shook his head, discomfort evident on his face. "The authorities are involved, as you'd expect—it's our beloved family jewel and priceless—but beyond that, no." He paused. "I'm delighted you came to our fair city. This might seem abrupt, and we've known each other only a short time, but you're already involved in the investigation in a manner of speaking . . . What if I retained you? What if I asked you to catch the culprit who ripped off my most important property? Would you consider taking such a criminal inquiry on? I'll pay you handsomely."

Maya seized a split second to consider this proposal, in what seemed like an interesting turn of events. She pictured Uma—how hurried she'd appeared the last time she'd seen her. It was as though she'd forsaken Maya and taken away the support needed to see the larger issue—that of the missing stone—brought to a satisfactory conclusion. With Neel back in her life, Uma seemed to have lost her motivation in that regard. She no longer needed Maya to stay involved. Even worse, she didn't even wish to speak with Maya. That hurt. Now, Rana, sitting across from her and holding a gentle expression, sought her help in recovering the ruby.

Although pleased, she kept her expression neutral. "What do you want done?"

"Never thought I'd hire a P.I. First and foremost, I would like to get the heirloom back. The real thing. To me. Safely, without damage. It'd also behoove me to know *why* someone confiscated it."

Maya gave a glance at Rana, at his thoughtful face. There was more to him than he'd revealed at first. "The *why* issue is, usually, the province of us detectives," she said lightly.

"A few other questions bug me: Why were they after my ruby? What was the motivation, other than to sell it and make a killing? Where is it now?"

"I'd be happy to help you," she said. "This case intrigues me. Our conversations will remain confidential. But I must make it clear that I'll need your cooperation in order to crack the case."

Rana smiled, made a note on his cell phone, asked for a price-quote and contractual details. She estimated the number of hours that would be required to do the job. They discussed the matter thoroughly. All sounded satisfactory to Maya.

"My assistant will get in touch with you for contract-signing. Welcome aboard." He paused. "So, how can I be of assistance?"

"First of all, I must examine the safe box where the ruby was stored."

"A police officer did a scene search and found no sign of break-ins anywhere. He processed the evidence—fingerprints—and I had high hopes, but it didn't lead anywhere." Rana's gaze darted to a point a short distance away. "The crook wore gloves, it seems."

She noticed his hesitancy. "Even so," she said, "it'd help me to conduct as assessment of my own."

"Ah, yes, well, Maya, it'll be a pleasure to invite you over. I have a good Indian art collection, by the way."

That old trick. "Thank you, generous of you. Should I share my detailed plan of action with you in due time?"

"An occasional update will be sufficient."

"When do I get to see the safe box?"

He glanced at his watch. "Good grief, I didn't realize how late it is. I must get back to the office. I'll have to pop over to Delhi the first thing tomorrow morning to attend a trade convention. Can you wait a few days?"

She couldn't, but having no choice, nodded.

What she'd grasped from this meet-up was that he hadn't given her the full story. His occasional evasive eyes and a weak voice signaled he harbored confidentialities of his own. Yet even though they hadn't developed full trust and it might need more effort to get him to confide in her, he was on her side. They'd formed an alliance of sorts. After all, he'd hired her. She'd officially began her assignment.

"I'll ring you." A flicker of emotion showed in his eyes, even as his voice thickened. "As soon as I get back."

NINE

DAY 2

RETURNING TO HER HOTEL AFTER MEETING with Rana and churning over their conversation in her mind, Maya decided to explore her neighborhood. She started walking down the boulevard. A radio buzzed. From the children's playground on the right, a bright orange quadrangle, what they called a small half-kite, popped up in the sky. Standing on the ground, a young boy, no more than ten, pulled on the line, a hum sound following. A pigeon fluttered nearby.

A glowing LED marquee sign mounted above the front door of an open storefront ahead of her drew Maya's gaze.

KiteWorld

Through a partially opened door, she could see a large showroom—no wonder—Jaipur being the kite capital of India and home for the yearly international kite-sport festival. Unbidden, Samir Gongo sprung up in Maya's mind. As claimed by Uma, Sam, a reliable domestic help, had vanished. Concern for his safety had put Maya in low spirits. Where might he have escaped and why? What knowledge would he be able to impart about Uma if he were to return? And about the relationship between Uma and Neel?

She remembered Sam so vividly. Whenever the domestic helper, a die-hard kite fighter, wasn't cooking, cleaning, or driving

Uma somewhere to run errands, he would hurry to the rooftop. His flying machine—a single-line flat kite, made of rice paper and bamboo—would accompany him.

"You can't help but chill out when your kite gets off the ground," he'd say. "It drifts up and up, the wind doing the lifting for you. You chill out even more when you snag your neighbor's kite down with your string. What a feeling. It's like you own the world."

Maya looked up at the marquee sign again. This kite shop might be a place to inquire about Sam. Her watch said six p.m., not closing time yet. She entered the room, cutting her way through the smell of papers and glue. A banner on the opposite wall said:

It's not just a kite, it's your self-image.

A blue-shirted young man, in need of a haircut, stood at the counter. His thick glasses gave him the appearance of a serious college student.

He did a namaste, saying, "How may I be of assistance?"

"I'm undecided."

"If it has anything at all to do with kiting, Madam, we'll give it our best shot," he piped up, proud eyes turning to the opposite wall. "Kiting is called wind art. We're a full-service shop, offering excellent workmanship, and catering to all fans of that art. You see that red one over there? It responds quickly and flies even when the wind is low. Perfect for beginners."

Her gaze rose to embrace the wide range of shades on the high ceiling—sky blue, royal blue, pink, silver, jade, and gold—diamond-shaped, with various patterns and themes. "A dazzling variety, I must say."

"The plain black and the plain white are considered the most auspicious. That orange, white and green one in that corner— Indian flag colors—is a tradition on our Independence Day. You might notice that many of the kites have social and political slogans, some outrageous, inscribed on them."

So, I see. Eyes on a kite that read, 'I got you,' Maya said, "What does that mean?"

"'I cut yours.' I won. I'm the king of the sky."

"Oh, I also see a picture of Goddess Durga."

"Images of deities are flying off the shelf. Lately, visual artists have jumped into the fray. So, we now have Picasso kites, appliqued kites, and kites with soft drink logo, FYI. We do custom designs. We can imprint a baby's name on a kite. We also have sport kites for operating in high wind speed." Perhaps seeing Maya half-turning, he added, "This week, we're giving a special. Half-price on a pack of twenty-five fighter-kites and three spools. Unbeatable quality, outstanding performance, cheap as it ever gets. Look around as much as you like. Ask any questions you like."

"You see," Maya said, with full attention to the clerk, "It's somewhat different. I need help in finding someone who loves kiting and who's playing hooky."

"Look no further, Madam. We're the biggest kite retailer in this region. Sooner or later, every kite-crazy pays us a pilgrimage. These hangers-on spend so many hours in this room with their playthings that we feel obligated to offer free chai in the back. We also have a separate room where we host a monthly kite club."

It's getting better. "I suppose you know the kite competitors by their names?"

"Not me, personally, Madam. My colleague is on a first name basis with all the elite players."

"Well, then, we call him Sam, short for Samir Gongo. He also goes by the name of Samir-G." *A breath-holding second.* "Might he be one of your patrons?"

"Samir-G?" The clerk knitted his brows. "Sounds familiar. Let me ask my colleague. Be right back."

He dematerialized through a side door. Maya made the most of his absence by further surveying the emporium. It was filled wall-to-wall with fighter kites: diamond-shaped, with a center spine, often made with bamboo, in various sizes. Displayed on racks were accessories: spools of brilliant threads covered with glass powder; handles; streamers; aerial photography kits, as well as souvenirs.

The clerk returned to his place at the cash register. "Guess what? Samir-G is a professional, a big name, and he's in fact one of our champion guys. My colleague knows him and respects him. He's on vacation, she believes."

Maya expelled a sigh of relief. "Happy to hear he's alive and well. Any idea where he might have gone for pleasure?"

The clerk gave Maya's question an instant of rumination. "Could be Jodhpur, Madam, where they had a major kite match last week. Two people were injured during the match, but Samir-G is fine. He'll be back tomorrow morning. He called here yesterday, spoke with my colleague, said he was out of supplies and reserved a few competition items." He took an instant. "Does Samir-G owe you money, if you don't mind my asking?"

"No, that's not it. I want to speak with him."

"A serious crush?"

Maya gave out a short laugh. "That's not it, either. He was employed by my mother until the day he dropped out of sight. She misses him, she's worried about him, and she's baffled. I'm eager to find out why he vanished like that, if he wants to come back to his job and if not, whether he wants his last salary."

"That's kind of you. My colleague said Samir-G didn't seem happy to be going away."

That was bizarre. As reported by Uma, Samir had gone missing while on a short break of a day or so. Now it seemed like there could be other factors involved in his disappearance. Did Samir leave because of Neel's political leanings? Did he become jittery because as a servant he might get caught in it, too? Or was he forced to leave for another reason, which might have to do with the hijacked gemstone? Mystified, Maya fumbled in her purse and pulled out her billfold.

Although she had no need for a kite, she said, "Let me buy your special."

The clerk's eyes came alive. He stepped toward a back room, returned in a few minutes, handed her a package, settled the bill, and did another namaste. "Come back if you need help with anything else."

"May I ask a favor?" she said. "Suppose I give you my mobile number. Could you ring me when Samir gets in here? Without his knowing. I'd like to surprise him. I'll be right over."

The clerk thought for a short time. "Yes, okay, fine. I'll chit-chat with him until you get here. Our new shipment of fast-turning kites in neon colors will keep him occupied."

Maya recited her number, which the clerk keyed in his cell phone. That set her mind at rest, if a little. "I can't thank you enough," she said.

"I don't know who you are, Madam, or what you're after," the clerk said, "My guess is you don't fly kites. That's not what gets your juices flowing. But I like being a part of your mystery."

TEN

DAY 3

A FEW MINUTES PAST ELEVEN A.M., Maya stood in front of her window. She watched the clear sky, a day full of promise ahead of her. A tiny yellow bird hopped from one perch to another.

She received a phone call from the clerk at the KiteWorld. He whispered on the line that Sam, "Our Champion," had turned up and was busy sorting through kites. "Would you like to stop by? Might be your chance to surprise him."

An unexpected bonus, a lucky break. This would be a perfect opportunity to speak with Sam, who could demystify a few things for her, such as his disappearance from the household of Uma and Neel.

She'd already buoyed herself with tea and toast. "Be there in, like, ten."

"One more thing," the clerk whispered. "Our friend seems to have made a large amount of fast cash, which he's carrying with him. Paid in banknotes for a bunch of expensive kites and accessories, talked about living it up in a fancy hotel in Jodhpur that I wouldn't be able to afford, and said he's taking taxis everywhere. Maybe it's nothing to make a fuss about and I'm happy to make the sale, it's profit for us, but . . ."

Who had paid Sam a tidy sum, a housekeeper with a meager income, and why? In her investigative work, Maya had come across

the usage of illicit cash in bribery and extortion cases. How handy
a tool to utilize that often left no trace of its origin or any indication
who initiated the process.

She sensed the tight spot she was in. She couldn't be too explicit
with Sam; she hadn't seen him in a while, and they hadn't built a
bond yet. After thanking the clerk, she collected her purse, flew out
of her room, went downstairs, and exited into the street. Given the
heavy vehicular traffic, it'd be best to hike, which would take her
less than ten minutes, and which would dissipate the tension she
felt in her guts. Easing into a comfortable pace on a sidewalk trembling in the late spring heat, she recalled a few facts about Sam,
affection in her heart.

Besides serving as a household help and chauffeur for Uma
and Neel, Sam, who was also an expert chef, prepared delicious veggie concoctions using his grandma's secret recipes. His
smokey, fire-roasted eggplant sauté perfumed the whole apartment complex and the hallways; it reportedly drove the neighbors nuts. An octogenarian grandmother, whose name was Ash,
short for Asha, had even asked Uma to fire Sam, saying, "Can't
stand all these spicy aromas. I have no taste buds left. Are you
trying to torture me or what?" Uma had smiled. She'd provided
Sam with room and board and a fair wage, almost double the
going rate. She described him as "Sweet and loyal, a person I can't
do without." Her apartment complex boasted separate quarters
reserved for domestics and Sam, a bachelor, occupied a tiny cottage, never too far away to answer Uma's calls. Uma offered him
a sense of belonging—a shy orphan boy from an obscure village
near Kolkata who'd never graduated from high school and who
had few friends. Which was one of the reasons Maya believed
accounted for his loyalty. The only luxury Sam indulged in was
buying kites and paraphernalia, and someone had taken advan-
tage of that vulnerability of his.

Upon noticing Maya enter the shop, Sam, standing by the cash
register, turned and drew nearer. A pleasant expression of amazement lighting up his face, he did a namaste. His tone turned happy

and light as he said, "So good to run into you, Maya-di, and in a kite shop, no less. When did you arrive?" Although they were about the same age, Sam always added the suffix "di" to show his respect.

"Two days ago," Maya said. "Let's go sit down and catch up, shall we?"

They shared a bench in the back of the store's high-ceilinged showroom, where a faint scent of glue infused the air and where they could hear conversations of other shoppers. Maya turned to Sam. Strong of build, compact in size, his height average, Sam sported an oily skin, a mustache, and an endearing face. He carried a jovial air about him, a man easy to get along with. From his lean toward her, his sparkling eyes, and a pleasant smile, Maya could tell that he liked relating to people. Yet there was a sense of holding back—of not being completely candid—a hesitancy. Next to him rested a large package, proof of his purchases and the wad of cash he must have exchanged for it.

"New toys?" Maya asked.

"Yes and a few accessories, like carabiners. Those things come in handy when anchoring a kite." He waited a moment. "I'm surprised to see you here, by the way. Should I assume you're on a case?"

Maya nodded. "I was hired to find a ruby of enormous value." She checked for his reaction. A small shock rippled through him, while a quiet tension pervaded the room.

Through the window, Maya observed an automobile, which initiated a brake at the last minute for a lumbering, thick-horned bull and allowed it to cross the street before proceeding with its journey. It was a near-miss, enough to unsettle her. She took a second to blink, swallow and pull herself together. "How're things going for you?"

"We kite-freaks are the happiest people on earth, Maya-di. We have our feet on the ground, but eyes high up on the stars. Our paper airplanes take over the blue beyond, a joy for us."

"Is blue your favorite color?"

"Beyond doubt, Maya-di. Blue, infinite consciousness, God Krishna. What could be better than taming your blue bird, listening to the buzzing sound it generates, even if my uncle calls it a childish obsession and asks me to give it up? For me kiting is an expression of joy and freedom, a form of empowerment, so much so that I consider me and my kite as one. Other kite pilots, operating alongside mine, must feel the same."

"Does it ever get cutthroat, pardon the pun?"

"Funny you should ask, Maya-di. Yes, it does. Lately, I might as well confide in you, I've had a few off moments."

Maya noted his guarded tone. "Such as?"

"Someone's on my tail." Sam blew out a sigh. "It could be a rival or, more likely, someone's accomplice, quite likely a shady character. Dark clothes, sunglasses, bulky, with a bad body odor, projecting a malevolent intent. Never too far way. I feel a shiver on my back whenever he's in the vicinity, even if I don't spot him. For all I know, he's waiting outside this store."

Uh-oh. We're on to something here, even though it sounds creepy. "Go on, please."

"My hypothesis is this. That lad has been sent by a competitor, whose game is 'Who's the alpha kite captain here?'"

"In other words, someone who wants your glory?"

"Could be. You see I won the regional championship two years in a row. That's partly on account of the wind goddess who favored me. Hell, I won also because I'm dedicated, I practice hours on end, I love the sport. That has pissed off a few people. Believe me, I can't help it. When I shake a kite, it comes alive, my hands throb and soon I give myself and my kite over to the vast open space, to the sky goddess. I become bigger and lighter, pure contentment flowing through me. Another incentive: If I win the regional five years in a row, then I'll pick up a special gold medal. So far, no one has achieved that."

"Impressive. Are you on guard?"

"You bet, but not too much. My kite, my daily practice, occupy my waking hours."

Upon noticing that Sam was fidgeting, Maya decided to change her approach. "Tickled to hear you enjoy your hobby, but why on earth did you vanish like that?"

Sam looked puzzled. "Vanish?"

Maya observed him closely. "That's what I heard from Mom when she phoned me in Kolkata. She said you'd disappeared—she was quite distraught."

"Distraught?"

"Yes. Not only do you manage her household and drive her around, but also you mean much to her. She cares about you, she's happy to have you around. It upset her that you asked for a day or two off and got the time off, but you didn't come back. Let me ask you this. Were you unhappy working for my mom and Neel? You've been with her a long time."

"I work for her happily. Most domestics can't stand their bosses. The stories you hear—how they're underpaid, treated like dirt, and given only leftovers to eat. How their salary is withheld if there's the slightest disagreement. How they get beaten up by the kids. Me, I never complain. Nothing of that sort ever happened to me. My condition is excellent. I work when I work. In return, I get caring and respect, earn a good salary, even get medical coverage. Best of all, I get time off to go kiting whenever I like. I'm always euphoric when I get back home."

"Then why didn't you return from your mini vacation?"

"Hang on a minute," Sam said. "There must be some misunderstanding here. I was told to go fly my kite, so to speak, and paid to leave town."

Maya was getting somewhere. Her breath on hold, she said, "Who paid you? My mom?"

He almost gagged. "Negative. She's the sweetest lady on earth, although she has plenty of issues at home. There are times when she looks upset and I'm not sure why, but she's always been kind to me."

"Her issues with Neel? What can you tell me about it?"

"Well, people change, and Mr. Neel has changed. He used to be open and friendly. Lately, he seems distracted and short-tempered.

He's broken bad. He must be doing something wrong. The flat becomes dark when he's around."

Sam had avoided answering her question fully, although provided worthwhile information. Maya would travel another route. "Would you mind discussing the ruby?"

"Don't mind at all," Sam said. "All I can say is this. I don't know about your belief system, but to me an object that's gone from you no longer belongs to you. You must let it go. With all your heart and soul. That's what Mr. Rana should do. He should forget the whole burglary episode and go on with his life."

Another superstitious person—or perhaps it was human nature to justify a loss. It could also be smoke screen. Now Maya caught on. Nobody would tell her the true story. She bit her bottom lip in frustration. "There's a difference here, wouldn't you say? For the Adani family, the ruby was a treasure, a family icon. They can't let it go so easily."

"Difference? I'd say that we're not that different from each other. We're each nothing but a gust of air."

"What does that mean?" Maya asked, aware that he was talking in riddles, perhaps in an attempt to distract her.

"Pardon me—it's a kiting metaphor. To be blown away. To be done away with. Never to reappear."

"Metaphor aside, who sent you on vacation?" Maya asked. "Who are you in contact with?"

Picking up his package, Sam hopped up from his seat. "Oh, darn. I have to leave now, catch a train to Jodhpur."

Maya stood. "Didn't you just return from Jodhpur?"

For a bit Sam eyed a pair of customers at the cash register, arguing about their bill. Voice low, he replied, "Got you. You see I'm not supposed to show my face in this town."

"Who asked you not to?" Maya asked, bursting with both dread and curiosity.

"Like that only."

That local expression was a way of not wishing to answer a question. His artifice indicated that he was much more enmeshed into the mystery of the whole state of affairs than it had initially appeared.

"What would happen if you did?" She stopped speaking when she caught him holding up a hand, palm facing her and smiling.

"Ah, that's for the next time, Maya-di."

"Please be extra alert," Maya said. "Don't let a gust of air knock you down. That's also a kiting metaphor, isn't that so?"

"Yes, I'm honored that you looked for me, found me, and expressed your misgivings." His gaze floated toward the kites on the wall. "I can see you're doing your best to protect me and others. For your sake, I promise to be back in a few days, at most a week, trouble-free, if my luck holds."

Was this man standing before her and not quite able to meet her gaze in trouble himself or was he a source of trouble? Maya produced her business card. "Ring me when you're back. Let me have your number as well."

He recited his number and she keyed it in her cell phone. Bowing slightly, he did a namaste, then said in a shaky voice, "Please be careful, Maya-di. I mean this. This town . . . well . . . And please watch after Mrs. Uma. She could be in danger. I beg you. Okay?"

Maya, caught off-guard, said, "What? What are you saying?"

Without offering a reply, he trotted out the door into the bright sunshine. Maya experienced an odd feeling in her gut—that a skeleton lurked in the closet, that he might be in a jam, that Uma might have a trying situation at home. Maya herself might be in a fix and that he was trying to help her, and she shouldn't let him go.

As an afterthought, she extended a hand and called out after him in a desperate voice.

She received no answer. He merged into the crowd, soon swallowed by a sea of dark hair.

AFTER TAKING A FEW MOMENTS TO calm herself, standing on the sidewalk in front of KiteWorld, Maya texted Hank. She asked him to do a web search on Samir Gongo—anything he could find. She needed to understand Sam better and figure out his role, if any, in the ruby burglary. Why did he hint that Uma might be in danger and that she herself was vulnerable? What should be the next step?

Then and there, Maya called Ash, Uma's next-door neighbor. She hoped to pump Ash about Uma's home situation.

Ash sounded pleased to hear Maya's voice and exchanged a few polite remarks with her. "Haven't seen you much," Ash said eventually. "Now that you're in Jaipur, I thought you'd be over at your mom's place all the time."

"Wish I could have," Maya said, suppressing the sorrow in her voice. "But my mom . . . strange she doesn't seem to want to see me, doesn't return my calls. Not sure what's going on, but it hurts."

"Since you mention it, I've noticed a strange phenomenon also." Ash paused, as though to collect herself. "Okay, I'll share with you. That beautiful blue sapphire ring Uma wore, and which looked gorgeous on her . . . have you noticed she's not wearing it anymore?"

"Yes," Maya said, without revealing her concerns about it.

"Are you aware that sapphire is governed by the planet Saturn?"

"And so?" Maya asked, unsettled.

"You may find it hard to believe, but many of us dread that planet. It's dark, moody, troubled. It brings disharmony. And who knows what else?"

Maya said, "I'd appreciate it if you'd tell me more."

"I'm an old woman and these are ancient facts, often overlooked by the younger generation. In my mind, they're valid—as true as the rising sun. Over time, Saturn could get disenchanted with the wearer and cause mischief. As a result, a person could court terrible trouble. They could lose their job. Their daughter could run away from home."

"The sapphire aside, Saturn aside, is there anything else you've noticed? How does my mom seem?"

"Yes, I've noticed a good deal. Uma and Neel have been quarrelling lately. I hear their raised voices from my flat, especially Neel's. Oh, the foul words that come out of his mouth. Then, too, I hear doors slamming and someone stomping out. What a shame. They got along so well in the past. They were an ideal couple."

Maya's mouth twisted in sadness. "What do they quarrel about? Do you have any idea?"

"My hearing is going down, so can't tell you." Ash's voice had a trace of hesitancy in it. "I've noticed though that Neel steps out by himself in the evening, leaving poor Uma all alone."

It pierced Maya to discover that their relationship had soured. "Well, Mom loved to invite friends at mealtimes. Her flat would be filled with happy chatter. Does she do that?"

"Not anymore." Ash said, her tone sad. "I'm sure she misses it. I see the melancholy in her eyes. She seems so down, so desperate, but she doesn't say a word about it, doesn't ask for help."

Maya couldn't be sure about the implications of all she'd heard; her stomach turned over. "My mom's used to being a care giver, not a care receiver. Will you keep an eye on her?"

"I will. Uma is one of my favorite people. I don't want to see anything bad happen to her." Then as though to inject a lighter mood to this conversation, Ash adopted an American accent. "Hang in there, Girl."

ELEVEN

DAY 3

MAYA REACHED HER HOTEL, APPREHENSIVE after her brief talk with Ash, distracted even. She consulted her watch: six p.m. Near the entrance she caught sight of the loiterer, a man who fit Hank's description: Caucasian, 5'9", sunglasses, ginger hair. He watched all comings and goings. Upon noticing her curious gaze, he turned and began striding in the opposite direction. Maya followed him for two blocks until she lost him at an intersection. Why did he flee?

Looking around but seeing no sign of him anywhere, she stationed herself at an alleyway. Her ears rang with vehicular noise. It struck her that even after being in India for a few days she hadn't acclimatized herself to all the tumult around. An airplane rumbled overhead, jarring her nerves even further. A few scattered clouds in the sky were tinged with red, purple, and orange shades. The top branches of a sheesham tree on the sidewalk shimmered in the late afternoon light. She scrolled through her phone messages.

Upon receiving a text from Hank, she called him.

"I hunted for info on Samir Gongo," Hank said. "Not much is there, other than him winning the Kite Fighter Championship several years in a row. And a short interview with a newspaper reporter. Sam, the champ, said that his goal was to save up enough funds so he could open a kite shop of his own. He also said it's unlikely to happen in near future. 'I'm a guy who's perennially broke.'"

Maya filed that statement away in her mind.

Sophie came on the line and said, "You know, Maya-di, I dig in the web, too. What makes early-morning kite flying so popular? Well, it's the healthful sun exposure you get. I'll have to ask my dad in Sydney to get out every morning, with or without a kite."

"Thank you, guys," Maya said. A text from her boss Simi asked for a call back. Talking with Simi always helped, and Maya searched for every opportunity to do so. She punched Simi's number.

Simi came to the line, extended a greeting, then asked her to hold. In the pause and because Maya couldn't hear her too well over an old Bollywood film tune, Kal Ho Naa Ho, blaring out of a window, she made a right turn and strolled down a dusty narrow lane. At first, she resented having to move. Then she refreshed her memory: The sidewalks and alleyways in this city, as in other Indian cities, often doubled as workplaces and contributed to its "informal economy." An instant later, she came face-to-face with a loud hawker, who seemed familiar. Rolling his rickety cart through the lane, he sold cotton candy and called out to passers-by. On closer examination, she recognized him; the same stout, acned blind man who had kept his attention on her at the yogurt stand and made her tense. Now he threw her a glare. The man was, without doubt, sighted. Before she could have a word with him, he turned, rolled his cart away and vanished into the shadows.

Who was he? What was he up to? That conjecture troubled Maya, now standing in a dingy lane next to a trash can. A homey, gingery aroma emanated from a nearby cottage.

Simi's voice broke through her preoccupation. "Got a copy of your contract with Rana and looked over it. All seems fine. You're officially on the case. Congratulations." She paused. "Now going back to Uma. From the report I get, she goes in and out of her flat on a regular basis. Hires the same taxi service, the same driver, but she and Neel hardly ever dash out together."

"Whatever the reason is . . . I can't get face time with Mom. She's cut me off from her life. There could be a whole slew of reasons, but I can't seem to zero in on any of them. I fear losing her—I'm having a hellish time. Also . . . I'm wondering and this is hard to believe if my mom's relationship with Neel is in jeopardy. They don't seem to socialize together. Their couple-ness is in doubt." Maya swallowed, ambled toward the other end of the alley. "Could you give me the name of that taxi service? I'll hire the same driver when I venture out. Will pay him extra, so he fills me in about my mom's exploits, but keeps his lips buttoned with her."

"Atta girl," Simi said. "Will get back to you with that detail. I have another call coming. Give me a minute."

Maya's gaze descended on a street vendor. In his sidewalk stall, he sold ornate, hand-crafted sandals, *mojaris*, made from camel leather. Among his offerings was a pair of slip-ons decorated with shells, beads, mirrors, and golden threads, making for an attractive leaf design. What a fine gift they'd make to sandal-loving Uma, if Uma would receive her, that is.

To manage the sadness welling inside her, she stared at a spreading banyan tree a short distance away. Its intertwined branches conspired to tumble like a waterfall on the ground. "Something else is going on here," Maya said to Simi when she returned to the line. "I might as well tell you. A blind man, who's not blind, seems to be keeping tabs on me."

"That tallies with what one of my sources has noticed," Simi replied. "That you're often shadowed."

"Why might I be the subject of a surveillance?" A ferocious-looking stray dog ran past Maya, brushing against her leg, causing her to wince. "Whose toes have I stepped on?"

"It's a common practice around here to exploit a handicapped person to get certain jobs done. You know how sympathetic our people are toward them? They can get away with murder." Simi's voice was laced with concern as she went on with, "Let me ask you this. Who knows you're here?"

"My mom, Neel, Bea, and Rana."

"And Alain."

The very sound of that name pressed against Maya. "You're kidding."

"He's in Jaipur."

The lane disappeared before Maya. A former live-in partner, who had professed to love her, had vanished from her life six months ago. How many sleepless nights had she spent wondering what happened to him? She braced herself for what she might hear next. "Jaipur, of all places?"

"I'm afraid so."

Maya tried to feel the rocky ground beneath her feet.

Simi's sigh was audible over the line. "Are you there?"

Maya steadied herself enough to mumble a yes.

"My informant says," Simi replied, "Alain is trying to contact you."

Eyes stinging, voice turning hoarse, Maya said, "Why doesn't he call?"

"He's afraid you'll hang up on him."

"Why did he decamp in the first place?" Mays asked. "Why didn't he reply to my emails or phone calls? Why did he wait this long? Not that you can answer any of these questions."

"You're right," Simi said. "I gathered this much. He misses you or so he's told his colleagues. He's been miserable these last six months. He can't live without you, et cetera. Let me ask you this. How do you feel about him? You want to see him?"

Maya couldn't steel her angst, nor could she forget the humiliation. "No way."

Simi's sigh poured down the line. "My ex-husband always charmed his way back into my heart and I'd fall for it, but the last time was it. He put me into a bummer. My sinking sense is this: Alain will call you, will want to get back together, he'll be persistent. You'll know what to do." She paused. "As far as it relates to the legwork for the ruby case, where are you? What's your next step?"

"I'm going nowhere with my mom and Neel," Maya said. "Bea has almost disappeared, but I'll keep trailing her to see what she's up to, if she's in touch with Rana. From what she'd suggested I'd have to go deeper with the Adani family. I've been curious about Anita Adani ever since I saw her name on a package to be mailed with Neel's return address. What do you have on her?"

"A fair amount. Anita is the family matriarch, a take-charge type of a lady," Simi said. "Six feet tall, about fifty years of age and thin as a stalk of kalmi saag, and she's similarly bitter. Not the nicest person to have tea with."

Maya allowed the facts to sink in. "Well and good, but what connection does she have with Neel?"

"The lady is hoity-toity and over the top but is also a connoisseur of fine gems and jewelry. She's a fountain of neighborhood gossip. Wait a minute, please."

While waiting and considering the implications, the sun's rays on her shoulders, Maya took a left and strolled down an alley. She noticed a shrine carved out of the rotund trunk of a tree, complete with a miniature statue of Ganesh, a leaf garland placed around its neck. A passer-by, hands folded, lingered before the statue, allowed a beat of silence, then strolled away.

Maya brought her attention back to Simi's voice saying that she was back.

"As the matriarch," Simi said, "Anita controls much of the Adani family's gem stockpile. The family has retained a private jewelry designer, Madan Lal, one of the best in Jaipur. Can you imagine a layered ruby necklace supplemented by 500 diamonds? A sword made of steel and gold, also studded with diamonds. Or a sapphire-dotted turban ornament, highlighted by a 60-carat emerald?"

"All these, but not the Meree Ruby? I suppose, there has been many a family-squabble over it?"

"An interesting angle, which would put Anita on your suspects list, wouldn't it? She could have pirated the darn ruby back from Rana to complete her collection."

"Any other facts about her?"

"A physical fitness buff," Simi said, "she specializes in a form of ancient Indian martial art maneuvered by women warriors in

the past. After studying that discipline with her guru, she claimed
to have gained magical powers. To make the art suitable for busy
modern women, she's modified them."

"Fill me in if you would," Maya said, "about how she's putting
it to practice."

"This is what I got. Thrice a week, she hosts a clan of women
in her house. She teaches them stylized strikes—kicks, punches,
and footwork, all coordinated with breathing—all the while
channeling 'energy' to them. Quite a workout, her students
claim."

"Is it her goal to empower women, given how many rape cases
are reported each year by the Indian press?" Maya asked. "I've
seen headlines."

"Quite. Our women are desperate to get self-defense skills
to better equip them with any physical assault. You can imagine
how popular Anita's classes would be. Hundreds try to get in, but
she's selective about whom she takes on. She can tell by a glance
at a person, or so she claims."

"And the end result of this toughening program?" Maya asked.

"You don't want to mess with her graduates." Simi's voice
was edged with seriousness. "None has ever been assaulted. The
program doesn't mean doing simple floor exercises, either. It
includes footwork and fighting practices. After the students have
completed that part and gained a bit of skill, they polish up on
how to wield a knife and a bamboo stick. I hear they even practice picking up a ball point pen, if nothing else is in sight, as a
weapon. Can you imagine that?"

"I can," Maya replied. "The innocent tip of a sharp-pointed pen
can be employed to strike a soft object, like an eye. Or it can be
thrust into the abdomen."

"No doubt," Simi said. "These ladies are fired up by folklore and
legends about India's warrior princesses of the past. They want to
feel equally strong and powerful. Anita helps them in that regard."

"She sounds like a formidable person," Maya said. "I'd be super
excited to meet her."

"Your mom happens to be her student. They live in the same neighborhood, so it could be a word-of-mouth connection."

Maya swallowed. "My mom is wrestling? That's not typical of her. Do you know how long she's been doing it?"

"A few weeks."

"That's recent enough to make me think she might be trying to protect herself from abuse at home," Maya said. "I also see signs that she's trying to hide something from me. Sooner or later, I'll figure it out and repair our relationship. Anything else about Anita?"

"Although she's mellowed over the years, you mustn't cross her. She's the type who could even set a booby trap to get you, if she becomes suspicious."

"Noted." Maya looked around, no longer at ease.

TWELVE

DAY 4

"**D**O I HAVE A NEWS FLASH FOR YOU?" Hank sounded excited on the phone. It was ten a.m. "Guess who is it about? "Neel?"

"Aye, aye."

"Can't wait to hear it," Maya replied from the back seat of her taxi. "I'm about to drop in on the elusive Bea Adani. Let's talk later in the day. Okay?"

As the taxi reached Bea's apartment building, Maya spied Bea climbing in her Maruti Suzuki and turning on the ignition. On an impulse, Maya asked the taxi driver, whose name was Boman, to tail Bea's automobile. It behooved her to shadow Rana's estranged wife. Even though she'd called her frequently since their first meeting a few days ago, they'd never spoken at great length. Bea always had an excuse. She never revealed much about her daily excursions. Questions churned in Maya's mind: What was Bea's connection to the mislaid ruby if anything? Who or what she might be hiding from?

"Very well, Madam." Boman beamed, pleased to be part of a conspiracy. A man in his fifties, he appeared traditional but wasn't out of it. "I won't let that red beast get away. I have the eyes of a hawk."

They drove in silence, navigating through a maze of crowded

streets. They passed by an upscale white marble temple—pure, pristine, and embellished with gold.

Boman announced that they'd reached the C-Scheme area. "It's a posh colony in the heart of our town," he declared. "Old money, high profile, and mischief galore, just the place for our economic crooks."

All around her Maya could see pastel-washed luxury villas fronted by lavish gardens and shaded by huge leafy trees, although no sign of any mischief right off the bat. Upon noticing Bea parking in front of a multi-story mansion with several balconies, she asked Boman to stop. Leaning back, she donned her wrap-around sunglasses so she could surveil from the privacy of her taxi. Her black jeans and black cotton blouse would also help in making her less visible.

With the confidence of someone well familiar with the surroundings, Bea marched through the gated entrance shaded by a large peepul tree. The white mansion, stylish and modern, towered over the sidewalk. It was fronted by a narrow strip of a formal garden blooming in reds and yellows. Bea strolled to the front door, her feet crunching on the pebbly path. She looked stylish in striped black-and-white palazzo pants, a short-sleeved white top, and ankle-strap sandals with ultra-high heels. A golden scarf shimmered at her throat. She'd prepared well for this encounter.

Her senses awake, Maya watched every detail from inside the taxi. Bea jabbed her finger on a keypad on the wall, then stepped back and waited. A few seconds passed, the front door swung open, and a handsome man, silhouetted by the heavy dark door, answered.

Maya gasped. It was Rana Adani, hair tousled, dressed casually in denim, appearing as though he was spending the morning in the house. He'd lied to her about his out-of-town trip. But then, what did he owe her? Maya swallowed her annoyance. They'd met only twice and even though he'd retained her and given her a green light, he might have reasons to hide from her.

Rana waved Bea in, without seeming jolted, and closed the door behind them. The rendezvous had been pre-arranged, Maya guessed.

She dug out her cellphone and checked the house number on the gate against Rana's address. *I might have known, they match.* So, this was Bea's residence, too, before she became estranged from her husband. What an unexpected development. Bea calling in on Rana, with whom she had had a serious disagreement, ending in a fist fight, and caused them to split. It became apparent: Bea hadn't severed all her connections with her husband, as she'd reported. Or the circumstances had changed. Regardless, Maya had a dismal feeling about that headstrong woman's role in this mystery.

She sat back, trying to reconcile the disparate facts in her mind, but found herself not making much progress. Before long, Bea emerged. Appearing distracted and carrying a small object, she strolled out of the gate. From across the street, Maya scrutinized the object: A wooden box, hand-carved, gem-encrusted, and sporting a floral motif, approximately 6"x8".

What did it contain? Maya caught another movement outside her car window. A masked man materialized from the shadows of the peepal tree and stepped onto the sidewalk. He couldn't be more than thirty, this tall muscular man, done up in a leather vest and a black mask, who took long quiet strides towards Bea. Maya's body tingled as he snuck up behind Bea, slid an arm around her neck and, with a quick motion, snatched the box from her hand.

Bea gave out a small scream, saying, "Hey, you, bastard, give my box back."

The assailant glared at her. "It's mine, bitch."

He was about to throw Bea to the ground when Maya jumped out of her car.

Her stomach heaving, she ran to him, positioned herself, and delivered a karate punch to his temple. Stunned, he lost his balance, staggered, and let go of Bea, who tumbled to the ground. "Give the box back to her," Maya commanded.

The attacker's nervous gaze fell on Maya. He straightened, while managing to hold onto the box. "A tough broad, huh. Stay out or you'll pay for this."

A tug-of-war resulted as they both struggled over the box. Within minutes, the attacker, taller and stronger, won. Smirking, the box clutched in one large sinew hand, he broke into a run.

"Motherfucker," Boman said as he joined Maya in pursuit of the quick-footed bandit, who soon melted into the crowd.

"Drat!" Maya halted, breathing hard, and feeling the disappointment in her tightened chest. "We lost him."

"*Badmas*," Boman said. Bad guy. "Good thing he didn't have a gun."

Maya returned to Bea who was lying on grass, crying, moaning. She squatted down and offered a hand. "Bea!"

Bea blinked, rose from the ground, dusted herself off, and mumbled, "Shit, shit, shit."

"You, all right?" Mya asked.

"That was crazy. Yup, I'm fine, a bit freaked out, only a couple of minor bruises on my hips." Bea allowed an instant to pass by. Hair tousled, tears tumbling down her cheeks, she rubbed her hips. "Heard footsteps behind me. Then came the attack. So sudden, I must have seemed like an easy prey."

"Have you seen the guy before?"

"Maybe, but I can't be definitive."

"That box you were carrying—did your husband give it to you?" Maya asked.

Head low, Bea nodded, wearing an expression of bewilderment.

"It mustn't have been easy seeing him again."

"Right, right, Detective Maya."

"What was inside the box? I could hear it rattling. What were you supposed to do with it?"

"It was a gift." A hint of horror crept into Bea's voice, even as she stared at Maya in amazement. "But . . . but what brings you here? How could you—how could you appear at the precise hour I needed you? When disaster sought me out?"

"Let's talk about that later."

Bea, trying to regain her poise, remained quiet for an instant, then said, "Thank goodness, you saved my life. That *goonda* could have killed me, at least hurt me. He made off with my stuff, that miserable S.O.B. I'm mad as hell."

"We ought to call the police, don't you think?"

"No, you'll have to wait hours for the constables to show up if they even show up—it's only a petty theft. They say, 'We serve, we care,' but they drag their feet. They don't give a shit. They're corrupt—will ask for, oh, a large bribe. Besides, have you heard of police torture?"

"You mean . . . ?"

"Yes, they . . ."

"Tell me then what was in that box."

Bea looked as though a reply was stuck in her throat.

"Look, I can't be of help, if you hide facts from me. Why did you go to see your husband? Did he contact you? Or did you make the initial call?" Seeing Bea stand there with tightened lips and a blank stare, Maya added, "If that mugger keeps track of you and shows up again, it might be worse the next time."

"Detective Maya—it's all hitting me now. Please give me time. I'll explain everything."

"How much time?" Maya couldn't hide the edge of frustration in her voice. "When do we meet? And where?"

"Wait for my call, please." Bea sobbed, plucked out tissue from her dress pocket and wiped her eyes. Slowly, she released her words. "I'm in so much trouble, you won't believe."

Maya eyed the mansion in front of her, the pebbled driveway, the exterior that shone in the arrows of fierce sunlight. A peacock emerged from nowhere and strutted about the lavish lawn, spreading its tail, fluttering its wings. Rana must not have been watching from inside or he'd have come out. "Should we go speak with Rana?"

"No," Bea said in an emphatic voice.

"How would anyone, other than Rana, have the knowledge that you'd be coming over at this time?"

"Easy. That bastard has been stalking me. I'm frequently stalked." Bea checked her watch. "Goodness gracious me. I'm late."

"An Order of Protection is what you need, Bea. It's as simple as that. I want to double-check—"

"I'll be fine, Detective Maya. Forget about that petty crook. Not much we can prove to the authorities. As a complainant you'll never get too far with them."

"Remember there's no time limit in filing a complaint, although the sooner, the better."

"I can't believe you turned up. I don't know how to express my appreciation." With that Bea hustled over to her parked vehicle, climbed in it, and drove off.

A flurry of frustration moved through Maya. She stood for an instant, then mulled over the situation: How to catch that thief who was still at large. How to figure out his intentions. Why was he following Bea? What connection, if any, this incident had with the missing ruby?

She signaled Boman, got into the passenger side of the taxi, and asked to be dropped off at the nearest police station. She had forensic evidence—DNA samples—on her hand, clothes, shoes, and fingernails from wrestling with that mugger, evidence she could turn over to the police and which would be proof enough. Inspector Dev would be back from his vacation in a few more days—the very thought gave Maya a boost—and they would be able to dissect the situation.

THIRTEEN

DAY 4

AN HOUR LATER, MAYA SAT IN THE LIVING ROOM of her hotel suite, dressed in white yoga pants and a mauve blouse. She'd had all she could handle for one day. On the coffee table in front of her stood a vase displaying a floral arrangement in whites and yellows, intermingled with green leaves. The hotel clerk who'd delivered it, said, "A service man dropped it off. Said it was a gift from a friend of yours."

The bouquet added serenity to the room, but also led Maya to wonder who had sent it, and why? Hank and Sophie positioned on either side of her, keeping her company, asked the same question. If truth be known, Maya didn't feel at ease, not after witnessing Bea being assaulted a short time ago, despite receiving these beautiful flowers.

Hank appeared to be well-rested, clad in jeans and a taupe T-shirt that said, *Should I have gobbled that curry?* Pushing his laptop away, he leaned back in his chair. A pink blush on her cheeks, Sophie was attired in a white lacy halter dress, snake-print sandals, and a pearl necklace, a getup stylish enough to go for lunch at a fancy spot.

A ray of sun peeked out from the side of the open window. A flock of black-winged birds made a peaceful arc on the sky. Maya could hear a pig grunting nearby. She shifted her position, hesitating to pull Hank and Sophie out of their reverie. Then, after a suitable pause, she recapped the entire mugging incident involving Bea, all she'd witnessed, and her trip to the police station. Tension mounted inside her as she spoke, her throat constricting.

Sophie's slanting eyes widened. "That's mind-blowing."

"Holy shit." Hank sat upright. "You had to tackle a mugger in broad daylight? Awesome. I wish I could do that."

The enthusiasm shining in his blue eyes boosted her mood. His job as an office helper didn't require direct involvement with a crime-prone locality. Then and there, Maya decided that henceforth she would encourage any initiative he showed in that regard.

"Given some training," she said, "there's no reason why you won't be able to do what I do. When I started out as a rookie, I took on every little job I could get my hands on to learn the ropes."

"I should try that," Hank said, "rather than hang around here. Get a smidgen of experience. I want to make a difference."

Sophie shot up from her chair, swirling her silky black hair. "You're thirsty for adventure," she said to Hank, "you're not up for it. You know your way about cyberspace, I'll give you that, but—"

Hank made a face. "Soph . . ." He turned to Maya and began chatting about the mugging incident.

"Let me order some grub." Sophie skated past them, pulled out her cell phone, and embarked on ordering lunch from the room service menu. "Chole bhatura and alu gobi for four, double order of pakoras. And don't forget eight cham-chams." Pacing the room, she threw out the names of the dishes as though they were her pals. "They must be fresh. What? No kale chips? You don't know how to make them? Okay, okay. Not a disaster. Please send a big pot of chai. Must be extra-hot."

As usual, the darling girl had ordered a feast enough for six. Maya couldn't help but chuckle, now feeling hunger pangs. In times of stress, she paid no attention to mealtimes; this was an exception.

"Sounds like you're stuck on that trail with Bea," Hank said to Maya. "What's next for you?"

"To get hold of Inspector Dev. He should have returned by now."

"Any word from your mom?" Hank asked.

Searching her mind, rediscovering that this was the longest she hadn't spoken with Uma, Maya swallowed, the pain of her mother's neglect reawakening in her. "Nope."

"That's freaky. Not that you need to pile on more complications," Hank said, checking for Maya's reaction. "It's like this . . . I have some scoop on Neel if you're ready to consume it."

From his cracked voice Maya could tell the story about to be delivered wasn't pretty. How much worse could it get? "Shoot."

Hank cleared his throat. "Our Neel was a teenager when he joined L.L.A, which stands for Lakhsman Liberation Army. Which I guess is named after the army of an ancient deity by the name of Lakhsman. Am I correct?"

"You are, but L.L.A?" Maya touched the arm of her chair, unease growing. L.L.A, prominent among India's far-right extremist factions, had been accused of inciting communal riots, among other illegal acts. They'd also been linked with a separatist, ethno-nationalist movement. "Heavens! People are fearful of them, don't want them around. They victimize people in their neighborhoods, hunt for targets of opportunity, and cause property damage. You're saying Neel is involved with them? I'm getting goosebumps."

"It's true. I've cross-checked. They all tally."

Maya shook her head. "Neel and I have talked about all sorts of things, but he's never, not even once . . ."

"Brought up the subject?" Hank said. "Is your family progressive?"

"Very much so." Maya's voice rose in excitement. "When I was growing up in Kolkata, both Mom and I joined in protest marches. We were activists. We supported farmers, teachers, small-business entrepreneurs, and the elderly. Progressives we were, and I assumed Neel was, too. After all, he teaches in a liberal college. That being the case, he couldn't very well show his support of extremism."

Sophie, finished with ordering, pushed her cellphone into her purse, and rejoined them. "You look like you've received some terrible news, Maya-di."

"I'll survive," Maya replied. "Even though it troubles me that Neel belongs to a far-right faction which might be linked to terrorist activities, what's equally worrisome is he hid it from us."

"You're wondering what else he has hidden?" Hank said.

"Without any doubt. Even my mom might not be aware of this bit of history about Neel. Mom would've told me if that were the case. Of late, we haven't spoken and that's a pity, but in the past, Mom never kept secrets from me." Maya sighed deeply. "And Neel—good heavens, he gives the impression of having been goody-goody, a bookish kid, someone for whom life was one long study."

"Quite the contrary." Hank smiled. "The info I dug up shows him as a naughty kid. His family sent him to L.L.A to join their youth brigade."

"Okay, yes, you have a point," Maya said. "Organizations like L.L.A often take in children from disadvantaged families and those who are orphans. In exchange for loyalty, the children are given training in toughness and discipline. Not to mention, they get meals, clothing, pocket money, and quality classroom education."

"It must have been a good match," Hank said. "Growing up, Neel became a body builder. Then he got admitted to the university, topped his class, and showed up in the classroom as a straight-up, funny history prof."

"But his past didn't leave him. He had debts to repay. Is that what you're suggesting?"

"Yep. He stayed in touch with L.L.A, donated a tidy sum from time to time, quietly, as you might expect. He maintains that practice, from all the reports I read."

"Where does the money come from?" Maya said, thinking out loud, concern rising in her mind. "As a college teacher he isn't scraping by, but he doesn't have loads of cash to throw around. And how does he manage to keep his L.L.A affiliation a hush-hush from the love of his life?"

"You're spooked about your mom?" Hank asked.

"To say the least." Maya shut her eyes for an instant. "Mom's so unsuspecting and she's so in love with Neel. He could destroy her."

"What about the ruby?" Hank asked. "And Neel's part in its missing?"

"This is where it gets interesting." Maya frowned. "I don't fully crack it. The lie-detector test he was administered at the police headquarters didn't raise red flags. With no other evidence in sight, the police pretty much winnowed him out as a suspect."

"The whole thing is bloody awful, Maya-di." Sophie's face glowed from the prospect of the upcoming feast. "You look pale. You totally need lunch. They'll deliver the food any time now. Dang, they have a good restaurant here."

"I'll keep searching for more answers," Hank said to Maya. "Believe it or not, I have a good lead on L.L.A. I've managed to contact an informant, who's tight with a bigwig at L.L.A and who'll give me tips."

"An informant?" Sophie shuffled in her chair. "That's dope."

Sophie resorted to the word dope for cool, Maya was aware. "That fast?" she asked Hank. She didn't like what she was hearing. "Where did you find such a person?"

A sudden clunk from the hallway caused Hank to pause for a beat. "You wouldn't believe this," he said. "The loiterer, whom I've spoken with, sent me an e-mail out of the blue. He's a cyber freak, who's aware of my cyber whereabouts. Tomorrow, I'll meet him for a bull session at The Third Cup and find out more."

"Be extra careful." Briefly Maya considered the prospects for fraud in the cyber world. She didn't need extra trouble that might involve her assistant. Now she mentioned her encounter with the loiterer, how he avoided her by running away. "You can't rely on everybody, especially someone you've only met on the street."

"Come on, boss," Hank said. "What harm will there be schmoozing with him over a cup of Joe? The chap is a Westerner. He'll be straight up with me."

"This is India," Maya said. "It can be a jungle when you're a newcomer."

"Like Sydney?" Sophie scooted closer to Hank and rubbed his back. "My chums called me 'around the way girl,' someone who'd mastered her way around. Would it kill you if I tag along? I'm damn curious; I could engage him. Or I could be a gecko on the wall and listen."

"No, Soph. The dude wants to see me alone."

"That's savage," Sophie said, which Maya grasped meant bold.

"Cut it out, you hard ass," Hank said.

Sophie crossed her arms. "Okay, whatever," she replied, pouting.

"Lighten up, both of you," Maya said.

"I've acquired a new word, *achcha*," Sophie said in a silvery voice. "It means yes, or very well, and much more. The word sounds reassuring. *Achcha*, Maya-di."

"*Achcha*," Maya said to Sophie, in a light-hearted mood.

Even though Maya's palm sweated. *For Hank going alone is not a sound idea.* This wasn't an assignment for the inexperienced, but she'd have to let Hank follow his instincts, make his own way. Only minutes ago, she encouraged him in that direction. She noticed a gray shadow pass over Hank's gaze; he must be rethinking, assessing the risks.

"Keep me posted, will you?" Maya said to Hank, her protective instincts rising. "And back off at the first hint of trouble."

FOURTEEN

Day 5

WITH MUCH EAGERNESS, AT ABOUT TEN A.M., Maya called Inspector Mohan Dev at home. Only yesterday, he'd returned from his vacation and gone back to his job. As reported by one of his subordinates she'd spoken with, he had a morning off, having stayed late at the office the prior evening. When he heard Maya's voice on the phone, he said a British-accented cheery hello.

She asked if they could meet in person. After all, he was an old acquaintance with whom she'd worked on a criminal investigation for several weeks in the Andaman Islands. They'd hung out together a few times and kicked around ideas. It was his email that had brought Maya to Jaipur in a hurry five days ago. Even so, she wondered if the police were really interested in the missing ruby case.

"I'd love to have a chai morning with you and catch up," Inspector Dev said. "You've been here five or so days and I'm sure you have a lot to share. Where and when can we meet?"

At eleven a.m., Maya joined him at a small table in a widely esteemed, rooftop, open-air tea joint, named Tea Harmony. It had a view of a nearby park, an expanse of green. On this clear day, white, fleecy clouds hung overhead. A sparrow chirruped. Maya could easily kick back here, in this perfect spot: cozy, fragrant and not too loud, with only a few tables occupied.

The inspector, well-groomed and dignified, wore a checked shirt and denim pants, not his usual khaki uniform. The three-star insignia on his shoulder as well as his khaki beret were missing. He had dark circles under his eyes. He seemed to feel at home from the way he sank into his chair. "You order."

What a pleasure to peruse the menu, which listed a wide selection of teas sourced from the finest tea gardens in India. Maya ordered for both: an aromatic, first flush Darjeeling, a gently sweet, light brew, as well as an accompaniment of savory dhokla squares, made with chickpea flour.

Their order came. Maya tucked into a piece of yellow-hued dhokla, a steamed, spongy, fermented cake, which overwhelmed her senses with its spicy, fluffy, and sour taste. As they exchanged niceties, sipped, and munched more, Maya further scrutinized the inspector. He had a few additional lines on his forehead, more silver streaks in his sideburns, and he'd put on a few extra pounds. Without his uniform, he appeared to be less intimidating, an everyday person. Yet his mustache, which had greyed even more, gave him respectability.

"I worked till two this morning," he said. "I needed this low calory, nutrient dense pick-me-up which, I must say, is also tasty."

Listening to the tinkling of silverware from another table, keeping with the local tradition of not rushing into a business discussion, she eased into the topic. "So, how do you like the Pink City so far?"

"Superior to Delhi." The inspector caressed the top of the table, seemingly in high spirits. "I was offered a transfer to our great capital for a higher-level position. That job didn't feel right. So, I took a salary cut and relocated here. That was four months ago. Jaipur is not a party town. Nor does it have that many 'happenings.' But my kids like it. They've 'anchored' here, or so they tell me." The inspector patted his belly. "The cuisine is delicious. My wife also likes it that there are fewer crimes. Mugging, pickpocketing, harassment, and occasional homicides are about it. This city is safer for women than Delhi, a big deal for her. She feels safe driving home alone late at night."

"Not so fast." A chili-ginger taste played on Maya's palate. "Picture this: a young woman being mugged in broad daylight in the C-Scheme neighborhood."

A look of unease passed across the inspector's face. "Mugged?"

"You better believe it. She's an acquaintance and I witnessed it." Maya recounted the entire episode, continuing to feel shaky from the memory of it, and updated the inspector on her visit to the police station. His expression remained unchanged. "You don't seem too bothered?" she asked.

"Ah, you bet we need to pay more attention. Gang activity in this area has picked up. And so, allow me to compliment you. You reported the incident and submitted the genetic material to my staff. We'll send the evidence to the forensics lab and a DNA profile could result, but it might be days or weeks before we hear from them. The lab is trying to cope with a backlog. Sometimes DNA samples degrade."

Maya steeled herself. She then brought him up to speed on her efforts on locating the nowhere-to-be-found ruby. Eyes wide, the inspector listened to her. She left out Neel's alliance with L.L.A., but otherwise spilled out the details, hoping to be able to tap the inspector for suggestions.

"Yes, the ruby case, Maya, what we call a 'high value' theft case. Even though that ruby is a status symbol, it's more likely an ordinary theft."

"Why was Neel taken into custody?"

Inspector Dev stayed silent for a split second. "We're keeping a watch on him due to his association with an extremist group. I'm not at liberty to talk about it."

So, the inspector was aware of Neel's allegiance to L.L.A. "If the ruby heist is so ordinary, then why haven't you located the freaking object and/or caught the rascal yet?"

The inspector cleared his throat to buy more time. With Maya staring at him, he relented. "Well, since you live abroad and may have forgotten our customs, allow me to do a refresher. Are you aware that our society is a bit superstitious when it comes to precious and semi-precious stones?"

Maya smiled. "Such as, a curse could fall on you, if you mess with a gemstone. Or if you damage it or lose it?"

"Laugh as much as you like, but quite a few of our police force believe it. A ruby is the gemstone of the sun, the 'Lord of the Day' who offers good fortune. Our officers are reluctant to take on the case, afraid that they'll attract bad luck. Their house could be on fire. Their daughter could run away. They might invite a snake bite, get struck by lightning, be hit by a lorry, or be poisoned. For safety's sake, one of my staff wears a *navaratna* necklace. Are you familiar with it?"

"Indeed. Nine gems placed in a piece of jewelry, with a ruby at its center. Often gifted at a wedding."

"That's right. It's the most common example. Let me add a little more if I may. To ensure cosmic harmony on your body, you wear a piece of jewelry on which nine gems are mounted. Our deities are supposed to reside on those gems, their physical places on earth. And, if not found . . ." The inspector raised both arms up in the air and looked up to the sky, as though indicating punishment from above might descend. "No one can predict what'll happen. Do you now see why we're at an impasse?"

Maya averted her gaze to hide her disbelief, the smile appearing once again on her face. *Superstition? Cosmic curses? Deities residing on a piece of jewelry?* A light breeze blew through her hair and distracted her. "For the sake of these deities, if nothing else, who, in your opinion, pocketed the ruby?"

"Perhaps a family member, a person going mad because of the loss of the ruby, acting on an impulse."

"A crime of passion is still a crime."

"Beyond a doubt. Since we aren't convinced at this point of what's going on, we're staying in watch-and-wait mode. Sooner or later, something will break. I haven't checked with my people lately."

"Are you saying you're not as involved as you could be, or this burglary is not your current focus?"

"I have much on my plate, short-staffed as I am." The inspector peered at her. "My highest priority is violent crime—murder, domestic violence, physical assaults. This case . . . well, I do keep track of key events related to it, such as your recent date at Delia's with Rana Adani."

Paralyzed for one tiny instant, Maya reclaimed her presence of mind, concealed her expression, and pasted a pleasant smile on her lips. "Oh, no, ours wasn't a date as such. How did you even hear about it?"

"These days all high-end restaurants have surveillance cameras. We reviewed the footage. You were spotted."

Maya instructed herself not to react, even though she considered this an invasion of privacy. "You're keeping tabs on Rana?"

His tone grew more severe. "Yes, for a different reason, ever since he reportedly knocked his wife down."

Maya, about to take another bite into her dhokla, coughed. After a pause, "The story I heard was she's the one who—"

The inspector frowned down at his tea. "Another version is he hit her first, she retaliated in defense. We don't know for sure. She's newly separated. Her intention might be to hurt his public image."

A rush of wind struck Maya's forehead. "So, Bea might have stretched the truth in her talk with me?"

"Her pride. She couldn't admit to the reality. That woman is a pain in the butt, pardon my language. I suppose she's trying to stay alive."

"What kind of safeguard can she expect to get from the police?"

"Good question. Our motto is we protect and serve. We also honor the Protection of Women from Domestic Violence Act. But let's be realistic. We can't provide round-the-clock security for someone unless there's an immediate threat."

"Are you saying she should hire a personal bodyguard?"

"Exactly. But we're keeping a watch on her for other reasons. She was a dissident in Singapore, had a gang connection there, or so the police there insisted. She hasn't been troublesome in India, so to speak, but it's a precaution, someone to keep under observation." The inspector leaned toward Maya. "On another topic and I don't mean to dole out advice but, if I were you, I would not . . ."

"Please go on."

"I would not meet with Rana Adani again for a social get-together."

Noticing the inspector's shrewd gaze, she blinked back her concern. In a level voice, she said, "Care to explain why?"

"There has been a complaint about him, although nothing has been proven. This is a gossipy town. The current chatter is that our macho guy is a womanizer, charming from all I hear. And he's charmed you from the monitoring footage we came across."

Although a wave of embarrassment washed over Maya, she snapped out of it. "Seems like you're digging around Rana Adani's private affairs?"

"He's also been reported to have slapped one of his dates. She said he's a hotheaded bloke, who loses control, becomes aggressive. You can imagine the rest. We have no proof, however, and the report might turn out to be false. She's a jilted lover."

Again, Maya suppressed any sign of discomfort. She wanted the inspector to continue dishing out vital information about Rana. A direct question would be best. "What do you think Rana's reaction was when he found the ruby missing?"

"I imagine he was devastated. According to Anita Adani, Rana's aunt, the stone belongs to her."

"She entrusted it to Rana for safe-keeping?"

"Yes, and he lost it. He's afraid of her wrath, not to mention embarrassed. She's an elder and he's failed her. He appears to be westernized, but deep within he's like any chap from a conservative family." The inspector threw a sharp glance at Maya. "As I've already said, I would keep that dude at arm's length. Until we gather more information about him."

He'd hit a sensitive point. Her stomach knotting, she said, "Look, I'm a private detective, involved in the ruby case, retained by—"

The inspector cut in. "You're also a beautiful young woman and a foreigner. You don't know your way around here. This is a tough town far as far as it has to do with crimes against women, such as rapes. For your own reputation and safety and my peace of mind, at least for the time being, please don't hang about with Rana Adani. Promise me?"

FIFTEEN

DAY 6

MAYA MADE IT TO THE CENTRAL PARK, located at the heart of the city, before eight a.m. Outside the park's gate, a row of vendors, already positioned in their respective concession stands, sold pastries, chilled drinks, and an eclectic variety of trinkets. A young barber, clad in white, had set up his chair on the sidewalk, his wares—combs, brushes, towels, and scissors—in full display. A cow lazily lay next to him.

She strolled under a dense canopy of evergreen trees, hearing the gravel path crunch under her feet. Although the inspector's words buzzed in her mind, she remained firm in her resolve to speak with Rana in person. The proprietor of the ruby, the man she should stay away from, as claimed by Inspector Dev. With the new development of watching Bea enter Rana's house, not to mention the incident of her being mugged in broad daylight, Maya needed to question him. She assumed Rana still ran here twice a week at eight in the morning. If so, this was the right day of the week at the right time. Would he make an appearance? If he did, would they get a chance to talk? Most likely, yes. In general, runners liked to exercise at a conversational pace. That combined with the natural scenery would be ideal for her to introduce a few potentially upsetting matters.

She made a beeline to the running track—Inspector Dev be damned. The gentle morning sun glowed through the haze; a light breeze tickled her forehead. Yet, despite the pleasant sensations, she felt a deep unease about Dev's insinuation that Rana might be a batterer. She inhaled and assured herself: Until proven otherwise; and time will tell. For now, she'd continue to carry out her tasks as far as they have to do with this crisis.

Upon spotting him, her body flushed with excitement, she took a step back. He ran toward her, clad in a lightweight black T-shirt and camel shorts, face shielding his intense concentration. He didn't move as smoothly as the last time. More than likely, his hamstrings were tighter. Maya, although dressed in a sweat suit in her favorite light blue shade, had no intention of running and colliding with him again. Instead, she positioned herself at the edge of the track, watched a flock of birds flying overhead and drank in their feeling of freedom.

"Maya!" Rana's strong, muscled legs slowed. Awe and delight bloomed on his face, as though he'd half-expected to meet her there.

She stood stock-still. He stopped and faced her. In a voice heaving from the exertion, he said, "Here you are. What a coincidence."

From somewhere came the sound of an auto rickshaw passing by. "A coincidence, indeed."

"Haven't had a chance to call you. Something came up. A crisis in the extended family." He rubbed his eyes as though wishing to erase the incident. "I had to take care of it."

"Shall we do a fast walk?"

He wiped his forehead with a handkerchief, hair tousled by the light breeze. "Perfect. I'm almost done. Finished a fast run."

They speed-walked on the pathway, matching their footfall, a woodsy aroma about them. "Pardon my nosiness," Maya said, "but—but did this family crisis, by any chance, have to do with the ruby?"

His black shirt intensified his dark eyes. "You guessed it right."

"May I ask which family member, if that's not too personal?"

"It's common knowledge. Anita Auntie, the oldest of my paternal aunts and the family matriarch, a volatile person, to say the least. Now she's losing it." Rana went silent for a long moment. "You should have seen her. She had a fit because the ruby hasn't been found. She chewed me out, up and down."

"Did the treasure belong to her then?"

He kicked a pebble in an agitated manner and furrowed his brow. "Definitely not. It belongs to me, the heir to the Adani fortune. And, so, the loss of it—is the worst thing that could happen. Not only do I create the impression of being irresponsible, but also there's a more serious factor here to consider. A gem, as you might know, has tremendous power. It absorbs beneficial rays of the planet it's related to and passes that energy to the owner. The common wisdom is: Don't trifle with this so-called power. It can bring a windfall to the owner but can also turn his or her life upside down, if mishandled, or if underappreciated."

Off in the distance, a dog barked. Good heavens! Yet another party who believed in the supernatural power of a piece of rock. Planting her feet on the gray pathway, she turned toward him and studied his eyes. "You believe that?"

Rana went silent as a knot of three young women, coming from the opposite direction, wandered past them, chatting, and laughing. He appeared as though he was attempting to eavesdrop on their conversation. When they were no longer within earshot, he replied, "Let me put it this way. I've gone to school in England and the U.S., seen the world, been part of the social scene. Our family firm employs people from all over the world and I stay in touch with them, even befriended a few. But I've observed happenings here at home that aren't explainable."

As she took another step, a leaf from a tree dropped in front of her. "Where did your family purchase the ruby from, if you don't mind telling me?"

"Not at all. My late father was always on the lookout for trinkets when he traveled abroad, which was often, and brought back unusual souvenirs. Oddly enough, once when shopping here in Jaipur, his hometown, on a Saturday evening at a jewelry showroom, he spotted a large, priceless, blood-red ruby. *A ruby should be purchased on a Saturday evening; and only if you're in a tranquil state of mind*, he told me later, due to the position of the planets. All of that had coincided."

Maya viewed a wash of amber sunlight spreading over a flower-bed. "What else did he watch for?"

"Brilliance, hardness, and a lustrous quality," he said. "The color should be deep, rich, and intense, but transparent—red with a blu-ish tinge. Red as a color is revitalizing, he believed. Sitting on a stool in that jewelry showroom, he felt energized. Also, observing the stone under proper light, he caught sight of a six-pointed star, an optical phenomenon called Asterism. He fell in love with the stone—'the fire in my heart' and the visual effect it had created, he'd tell me later. The stone had been mined in Myanmar, hadn't been treated with heat to improve the color, and had been owned by a single family."

"Which family?"

"Oh, Maya." He shrugged, sighed, blinked. "I don't have an answer to that."

Wondering whether he might be hiding any facts regarding the ruby ownership, she posed a direct question. "Why would that family trade such a precious item?"

Rana sighed. "Okay, I'll tell you and you'll be the only one other than me who'll know this story. After my dad's death, I happened to locate one of his personal journal notebooks. Buried in the attic under a stack of papers, it was marked Volume Five. A page in the notebook revealed that the ruby was a loan, only a loan, from an unnamed family. They needed the funds, being in a desperate finan-cial bind, and leased it out, with the assurance that they'd get it back."

Exciting discovery, leading to new questions. "It was a loan then," Maya said, "not a purchase."

"Correct. My dad put the gem in a safe box at home. Every so often, he'd sit in a chair, hold the 'red beauty,' and contemplate its qualities of energy, passion, and motivation."

A bird danced through the branches of a tall bush. "Did he get benefits?" Maya asked.

"Lots. I was young then. He'd tell me that soon after he acquired the gem, he found himself fired up. He'd put in long hours but didn't become fatigued. His business doubled almost overnight. He'd laugh and add that ghosts and evil spirits stayed away from him. He attributed these takeaways, as you can guess by now, to the gem's supernatural powers."

"That's why he decided not to return it to the rightful owner?" Maya said.

"That'd be my guess."

"What about you? Have you ever considered giving it back if you could locate the right person?"

Rana exhaled bleakness and frustration. "Yes, I'd considered that option when I had the ruby in my possession. It tore me apart to think how much that family must want it back. How they must have been struck by one mishap after another. Deep down, I felt their pain, their suffering, what they might be going through. The truth of the matter is the ruby belongs to them. Not me. I'm only a temporary safe keeper. Yes, I'd give it back.

"However, I have no idea who that family is, where they live, or why they had to 'loan' the ruby. I never was able to locate my dad's complete set of journals. Regardless, I quietly contacted a few premium gem dealers in the state and offered a reward for any effort that led to locating the original ownership. Since the transaction took place years ago and the details were neither put in a record book, nor digitized, they found it impossible to trace. In any case, the transaction details are legally required to be maintained for only three years. It's way past that. That put an end to my search. Not sure why, but I haven't given up hope."

Here was a different side of Rana, more trusting of her in sharing this confidential information. He sighed deeply, a tender look in his eyes, a man less preoccupied with his business endeavors, seemingly possessing compassion and kindness for others. Could this be the real person beneath the Adani glamor? She changed the discussion to another topic. "Did your dad ever have the stone mounted?"

"No. That'd be an impulse, wouldn't it be? Dad believed that a loose stone allowed you to appreciate it better. He would open the safe, stare at it, pick it up and caress it. He washed it in milk for a cleaning ritual and meditated on it. He kept the safe box open, so he could stare at it throughout the day, so the ruby would wink at him, whenever he happened to pass by it. A direct contact, even a split-second eye contact, transferred the stone's power to the viewer, he believed. On special occasions, he'd do a puja worship service by placing a lamp, fresh flowers, and an incense burner near the stone." Rana gave out a long sigh. "He followed that routine till the end of his life. When he passed, I assumed his business responsibilities. I also became the custodian of the stone.

"As mentioned by my dad, an important aspect of gem ownership has to do with how to match a gemstone with a person. Dad believed that a person's date of birth suggested the selection criteria. I'm a July baby. Ruby, the sun, happens to be my birthstone and so Dad was more than happy that I'd own it someday. Ruby has the color of love and passion. It's also called Ratna-Nayaka, the top gem player. All other precious gems are considered side shows."

"What else does your ruby do?"

"First, it puts a protective shield around you." Rana smiled. "Second, it welcomes romance into your life. They say that if you're a lonely soul or have a broken heart, wear a ruby. You luck will change overnight. Your phone won't stop ringing. Love notes will pile up on your mailbox. Women will chase you no matter where you go. And you'll get gifts galore. There is a flip side to it, however. Lose your ruby and in no time your relationships go down the drain."

You want me to believe this? "Did Anita Auntie ever possess the Ratna?" Maya asked.

"She did, for a period after my dad's death. Said she believed only women in the family should inherit family jewels. Also said the piece was promised to her. Not true at all. Too worn to quarrel with her, I let her have my ruby for a short time. She wouldn't return it. As the lawful heir I claimed it back after several months of legal battles in accordance with the law."

For an instant Maya listened to birdsong. "Your aunt—how's she been affected by the loss of the stone?"

"I don't mind telling you, Maya. Anita Auntie—a fit lady in her middle years and attractive—is famous for the exercise sessions she holds for women. They call her the 'Guru of work-outs.'" A brief smile appeared on his face. He seemed to both admire his aunt and hate her. "She's busy in her spare time as well. A single woman, mind you, the lady has more lovers than anyone can keep track of. Carries at least two cell phones in her purse. Neighbors gossip. The whispers, the wackiest ones I hear, are she's insatiable. My aunt! Chatting with her the other day, I found that for reasons unknown, her lovers have receded from her life. They don't call, email, or pop up at her doorstep like before."

"And?"

"She's going nuts. Wants to get the ruby back to her own vault. Could kill someone, if that was required to get the stone back, or so she insisted. But I can't help her. I don't possess the ruby anymore."

"I suppose she blames you?"

"Precisely." He narrowed his eyes. A tremor passed through his body, as though his veins were throbbing in anger. "'Find the god-damned gem,' she screamed at me. 'I'll have it mounted on a ring and wear it twenty-four hours a day.' When I said I had no idea where it went, she came at me, spat on me, and almost hit me. Hurled obscenities that I don't want to repeat."

"What about you?" Maya said. "How has the ruby's loss affected you?"

"You're asking about my love life?" Disappointment rang in his voice. "It's in shambles, a shithole, one might say, ever since my wife walked out on me."

Shrieks of laughter came from a short distance away, where uniformed school children tossed a ball around. "Didn't your wife stop by your house the other day?"

A stunned expression swept over his face. "How do you even know? That's my personal business."

"As a P.I., I make it my business to study other people's business. And since you've retained me . . ."

At first, he went speechless. Then, with a warm gaze at her, he said, "Yes, she did come to pick up her jewelry box. And, no, we didn't kiss and make up. I'm saying so on the assumption that you're curious. She stopped by for less than fifteen minutes."

"Would it astonish you if I said that she was mugged on her way out? Lost her jewelry box to a mugger?"

His eyes blazed with anger. "What the hell. Mugged in broad daylight in front of my house? Our neighborhood is considered a VIP district."

She breathed in the stuffy warm air, feeling the arid, rocky ground underfoot. "The police didn't come to your door and question you?"

"No, not for a petty theft. If it's any consolation, there wasn't much in that box. Only a piece of imperial jade, her mother's gift— one of sentimental value and the accompanying belief that it prolonged life." He paused. "Was she okay? Did you talk with her? Where did you meet her to begin with?"

"She's fine." Maya relayed the details of the grab-and-run theft, stressing the fact that she'd reported it to the police. As she spoke, she wondered once again if the assailant was a career criminal hired by someone. Was he motivated by greed? Or did he have another rationale for stealing, which might open a window to this case?

"Good heavens. I must warn Anita Auntie." Rana's eyebrows crinkled. "She's over-the-top, even goes to the market draped in jewelry. She says she has no idea whom she might come across. Doesn't realize it's not safe to be so ostentatious. But, as you can see, our Indian women weigh themselves down with jewelry— necklace, earrings, nose rings, bangles."

"Each piece has special meaning. Women get them as gifts."

He said playfully, "Any idea why a necklace is worn?"

"Yes. A necklace lies close to the heart. I'll let you finish it."

"It protects the heart," Rana said. "Your turn."

"Makes the wearer more loving."

"Right you are," Rana said. "Flowers and kisses. Tradition, devotion, or status symbol, whatever is the reason for wearing jewelry, the best is love. My auntie is no exception."

"Any way I could meet her?" Maya asked, turning a bend. "Maybe watch one of her classes, see her in action, speak with her afterward?"

"My aunt is pissed at everyone, including myself. I won't be blown away if she's rude with you if you try to drop in on her. Well, I suppose I could arrange an appointment for you. Might take a few days. She's visiting a cousin in Mumbai." He stopped, dug his cell phone out of a pocket, keyed in a note, and resumed walking.

A gust of air trembled the trees. "Without Anita Auntie suspecting that we've talked, I hope?"

He nodded, stopped walking, and stared at her. "This is where I peel off. Would you like to have dinner with me this week? We can continue our discussion. I must say I enjoy our talks." Receiving no immediate reply, he added, "What's the matter? You seem to . . ."

"If you must know, I've been warned."

Shock blanched his face, even as his steps slowed. Voice rising, he said, "Did you speak with your police pals? And those morons told you I'm a batterer? Oh, Maya, please don't listen to what they say, which is rubbish. They're always casting about for a scapegoat. This time it's me. Which is why it's important for me to have you involved in this undertaking."

In other words, he wanted her to be on his side. To protect him. To share all she'd gathered. To lead him to the ruby thief. Even more so now that he'd had a fallout with his aunt. "To dig deeper, I'll need your assistance."

"At your service."

"It'd be of interest to me to see the safe box where the ruby was stored."

"No sweat, it'll be a pleasure to invite you to my house. Let me call you later this week. Can I ask you something?" He paused. "Are you involved in a relationship right now?"

Maya thought for an instant about Alain. "Well, to speak the truth, I'm not sure. I know that's an odd answer . . ."

"I'm not ready for a relationship, either."

"Shall we be colleagues, who are also friends?"

Rana nodded, eyed her fully in the face. "Glad to have run into you, Maya. Cheerio." With that, he turned, waved, and headed toward the wrought-iron fence where the exit was located.

Watching him vanish, she harbored second thoughts: Should she meet with him at his house, where they'd be alone together? Well, she had had self-defense training. Despite that, Inspector Dev's warning screamed in her head: *For your own reputation and safety, don't go near Rana Adani.*

In the pleasant breeze that blew, she found herself somewhat disbelieving that warning. She was beginning to see a different side of Rana. In any case, did she have a choice? Both Rana and his house held secrets she needed to decode.

SIXTEEN

DAY 7

WHO GOT AWAY WITH THE RUBY AND WHY? How much trouble it had already caused. At nine that morning, Maya, her mind focused on how to retrieve the stolen good and from where, heard a knock on the door of her hotel room. She opened the door, said good morning to Hank and Sophie, and welcomed them in.

Hank was squeezed into a T-shirt that said: *Left unsupervised*. Sophie was outfitted in a flutter-sleeve yellow dress and intricate filigree gold bangles. In keeping with the Indian tradition, she'd tucked a white flower bud behind her ear. A smile flickered on her lips. "Hiya, Maya-di."

In the week, all three of them had been here, breakfasting together had become their tradition, a pleasant pattern. This was the hour during which they caught up on each other's daily activities. Only after that, they'd discuss matters related to the ruby case. Aware that Hank might have input, Maya remained extra alert.

They took their seats. Volume low, a Bollywood dance number played on the radio.

Sophie declared she'd already ordered a regional specialty called dal-baati-churma. "You haven't seen Jaipur until you've tried their signature chow-chow." She changed the topic then. "Indian women are so stunning. They dress so well. How can I dress like them?"

Maya named a few boutiques. She suggested that Sophie got herself fitted for lehenga-choli-dupatta, an outfit favored by young Indian women over a sari: Lehenga being a long A-line shirt, choli a fitted blouse, and dupatta a long scarf.

Before she could finish speaking, three white-clad boys from room service laid out the feast on the black walnut occasional table between them. Aromas from dal, a spicy legume dish, permeated the air, as did the scent of baati rolls, freshly baked golden wheat rounds. Luscious orange balls, the churmas, gave off a scent of cardamom. Hands reached out from all directions. Sophie, her hair shimmering under the ceiling light, poured three cups of amber tea. She did this slowly and meticulously, uncharacteristic of her, as though in the process of adjusting to the local pace.

"And before you say it, I don't think Gordon Parker is his real name." Hank looked more solemn than usual as he took a hungry bite of a baati. His eyes, appearing to be an intense shade of blue, burned with intensity. "The guy I met for coffee."

"What's his story?" Maya asked.

"The dude is from Oklahoma, been here a month, employed as a correspondent for a wire service, although he wouldn't reveal which one. Nor do I believe who he says he is or how long he's lived in India. I think he's been here for a while. He's well connected."

Maya put her cup down. She didn't like the sound of things. Her bookish assistant, younger than her by a decade, hadn't seen much of the world. How could she protect him from possible harm if something did happen? He had a mind of his own and, since his arrival in Jaipur, he'd turned a bit reckless. A sense of responsibility pressed down on her. "What does this Gordon want from you?"

Hank stirred his bowl of lentils with a spoon in a concentric circular pattern. "He's lonesome in a foreign land and wants to hobnob with other people. We hit it off, kicked around a bunch of stuff—travelers' woes and all. Had a pleasant time. I wouldn't mind being chummy with him."

Sophie lifted her gaze from her plate, a sigh of contentment following. "That creep?"

"What are you saying?"

"What the fuck," Sophie said. "He seems to be the type who looks at porn."

Hank cradled his cup in both hands and stared at Sophie. "How did you pick up such intelligence?"

"I secretly followed you." Sophie checked the pink polish on her fingernails. "I wanted to study the guy, see what he was about. And boy—"

"Wait a minute," Hank went. "I wouldn't have brought you here if I—"

"What do you mean you brought me?" Sophie's voice reflected an added firmness. "I came on my own."

Hank said, "You could be sent back—"

"Sent back?" Sophie tipped her tiny chin up. "Hey, listen, you're the one not following instructions. Maya-di has told us to watch our steps, so long as that rock is missing, and the crook hasn't been put behind bars. Haven't you, Maya-di?"

At Maya's nod, Hank said, "Don't be irrational, Soph. You've never spoken with Gordon. He's freaking interesting. I chatted him up, found out a bunch of things."

Maya stabbed a baati roll with her fork, even though her hunger had subsided. "Such as a few classifieds about Neel, I presume?"

"Right you are. Gordon claims that Neel attends L.L.A meetings. An old-timer, an active member, and a regular attendee, he's an influencer, so to speak."

"That's newsworthy, but how does Gordon know Neel?"

Hank, now in his second cup of chai, said, "I snapped a photo of Neel, strolling on the campus ground of the college where he teaches. A student of his pointed him out for me. I shared that photo with Gordon and told him that Neel and I have an indirect connection. Gosh, Gordon recognized Neel from seeing him at the L.L.A headquarters."

"Was that such a good move?" Maya asked. "What also intrigues me is the fact that the L.L.A folks would bank on Gordon with this type of intel. I mean to the extent of releasing the identity of their members."

"I'm dumbfounded, as well. Gordon says they want him to report fairly on their doings in the media. So, they open their mouths on most everything."

"In other words, they're trying to prove they're not a terror group?" Maya asked.

"On the dot. The charter of L.L.A, as attested by Gordon, is to do good for the poor. You should hear him talk. How every Wednesday they deliver free lunches to the needy and distribute clothing. How they dispatch a set of mobile medical units to remote areas to provide dental care, to do vision check, and to treat those in physical pain. How they've established schools for children. All of which, I might add, are free of charge."

"This type of a charity arm helps build their network, I suppose," Maya said.

"Righto. Gordon is also ecstatic that they've given him restricted access to their facility, located in the outskirts of this town, as well as to their events."

"What does 'restricted access' mean?"

"Means he has a pass to get in the building. He's allowed to walk into their general assembly held weekly and take part in their proceedings. He can rub shoulders with most of their members and officers, although not those in the upper echelon."

"A privileged position, in other words. Where is this facility located?"

"In a village named Anatpura, not far from here, rural but beautiful."

"Anatpura?" Maya said. "No kidding. My mom has a weekend cottage there. What a coincidence."

"Gordon has invited me to join him as a 'fresher' at their next forum, coming up in a few days. I'm supposed to act like his little brother and blend in. How cool is that?"

Sophie looked up from her plate. "Jeez, Hank, you're his kid brother? They'd believe that?"

Maya took a swallow of her warm tea, which failed to soothe her. She asked, even though she could divine the answer, "You're not going, are you?"

"Absolutely, positively, definitely, I'm going," Hank said. "How can I pass it up? You would if you were in my place, would you not?"

"I'm just saying." Sophie poured more tea into Hank's cup. "Isn't that the definition of danger?"

"What have you both got against it?" Hank, exasperated, curled his fingers. "This is the most excitement I've had since I came to Jaipur. L.L.A is a vibrant organization. They're on the side of commoners. They take in orphan boys, give them a home, feed them, and send them to school. How can you help but root for such an outfit? And if there's serendipity, I might run into Neel there. He wouldn't have the slightest about who I am. Can't wait to get a chance to chat him up."

Sophie's hand fluttered up to her throat, to the elaborate pearl necklace. "You can be so easily bluffed."

"Chill out, Soph."

Oh my God, Maya thought, feeling frozen. On the one hand, she'd welcome any information about Neel's connection to L.L.A. On the other hand, this sounded like a brain-washing job, could even be a recruitment effort. Hank had gotten involved with none other than the widely mistrusted L.L.A. Maya cared about him. What would be the best way to intervene in order to help protect him?

"I've never mentioned this to either of you," Hank said. "In college I was briefly a member of a student anarchist bunch."

A shadow filled the room. "Truly?" Maya asked.

"I'm deadass." Hank replied in a dead serious manner.

"Did you smash a window with a rock?" Sophie asked. "Did you hit a cop? Did you talk over a professor?"

"We did not. We only wanted to get rid of the existing

hierarchy, also called democracy. We believed in open discussions. We decided how to conduct our own affairs. We listened to everybody. No one held power over us. But my mom found out. She demanded that I leave that squad, or she'd disown me. So, after a few fights with her, I did."

"That experience doesn't make you danger-proof," Sophie said.

"It doesn't," Hank replied. "So what?"

"Would your mother freak out if she heard that . . ." Sophie trailed off.

"She very well could . . ."

"Should she get a call—?"

"No, Soph, I'm warning you. You mustn't call my mom."

"Let me tell you about a recent experience I've had." Sophie's bangles made a tinkling sound. "A blind man follows me around. The creep wears sunglasses and has a cane, but I think he fakes his blindness. Boy, he scares me by coming close. And does he smell awful? I yell at him to go away, and he laughs. Even though I wear high heels, I can power-walk. It's like, like, not sure, but I manage to get away."

"The same creep follows me," Maya said.

Sophie lowered her voice. "I spotted him slopping up his lunch alone in an alley, sans his glasses, while thumbing his cell phone. The eyes were cloudy, but normal—he's not blind. Could he be . . . I mean . . . a spy? Sent by Gordon?"

Hank repositioned himself in his chair, said with a disturbing note in his voice, "Now, now, Sophie, what gives you such an idea? In any case, I don't like the sounds of this. I'll bust the creep in the mouth if I come across him."

"No, no," Maya said. "Here in Jaipur, I wouldn't get into a street brawl, if I were you. They'll come at you with stones and sticks."

Hearing her cell phone beeping, Maya excused herself and stood up. Heart throbbing with misgiving, she crossed to the window and answered the call.

A deep male voice said a sexy low hello. That was followed by, "I'd love to get together, darling."

Memories came rushing, almost knocked her off her feet. Even though Simi had already alerted her, she nearly dropped the phone. "Alain?"

"Yes, it's me, darling."

She was both frozen and excited at the same time. "Where are you?"

"In Jaipur." His voice grew more intense. "When can we meet, my love? How about this evening at six? I have a nice spot in mind. Outdoors, safe, easy to get to. It's been so many months. I can't, I simply can't, go on any longer without seeing you."

This evening? Her pulse quickening, she wondered about the urgent nature of this call, somewhat of a suspect, given that he'd failed to be in touch for months. And to imagine he'd be in India. How did he find out she was here? Who told him? What brought him here? In an attempt to go slow, to figure it all out before making a commitment, she mumbled, "I'm not sure."

"I'll text you the directions." He hung up.

SEVENTEEN

DAY 7

SHE SPOTTED HIM FROM A DISTANCE. A broad-shouldered man, adorned in a pair of expensive trousers in a khaki shade, taking long, confident strides toward her, his gait familiar—Alain, her partner of the past. He'd added a few pounds and sported a new haircut, long on top, with a side part. As expected, he was perfectly on time for their rendezvous. All afternoon Maya had agonized over the prospect of this encounter, wondering if she should enter into the picture and how it might bring the past hurt into play.

Alain drew closer. Limned by the afternoon rays, he stretched out his arms. She stepped into his embrace, jaws tense, cheeks flushed, and a flutter in her belly. She couldn't escape the familiar scent of cologne, gentle smile, assurance he projected. The physical proximity, the attention helped to soothe her wounded heart, if only a trifle. It became clear to her, clear as the water gushing out of a nearby fountain, that she still harbored feelings for him. Only that there was hesitancy mixed in it, like a dash of salt not called for in a dish. A sigh escaped her as she looked up at him. The instant their eyes met, he kissed her lightly on the lips. "Love you, love you, my Maya," he murmured. For one foolish moment, she basked in those words, wanted to raise her lips to his again to feel the warmth.

On second thought, she released herself and took a few paces back. Catching her breath, she stood face-to-face with him. On a closer scrutiny, she saw that his eyes reflected a sense of weariness; he was no longer the happy-go-lucky man he'd once been. That touched her, alerted her, even infected her with a desire to comprehend why and what she could do to help him.

A child cried in the distance. Realizing they were in public, and a few heads were turning in their direction, she chose to swivel, stand back, and check out her surroundings.

She stood on the shiny new plaza of an office building, situated a short hike away from the main road, this being a secluded setting, a precious commodity in this noisy town. A vivid flower patch, a fountain, and a set of benches brightened the plot. Now that it was past six p.m. and the offices were closed, only a few people loitered: A pair of lovers holding hands, a couple with a small child, and two uniformed schoolgirls. The city sounds were muted save for a hornbill perched on a tree, pecking on an edible fruit, and making a cackling note—no surprise about the selection of this location. Alain, a perpetual traveler, had always had a talent for finding the hidden gems of a new town. She pointed at an empty bench. "Shall we?"

He inclined his head in agreement. Amidst an awkward silence, they settled on the bench, side by side, with enough space between them to make it easy for talking.

He peered into her eyes. "God, Maya, darling, you look well."

She wanted to say, "*Alain, dear, where have you been? How much I've missed you.*" She wanted to take hold of his hand. Instead, she mouthed a quiet but heartfelt, "Thank you."

"How is Jaipur treating you?"

"I'm adjusting to it." Even though his tone was distancing, his voice caused her heart to skip faster than usual. It also made her smile shyly, like when they'd first met, when they were falling in love; all those dizzying moments, the unexpected kisses. "I'm not here as a tourist, by the way. I'm here to crack a case."

"Ah, you're stuck on an investigation—searching for a huge red ruby, the reddest and the priciest in the world."

That gave her a jolt, broke the spell, made her swallow. "How do you happen to know this?"

"A ruby is a symbol of great love."

She reached within. During their time together, she reveled in the sunshine of his declaration of eternal love for her. It could have been silly or naïve on her part, but on those happy occasions, she didn't doubt him. Their love would last forever, wouldn't it? Now, after a separation of six months and the uncertainty about the reason for his return, she perceived how their emotional ties had worn out. And what about her connection with her mom, whom she visited once-a-year? Hadn't that suffered as well?

Gazing up, she witnessed the first evening stars shining through the violet sky. "Wait a minute." She kept her voice steady, so as not to show her inner turmoil. "You're aware of the symbolism, too?"

"I make a point of being aware of what you're up to, Maya."

His tone, overeager and mildly threatening, punched her in the belly. What might his intention be? She'd never doubted him like this. A strong gust of wind, blowing from nowhere, roared in her ears, even as a sense of unease skittered through her.

"And yet, you haven't been in touch." Seeing him stay silent, she said, "Tell me, if you would, since you seem to be up on it, where's the ruby?"

"No idea. I must say this, however. I wouldn't lose it if it belonged to me. Lose your ruby and see your life go down the drain."

She pushed a lock of hair away from her face, sneaked a good look at him, at his curled back, clenched hands, and lined forehead. What a letdown. They were so close once, for eight long months. A sigh escaped her. "So, you believe in . . .?"

"Superstition? Witchcraft? Folklore? Not usually, but when in Rome . . ."

"What else can you tell me?"

"I don't want to spook you, but if I were in your shoes, I'd forget about that darn stone. I'd get the hell out of here, catch the next flight home."

His warning gave her a temporary pause but didn't stymie her. She placed her feet firmly on the ground to feel its stability. "Why so?"

"Ah, my darling, it's common sense. You know better than I do that in India, jewels are a family's most important possession. It's a portable asset, part of a family's portfolio, one that can be kept private. Stock markets may tumble, currency could depreciate, but the worth of jewels go up over time. Which is why they're handed down generations and looked after. I'm told they're considered a person's fate. I can't get my head around that concept. Even more unbelievable for me, Maya, far beyond my comprehension is the assertion that there exist cosmic influences over gemstones—electromagnetic stimuli or some such thing. What I've gathered is you don't want to mess with gemstones and their forcefields."

"You said you didn't believe in supernatural powers."

"Look, I'm with you." His voice thinned, showing signs of an attempt at evasion. "I care about you. Don't go near these things."

He had too much knowledge, but wouldn't reveal the source, which aroused her suspicion. This was never the way their relationship worked. She would glance at him and intuit what he was musing, easy as that. He would do the same. Their thought processes would meld, with the result that they'd talk things over, see things together, as it were, in the same light, whether they were big or little. It hit her now that he'd changed—time, distance, trauma and who could tell what else—had come between them.

Although torn inside, a lump in her throat, she kept her face neutral. "How did you even hear about this case? So far it hasn't been reported by the media."

"Again, let me remind you. In Indian society, a rumor is a way of passing data. Not for nothing they call rumor a 'cosmology for the common man.'"

"A bit far-fetched, I'd say. How long have you been here to get an education on this cosmology?"

"A week or so."

"I must ask you if you're acquainted with Rana Adani, who's often a source of rumors."

He stared into the space. "You're playing with fire."

She was getting somewhere. "Do you, by any chance, report to him?"

"I can't reveal for whom I work. But I'll tell you this probe is doomed."

He was here for other reasons, not just her. She sighed and told herself not to be discouraged. "Well, I'm here with a purpose. When innocent people get involved and—"

"That's my girl," he said warmly. "Always trying to correct any injustice she comes across. I love that about you. In this case, however, has all this running around done you any good? You're nowhere near cracking the case."

The patronizing tone so ached her that she wanted to get away. Watching a crow circle overhead, she wondered once again whether Alain had intelligence about the robbery that could help her dig into the case better. Despite feeling tormented, she formulated a strategy: Stay dispassionate, hear him out, learn what you can, and be careful not to fall for his charming ways.

Noticing that his face had become an impenetrable mask, she said, "How did you locate me?"

He flashed a grin. As if for a split second, a smug sense of satisfaction shown in his gaze. "I have resources, contacts, network."

Great. That he'd have the knowledge of her whereabouts and who knew what else. He could disappear again and cause her distress. She looked up at the fleecy cloud overhead, moving, fluctuating. An awareness dawned in her, saddened her. She had changed, too. No longer was she willing to put full faith in him. She'd already shed too many tears. "I suppose the same resources, the same contacts—"

"That took me away from you? Yes, my darling, such was the case." His eyes were filled with pain. "I regret it, the mess I was in, I didn't want to leave you ever. No amount of apologizing could explain how badly I feel about how I was forced to treat you."

Is this apology enough? "Do you have any idea how many sleepless nights I've spent stressing over you?" She could have said more: how devastated she'd been for months, how many phone calls she'd made, always hoping that there was an outside possibility that he'd respond, that he was well, that they'd get back together again, that any misunderstanding would be cleared, that love would prevail. She gazed down and noticed the feather-like grass around her feet, save for a tall blade that looked sharp enough to stab her.

He hinted at his own discomfort by twisting his watchband. "I don't mean to sound mysterious, but . . ."

"There's more than a touch of mystery here, Alain."

Disappointment bloomed in the depth of his eyes. "You don't trust me anymore, do you?"

"Do you blame me?"

His lips tightened. "No, not at all, but . . ."

He was hoping against hope, and she was, too. At the same time, she could tell that he was here for other reasons, the man she'd been so in love with. "You jetted hundreds of air miles to get back in touch with me?"

"I mean, I thought I'd give it—"

"A try?" That voice, the expression of longings, the burning eyes, caused a pull at her heartstrings, even as a battle waged in her consciousness as to who he really was, what was he after. "I heard you changed your name after—"

"Being held at gunpoint by terrorists in Borneo? Yes, an experience like that can make you forget your identity, memories of your previous life, all you ever believed. I survived, but . . . let me emphasize this. I'll always want to be Alain with you."

Perfect. He wouldn't even share his name. Despite the excuses he presented and however believable they might be, she remained cautious. "What do you want from me, Alain?"

"Maya, my Maya, I want us to be together again. Yes, darling, I do. We've had a long separation. That doesn't have to spoil our future."

In the brief silence, a blast of warm air tickling her face, she pictured their life together in Seattle. So many happy occasions filled with laughter, so many shared activities, learning about each other and luxuriating in their common household, venturing out as a couple, all burned to ashes when he departed abruptly. She snapped out of her preoccupation.

"I could have traveled to the States and met you there." His gaze held intensity. "But it wouldn't have been the same. Jaipur is a romantic town. Palaces, gateways, and peacocks, Paris of India, as they call it. Here you find opulence and leisure at its best, the perfect spot for us to be reunited. Shall we spend a few days relaxing, sight-seeing, and catching up, then flying back together to the Emerald City? I promise I'll never leave you again."

She stopped listening, raised her eyes at a lone star in the evening sky. Could she go through with his plan? No, with the wisdom she'd gained so painfully, she had shut that part of her life out, had closed a door that now stood like an insurmountable barrier. They'd lost time, not easy to make up, also lost some of the feeling they had for each other. Furthermore, he'd introduced a new set of questions about himself. She glanced at him. Who was this man sitting next to her on this hard bench, eyes sad, lips trembling and shoulders slouching? He wouldn't come clean about his identity, much less reveal the source of his information about the pillaged gem. But he had enough nerve to ask her to get back together. And he was trying to tempt her to leave Jaipur, thereby removing her from the investigation.

Who was behind all that? Where did Alain's allegiance lie? If not Rana, who? Could it be Neel who hired him? If so, for what purpose? She saw the end of trust between them, the weakening of their bond. Like that broken branch of a tree at a distance, lying on the ground, stiff and dry, waiting to be hauled away.

She rose. With a sense of finality, she uttered her words. "I must be off now."

"Sit down, sit down, darling," he murmured. "I miss you; I need you; I think about you all the time. Do you realize how much it means to be together again?"

Once again, she stared at the fountain spouting out droplets of light, beautiful sparks that were temporary in nature. She mustn't allow herself to be swayed by his words of devotion and love. This time it didn't work to improve her feelings about him.

He sat taller and shifted the topic. "What does that piece of rock mean to you?"

"I'm invested in finding it. What's your connection?"

He said, "Please stay longer."

She could see they'd come to an end of their meeting. "I'd like to say a few words about the status of our relationship before I go. I believe you must have common values to build a partnership. Common values such as . . . such as bringing your true self, discussing any matter openly, and being honest with each other. Am I in the ballpark? Otherwise, a relationship will not stand on solid grounds. A house without a foundation. And love will not thrive. Am I making any sense? If this get-together proves anything, anything at all, it's that . . . I'm sorry that we're not in sync in the values department. Which precludes our being happy together ever again. Do you follow, Alain? However painful it is, and it's difficult for me to say it, but I must . . . break it off."

As though to compose himself, he sat for a moment in silence. Voice faint but serious, he said, "Catch up with you in Seattle. Yes, you'll see, I'll make you change your mind."

"I'm sorry—so very sorry, Alain. It's over. Don't try to contact me ever again." Tossing the words over her shoulder, registering the plea in his gaze, she waved a good-bye.

Then she walked toward the main road, with a feeling of bold determination.

EIGHTEEN

DAY 8

SETTLED IN A TAXI ENROUTE TO RANA'S HOUSE this afternoon, Maya once again went over in her mind her reasons for making this trip. She'd been here for over a week now, making slow progress, the Indian way of doing things. Yesterday, she'd broken down and called Rana, to remind him of his promise to show her the safe box where the ruby had been stored. At that point, he'd extended her an invitation to his house. *How perfect*. Although a crime could happen anywhere, the crime site, i.e., the physical reality of the location or the trail, often provided clues, especially in the event of a personal property theft. A walk-through would help. With the professional camera she carried in her purse, she'd be ready to photograph any evidence at a moment's notice. It'd also help to get a better handle on Rana: the real person behind that cool façade and what, if anything, he might be hiding from her.

Surrounded by the constant noise of car honking, which somehow provided her with privacy she confronted her feelings about Rana. It pleased her that they'd established a rapport. After her encounter with Alain only a day ago, one that had left her anguished, she relished the prospect of male companionship, however superficial it might be—but first things first.

As the taxi bumped along a road full of potholes, Maya checked the cloudy afternoon sky visible through the car window. Light drops of rain splattered on the sidewalk. Her glance fell on her watch: five p.m. It was taking far too long to reach her destination, due to rush-hour traffic and slippery road conditions.

Boman, the taxi driver, showing off a long crew-cut hairstyle, stopped for a red light. Perhaps intuiting her discomfort and trying to distract her, he said, "Do you believe that we exist in different dimensions, Madam."

"I've heard that there are many 'yous' out there."

"My guru says we're in past, present and future simultaneously."

"So, what you're implying is we've already landed at our destination?"

Boman laughed. "Only a matter of minutes."

Twenty or so minutes later, the driver wheeled the taxi into the winding driveway of Rana's mansion. Maya got out of the car, her heart pounding. In this lushly landscaped lawn, she breathed in the mild fragrance from a carpet of small white flowers. A line of well-maintained trees bordered the lawn's edges, a rarity in this town, given its desert-like climate. Needing a little extra time to prepare herself for the interview, knowing that Rana wouldn't expect her for another five or so minutes, she decided to give the landscaping a closer inspection.

A tree, about 20" in height, with oblong fruits, looked familiar. "Is that a castor?" she asked Boman, who had climbed out of the taxi and was standing by her.

"Yes, Madam, it's very precious, owing to the castor oil we get from it. Almost every part of a castor has a medicinal application."

As her gaze alighted on a thorny, evergreen, another question leapt out of her. "And that one?"

"That's khejri, our state tree, also called the 'King of the Desert.' Supposed to bring good fortune, it's also a folk remedy for whatever ails you. Talk about being drought tolerant. A khejri has a root system you wouldn't believe. It's as complicated as my son's mathematical equations."

Her attention on a tall, shading, broad-leaved evergreen, she asked, "That's a neem, isn't it?"

Boman beamed. "Yes, the popular neem, 'Good Health Neem,' 'Slim as a Neem,' that's what our girls say they wish to look like. I take an Ayurvedic medicine every morning that has neem in it. My wife throws a handful of neem leaves in her eggplant dishes. Delicious."

Heading toward the front entrance, Maya noticed that it faced east, locally considered an auspicious angle, for it would receive the sun's first rays. She liked it that Rana not only took good care of precious natural resources that were tolerant of the region's semi-arid climate, but also adhered to Indian cultural practices.

She hustled up the front steps, pausing when she heard Boman saying from behind, "I'll wait for you here. Call if you need me."

She turned, regarded him enquiringly.

"Well, you never know," he said lightly.

Even before she could touch the doorbell, Rana had opened the door. Voice slightly hoarse, smelling lightly of beer, he said, "Come in, Maya, please come in." Standing aside, he invited her to enter. Attired in a maroon vest over a pale blue shirt, a pair of black jeans, and running shoes, he appeared healthy and vigorous, although the spark in his gaze was missing.

All is not well. Maya sensed that much. She watched him shove his hands in his pockets, another sign of distress.

He led her to a well-appointed living room with a window facing a row of evergreens. The sun cast a golden sheen over the leafy branches. "Please make yourself feel at home." After a pause, "Feel like a chai?"

She pushed her concerns aside and said an enthusiastic, "Nice idea."

A moment later, she heard him speaking to a servant in the hallway, ordering him to bring refreshments. The mansion had at least fifteen rooms and would require a large staff of live-in house-keepers to keep it functioning, she surmised. She took her seat on a majestic wooden settee with a mahogany-colored cushion. Listening to the low sounds of tabla music drifting from a home theater system and finding it restful, she peered around. Several armchairs, each with a warm walnut finish, graced the room as did an oval glass cocktail table. The opposite wall displayed a rosewood hunting trophy. A shiny gold insert declared it had been awarded to Rana Adani. How proud and handsome he appeared, he, an accomplished hunter. She checked the rest of the room. An overgrown, cactus-like plant grew out of a large white ceramic planter on one corner, adding visual variety. Beyond that, a textile wall-hanging, depicting a summer garden, provided another lively touch. From the ceiling descended a cluster of lights shimmering like heavenly bodies. The room had a formal feel, indicating a professional touch. Rana, no doubt, lived in style.

Drops of sudden rain from a passing shower rattled the window. A young, white-clad servant with a sunbaked complexion appeared in the room, hauling a tray. Bending, he set down cups of steaming golden chai on the cocktail table. She smiled when she noticed the accompaniment: a serving of milk-based, cardamom-scented, and pistachio-garnished dense pastry—the popular "heart stealer" known as sandesh. He straightened and did a namaste in a shy manner.

She looked up at him. "Any sugar in the chai?"

Voice soft, he replied, "No sugar—mother promise."

Maya chuckled at the colloquial expression, meaning he was speaking the truth. After taking a bite of the sandesh, she asked his name.

"Bedi." He swallowed, as though trying to overcome his shyness. "I run this household. If you ever have any questions . . ." He paused and floated away.

His offer came as a jaw-dropper, an opportunity she hadn't expected. Maya grasped the warm handle of her teacup.

Rana returned and took a seat. She watched him closely, without making it obvious. He added an extra spoonful of sugar to his cup, and stirred with the spoon, without ever hitting the rim. They talked for a few minutes about their respective morning runs in the park. "I sleep better," he said.

"Puts me in a good mood," she said.

"That, too," he replied.

He finished his cup, waited for her to finish hers, and pushed himself up from his chair, perking up. Voice turning light, he said, "Shall we? I have no etchings to show, but the safe box is in the bedroom for your scrutiny. As you can see, I have a couple of housekeepers who are always about. No worries about being alone in a man's lair."

"What made you think I'd worry?"

He expelled a sigh, a hint of gravity showing in his dark eyes. "It's a peculiarity of this town. As a single guy, you can acquire reputation you've done nothing to earn."

"Tell me more about it, if you would."

"False rumors. Oh, God, I've had to suffer through a stream of them. Someday, Maya, I'll share with you."

He had a story there, which she wanted to hear, but it looked as though she'd have to wait. Her focus on Rana's back and his confident gait, Maya followed him down the hallway to the third door on the right. After fishing out a key from his pocket, he unlocked the door to a spacious bedroom, and stepped aside for her to enter.

Maya peered around, without making it obvious, her senses sharp. First, she noticed an open closet to her left. Following Rana's eyes, she saw a king-sized bed positioned against a wall, covered with a red-splashed katha quilt, and accessorized by fluffy pillows. A tall chest of drawers stood next to it. A handmade beige wool rug, quiet and unobtrusive, covered the floor. To complete the décor, there stood a leather wingback chair in a neutral color and a pair of hanging reading lights. The whole effect was earthy, yet dreamy. A strong air-conditioning system made the room feel extra cool. Maybe it had to do with the temperature requirement of the now-embezzled gemstone.

Rana turned to her. He sounded secure in his own element as he said, "Ask any question you like."

She posed one of the first questions that was mandatory for her at a robbery scene. "Who has access to this room?"

"Currently—just myself. It's off-limits to my domestic help. They clean it once-a-week, only when I'm around."

"Has the room been tidied up since the robbery?"

"Oh, yes. I was present."

That eliminated the need for photographs or a video shoot. Maya must take a different approach. A silver-framed photograph of a woman on the opposite wall caught her attention. She moved closer and recognized Bea, who struck a dramatic pose. "Your wife? Did she—?"

"Yes, she did the overseeing in my absence."

"I assume the stone was there when she left."

He knitted his brows. "Yes, on that day, it was there undisturbed. I discovered the misfortune only after she'd been gone for several days."

"How many days?"

"Three, four, five . . ."

She persisted, a necessary part of her job. "Makes a difference if it's three or—"

"Three."

Saying so, he veered left to the partially open closet and pushed the door open wider. Inside, there rested a sturdy, black, medium-sized, multi-drawer safe box. Three feet in height and of solid steel construction, it was anchored in place on the floor. The top drawer was open; it was empty. He peered at her, as though expecting a reaction.

She smiled. "I expected to be led down a trapdoor that opened on to a secret vault in which a safe box rested, unlocked only by a sacred chant and a hand wave."

"Sorry to disappoint you. However, this one is, by no means, a simple lockbox. Fireproof and humidity-proof, it can withstand high heat and high flames. It's also waterproof and gun-proof, the best overall home safe on the market. No sacred mantra will ever open it, only the right combination of digits set by me. I changed that combination often."

"Any safety features?" Maya asked.

"None. I disabled whatever was there."

"May I ask you why?"

"Too inconvenient," he said.

"No video camera or a recording system?"

He made a dismissive gesture with his hand. "Never thought I'd need such equipment."

"What about Bea? Did she have the combination?"

"No, never."

"Who else besides you then?"

He stayed silent.

"Do you have extra keys to the safe?" she asked.

"To be frank, I don't have *any* keys. Never once have I been locked out. I have a perfect memory for numbers—all those years of studying Mathematics in school."

Whoever pilfered the ruby didn't need the combination. That wasn't necessary, given that the safe was kept open. "Don't safety boxes often come with a fingerprint scanner?"

"Yes, you're right, they do. That feature—let me think—might have been included when I bought it. I never turned it on."

"Why not?"

Silence.

"So, overall," she said, "do you believe you had enough security for the box?"

"No, that was a lapse on my part and the police will agree with you."

An odd feeling pressed into her. "Yet another directive in the gem business is, 'Don't leave your gems and jewelry unattended.'"

"In hindsight," he replied, "I can see what a serious mistake I made by leaving the box open. But this is how we've lived for generations."

She sighed. "That tallies. I remember how my uncles and aunts wouldn't consider using bank lockers for their heirlooms."

"My dad said your home was where you kept your treasures. You could never guess when you'd have to celebrate a special day, whether it's honoring a deity, a wedding, or a child-birth, and what jewelry pieces you might need." His gaze conveyed a sense of genteel pride. "I follow the ancestral way of doing things. I do carry home insurance, however."

Another aspect of Rana's character. Despite his reputation as a jetsetter and party-thrower, he struck her as more sentimental and tradition bound than he'd at first appeared to be, a "hearth and home" type of man, grounded in an aristocratic tradition.

She decided to change the line of questioning. "Have Neel and/or my mom ever come to this room?"

"Yes, they were most welcome here." He sighed. "They'd come often. Neel would get the ruby out. There was a routine he followed. He'd do a maintenance check with a prong type instrument. The stone, tough as it was, accumulated dust. He made use of ultrasonic equipment to clean it. He removed any impurities and negative energy, which it could pick up from people in the house or the dust in the air and restored its luster. After his routine was complete, Neel would hold the gemstone before me. It'd dazzle my eyes, with its hypnotic brilliance. The more I stared at it, the more it'd make me forget reality, at least for a few precious moments. Uma-di, sitting next to him, would smile."

"My mom—I remember you saying that you liked her."

"Yes, I love Uma-di dearly. She's like an aunt to me, much nicer than my own aunts. We even have a distant connection due to an adoption of her cousin into our family. Believe it or not, I owe her a fair bit."

"How so?" she asked.

"Uma-di helped when my marriage was breaking up after only a year, leaving me devastated. Over time, it's only on account of her that I made peace with my wife. Together we pulled out of the hole. Uma-di is loving, kind and straightforward, not to forget honest and sincere. If I can't have full confidence in . . . someone like Uma-di, whom will I have any faith in?"

Maya bowed her head, agreeing with him on that point. She valued her mother for the fine human being she was. The moment vanished. Maya's emotions stirred. It reminded her of Uma's recent metamorphosis, her unwillingness to get in touch, and how much Maya suffered from that. They hadn't spent time together lately. How odd. She couldn't even remember when they last had a heart-to-heart. What had changed and why? How could they regain their mother-daughter closeness again?

"What was your first thought when you discovered the theft?" she asked. "Were you alone in this room?"

He blinked from confusion and went silent. Either he wished to buy more time to dig up a suitable answer or he was trying to hide the truth. "I was alone. I felt sick, I sweated, I might even have blanked out. I shuddered to think that my ruby might be changing hands at a pawnshop." After a pause, "I kept staring at the box, wishing my ruby would be back. Then, when I realized it would not return, I lost all feelings. Numb, I sat. The whole evening went by. I could hear stormy weather outside. I don't remember any more."

Yeah, sure. You don't remember. A sting of disappointment burned in Maya, even though he'd given her a few facts to run with. "It's a huge shock, no doubt. On another topic: What about Sam, the chauffeur? How well were you acquainted with him?"

"Pretty well. He had the responsibility of driving Uma-di and Neel here. I liked the fellow, always enjoyed chit-chatting with him about kiting."

She met his gaze. "Did he have any access to your safe box, the combination or any knowledge of the safety features?"

"Certainly not. He'd never stepped inside this house, I don't think. After parking the car in the driveway and letting them out, he'd disappear for a while. He'd return later to pick them up. Always he met them at the front door."

"Any other reaction on your part when you found the stone gone?"

"You mean besides feeling a huge void? Feeling as though the world is ending?" Anguish crept over Rana's face. "Well, I traced my way back to the days when my dad was alive. Papa depended on me. He gifted the stone to me and to generations after me. You should have seen the happy expression on his face when he made the gift. He was a serious man, hardly smiled. That was the happiest I'd ever seen him. Unfortunately, I dropped the ball. My carelessness did it. I can't forgive myself—I never can."

His remorse touched her. In the ensuing silence, she concluded that they'd reached a dead end regarding this topic.

Rana breathed deeply. "So, what do you think?"

Although Maya was beginning to draw a few conclusions, she wouldn't reveal them quite yet. Not until she'd reached some certainty. She gave the standard answer. "Inside job, limited number of players, but secrets run deep."

He sighed. "Well, I have faith in your ability."

"Need more time." She thanked him and turned toward the door. "I must run now."

It struck her, as she glanced at him, how downhearted he appeared from the way he lowered his gaze. He wanted to spend more time with her. She'd have liked the same, but it had to be another time. At the front door, they said brief goodbyes to each other.

She exited the building, walked down the gravel pathway, and headed toward the gate, where Bedi stood. "Leaving already?" he asked.

She gave thanks for his hospitality and said, "May I ask a question?"

"Yes, you may."

"Did Bea Adani leave this house before or after the ruby was ripped off?"

"Before," Bedi said. "Oh, days before. Mrs. Bea is quirky, and she didn't get along with Mr. Rana, but she isn't a thief. That's not who she is. Relatives suspect that she ran off with the jewel because she came from a down-and-out family. But take it from me, Detective Maya, she's straightforward." He looked up at her, as though expecting more questions.

"And those rumors I hear?"

"That Mr. Rana was violent with his dates?" Bedi smiled. "Don't pay any attention. A rich spoiled girl he didn't want to go out with spread rumors about him. Those rumors, I'm sure, will die down, especially since she's been caught shoplifting and had to pay a big fine to avoid a jail term. It was in the local newspaper. Take it from me, he's a good man, considerate of others." He paused. "That flower bouquet sent to your hotel room—it was from Mr. Rana. I delivered it. He wanted to keep it a secret, but I had to tell you."

Maya blinked back her surprise and delight. How fortunate Bedi was laying it all out for her. It made it easy for her to ask, "How is he as an employer?"

"He pays me a good salary, treats me with kindness," Bedi said. "There's more. You see I'm enrolled in an automotive training program, which I pursue during my spare hours. I can't afford the tuition, so Mr. Rana is paying for it, which is more than I can expect.

"Mr. Rana isn't without fault. He overschedules himself, forgets his appointments, doesn't show up at his cousins' birthdays. He can be short-tempered. Wants everything done yesterday. Even so, as a domestic servant, I couldn't expect better. I'm speaking the truth. My grandfather, who was a follower of Mahatma Gandhi, advised me to be honest. 'Honesty doesn't buy you a kilo of rice, but it makes you feel good inside. That counts for a lot.' I bow before his photo every morning."

NINETEEN

DAY 9

SEATED IN HER HOTEL ROOM, Maya sipped at a cup of chai, a mid-morning ritual, and sorted through her emails. An article about Singapore forwarded electronically by Hank drew her attention. It said that the government was adopting a more lenient attitude toward its dissidents. Which made Maya wonder: Might Bea consider moving back to Singapore? If so, any knowledge of the ruby she had would be lost. What could be done about that?

Around eleven a.m., a hotel clerk, bearing a tea tray, knocked on her door. He refilled her cup, handed her a plain, white, fine-quality envelope, and performed a namaste, saying, "A gentleman dropped this off for you. He said he was in a hurry and couldn't see you in person."

Who could it be? Her fingers frozen, she tore the envelope open. Inside, there rested a card, with a note scribbled by hand. She recognized Alain's handwriting.

Should she subject herself to more torture?

Dearest Maya,

I am on my way to the airport and will soon catch a flight out of Jaipur. After our talk, I concluded that you were right. Our relationship could never work. Too many things have come between us.

That slashes through me, leaves me sleepless at night but, in time, I'll accept it, and move on.

My parting advice to you (and please listen carefully): Leave Jaipur as soon as you can. This place is not safe for you. I've already warned you once. I must repeat it because you didn't seem convinced.

Know that I'll always love you. Know that I'll always be Alain to you. Know that I'll always wish you the best, no matter where I am.

With loads of happy memories and a bundle of regrets,

Love and kisses,
Alain

Maya sat with the note, cogitating on the good times they'd shared and what might have been but could never be. If she were to make a guess, Alain had dropped this note himself. She couldn't quite chuck it. There was his parting advice, words of warning that weighed in on her. Where were those warnings coming from?

About to put the note way, she received a call from Inspector Dev. From the disturbed tone of his voice, his low hello, Maya could tell something was up. Breathlessly, she asked, "What's up, Mohan?"

"You stay in touch with Bea Adani, don't you? When did you last see her?"

Her chest felt tight. She gripped her teacup. "That mugging incident was the last time. She hasn't returned my phone calls since. What's going on?"

"I'm so very sorry, Maya. Something terrible has happened."

She put her cup down with a clatter. In the process, she spilled a little chai on her index finger, which she rubbed off with the napkin, but couldn't make a sound.

"Are you, okay, Maya?"

Things weren't right, she could tell. She mumbled a yes.

"I'm afraid Bea is dead."

It was as though the walls crumbled. She sat immobile, troubled thoughts swirling in her mind and going in all directions. Would Uma be safe in this town? How about Hank and Sophie?

And Maya herself? Her heart dropped, with no sound coming from anywhere. At first, too shocked to speak, she managed to ask, "What happened?"

"Killed by a freaky kiting accident."

Maya gulped. "A kiting accident?"

"Yes, kiting is not as merrymaking a sport, as tourists believe. Not if you consider the number of deaths and injuries that result from the abrasive strings of stray kites. How does that happen? Okay, kites fly high up in the sky, between buildings, then flutter down and hit the sidewalk or cut through the flesh of a pedestrian. It tears me apart to report that Bea Adani happened to be at the wrong place at the wrong time."

"Can you elaborate?"

"It was late morning, sunny, the sky clear, with only a few kites floating about. Bea strolled on the pavement past a row of retail outfits, located several miles from her home. She was about to step through the doors of Radha Produce when a dangling kite that was floating high up above, raced down and landed on her head. A crazed kite flyer must have lost control of his kite."

Radha Produce: Maya remembered Bea mentioning her daily trips there, what must have become a predictable pattern. Sam, the skillful kite captain, also emerged in Maya's mind. She didn't like what she was hearing.

"Bea's throat got caught by its tail," the inspector continued. "Trapped in a loop, she struggled to free herself, tried and tried, but failed. In seconds, the kite string slit her throat. She fell on the footpath, screaming and bleeding, and lost consciousness. The cotton string, as it turned out, was coated with . . . the worst material you can think of, sticky, abrasive, powdered glass mixed with glue, manjha."

The words sunk in deep. Maya couldn't respond, eventually saying, "Haven't environmentalists and concerned activists asked for a ban of manjha? Isn't it considered illegal?"

"Illegal it is, but it continues to be manufactured. In the sport of kite-fighting, popular in Jaipur, an opponent's line can be cut with ease if you employ an abrasive string. The ruling against manjha hasn't been easy to enforce. We police can't often trace the flying line and therefore who was piloting the kite, the guilty party, in other words. We've recommended drone surveillance to determine who's flying a kite and from where, but its availability is not widespread yet."

The inspector was playing it down, trying to make it seem like it was a random event. However, Maya wanted to gather all the facts before making such a conclusion. In the somber mood that hovered over the space, she considered: If only Bea had listened to her. About the dangers she faced any time she ventured out in public. "And the sidewalk where it happened?"

Inspector Dev provided her with an address. "It's an ordinary intersection, which has now been cordoned off with crime scene tapes. We've 'frozen' it, so to speak. A constable is standing guard. Our initial screening having been completed, we've conducted a video walk through, taken still photos and documented all the evidence. There are likely to be fingerprints on the kite. We have an inventory log as well."

"Any witnesses?"

"Luckily, yes. A motorcyclist, who happened to be idling, photographed the incident on his cell phone and gave our station a tip-off. That was a shocker. A medical person and a coroner were rushed to the scene. Bea Adani was pronounced dead even before she could be transported to the hospital. The cause of death was reported to be excessive bleeding. We've ordered an autopsy."

"I suppose you haven't been able to trace the kite-flyer?" she asked.

"Not so far. My constables knocked on the doors of all nearby houses. No one was steering kites from any rooftop. Nor could anyone make a guess from where the killer kite had been launched. To answer your question: No, we haven't been able to track the culprit. We don't have reasons to believe it was an intentional act on anyone's part."

How tragic. Estranged from her husband, Bea hid in a dingy apartment, fearing for her life, and eventually met, quite possibly, her nemesis. "That remains to be seen. Has Rana Adani been notified?"

"Yes. He was attending a business meeting. Took the news hard. He broke down. You could hear it in his voice."

Maya held herself together as best as she could. "What color was the kite?"

"Sky-blue. The string was also blue."

Again, Maya pictured Sam, who fancied that color. Things clicked in place, even as sadness waved through her; Sam, coming into big bucks, staying at a pricey hotel in Jaipur, before taking off on another trip. Where did the funds come from? But what could Sam's motives be in killing Bea if he'd indeed done so? Was he, a free-spirited kite flyer, a hitman? As she began to contemplate the tragic consequences that could follow him, her legs buckled out from under her. How much she liked Sam. Who could have pushed him into committing a crime? Not Uma. No, no, that can't be. Who then?

Another fact sprang to her mind. "Isn't Hotel Rose Premier, a fancy guesthouse, located nearby? Did you check with its residents?"

"That hotel is, indeed, right around the corner. Good tip, Maya, but no, we didn't verify with the management. Usually, hotel residents don't take to the rooftop for a wild ride with their kites."

Downhearted, she said, "I suggest you confer with the hotel manager. And oh, what about Bea's apartment? Has anyone gone there to do a home search, to make sure that evidence, if any, hasn't been destroyed?"

"You have a point. I did send my team out to her flat. It was ransacked. An intruder rifled through her possession and left a mess behind, although her jewelry hadn't been touched."

"No evidence at all of whom the intruder was?"

"Wait a minute, yes. We did find an object outside Bea's door. A carabiner—it was lying on the hallway. Must have fallen from the intruder's pocket. I had no clue what the darn thing was. One of my staff recognized it as a tool that kite flyers reach for when they need anchoring."

Carabiner. Maya's heart twisted. Sam had mentioned buying several carabiners. "Does it seem likely then that the kite flyer also posed as a burglar and hunted for the ruby?"

"Why are you connecting Bea's death with the loss of ruby, if I may ask?"

"The burglar might have assumed that Bea had run off with the ruby and had it hidden in her flat. With Bea dead, out of the way, the burglar now could break into her place and comb it, taking for granted the ruby was there, finishing the job, so to speak."

The inspector's voice had a harder edge. "You seem to be making a wild guess. It's a developing story and, as of now, we have no proof of any foul play."

Maya sat straighter, seeing the complications before her eyes, which might turn tragic. "Suppose it's not a guess. Suppose it wasn't an accident. Suppose someone on purpose got his or her kite to—"

"Why, Maya, do you suspect someone?"

"Yes, I think so, I have a potential suspect in mind." She tried to take a deep breath. "Samir-G, who goes by the name Sam."

"God Vishnu. You mean our local kite champion? You're familiar with the guy?"

"He's my mom's cook and chauffeur." Sorrow found a nest inside her as she recounted the rest. "Spoke with him only days ago, as a matter of fact. He'd been paid to take a vacation. By whom, he wouldn't reveal. He did say that someone had been trailing him. He had no idea who that might be or why."

"Suppose Sam made things up?" Inspector Dev said. "To show how important he was? You don't live here and might not be aware of this, but we depend on our domestic helpers. And they squeeze every penny from us, exploit every excuse in the book not to show up for their duty—"

Maya interrupted him. "One hears of exploitation and abuse from the other side, as well, Mohan. There's a saying, 'You oil your machines regularly, but forget to provide your servants with food and drink.'"

"Not true, not true in my household. My housemaids get a good meal, a decent wage, time off, and periodic raises." He paused. "As an expert kite flyer, Sam could have maneuvered a murder like this. But . . . this is puzzling to me . . . why would he do so?"

"I can't decipher his motivation quite yet. However, it'd be of interest to me to question him before he leaves town. Is there any way you could arrange that?"

"Most certainly, Maya. My constables will get the approval of the hotel management, then knock on Sam's door. There is 'reasonable suspicion' on our part because of his kite competency. We would accompany him to our station for questioning. Would you like to drop by?"

"Yes, for sure, I would be there. Afterwards, I'd like to go through your video photography, the photos, and the inventory log."

"All will be ready for your perusal, Maya. Please wait for my call. By the way, we're keeping Bea's identity hush-hush until her family in KL has been notified. It'd be difficult to break the news to them."

After clicking off, Maya stood by the window, grief settling over her chest. How much she wished she could have protected Bea. Her eyes fell on the sidewalk. A crew of five or so dancers rehearsed an energetic free-style dance routine, with the accompaniment of a melodious recorded tune. In a transitory relief, Maya tapped her feet on the floor to the music.

A short time later, her phone vibrated. Inspector Dev was on the line. Disappointment rang on his voice as he said, "Guess what, Maya? Sam checked out of the hotel in a hurry before my team could reach him. The hotel clerk said Sam looked rather distraught, not his usual affable self, and slipped away with his carry-ons. He hailed a taxi."

Maya shuddered, picturing Sam, a man on the run and what he might face.

"We'll continue to search for him," the inspector said. "At bus, train, and auto-rickshaw stations. We'll inspect the passenger list of all flights taking off from the Jaipur International Airport. I've already spoken with the DGP, the Director General of Police, in our state. He's offered to help. We'll get Sam. Once we locate him, we'll detain him and escort him to our station for interrogation. Will keep you posted."

Mya disconnected the call, a question haunting her mind. Who had put Sam to this task, if indeed he was the culprit? Then, too, she envisioned how Uma might react to this news, how devastated she would be upon finding that her beloved cook of many years might be implicated in Bea's death. Even a risk-taker like herself, with a degree of tolerance for discomfort, Maya felt anxious.

Her heart washed with melancholy; she wondered: Who would be next?

WITHIN THE HOUR, PROCESSING the gut-wrenching news about Bea's unfortunate death, Maya paid a call on to Rana. They'd become friends of sorts and she was deeply sorry for his loss. She wanted to offer him any solace she could. And as a P.I., she'd be the right person to pop over, Rana being the surviving spouse of a homicide victim. She had yet another incentive. As stated in the Indian Penal Code, if a wife died of "unnatural" causes within seven years of marriage, the husband might be considered a suspect. Maya wanted to see the effect of Bea's horrific death on Rana with her own eyes.

Pale-faced, moving slowly, he ushered her to the living room. He motioned her to take a seat, his voice soft and low. They perched on the opposite ends of a long sofa. Seeing how dejected he appeared to be—back rounded, face crumpled, dark circles under his eyes— she allowed him time to reclaim his composure. The lacy curtain on the window fluttered in the light breeze, the only movement in the room.

"I feel responsible." Regret rang in Rana's voice. "And that responsibility weighs me down, crushes me. Did I drive her out?

Could I have been nicer to her? Or would we have broken up in any case? Ours was, unfortunately, a 'case of the mismatched couple.'"

Maya stayed silent, so he'd share more.

He gave out a slow breath. "I'm a business guy, which must have been boring for her, but I like to have a certain order in my life. Follow what I mean? She was too much of a free spirit, driven by the impulse of the moment, took chances without a second thought. At first, I thought it was cool and creative, then it became clear you can't live life that way. We couldn't be together—such opposites we were. Our world views clashed. We didn't agree on anything. My days became like an inky black screen, with no light anywhere. It was like someone was choking me, choking me until I had no words left." His voice cracked. "I lost my temper too often, neglected my business, stopped being social. However, once we separated and I came back to normal, I wished her well."

"Of late, did she share any . . .?"

He crossed his arms. "She did. Of being stalked by a masked man, which petrified her. That thug watched her every move during the day. At night, she'd see a shadow of someone outside her window, quite likely the same person. How could she have any peace? At the same time, she didn't want to involve the police. She has had bad experience with the cops in Singapore. As far as Jaipur was concerned: she told me she couldn't come up with any justification for continuing to hang out here. The fact of the matter was . . . her acting career didn't take off. Then, too, we'd initiated the divorce proceedings. She said her wish was to 'get the hell out of here and be back to the Lion City.' If only she'd done that sooner."

Maya closed her eyes for an instant, her heart hammering. Uma—what if someone, with a similar evil intent, pursued her? "Any idea who might have trailed Bea around? Anyone who disliked her? Who wanted revenge?"

He wiped his eyes with a tissue. "I have no idea. My relatives didn't take to her, but they wouldn't go to the length of . . . oh, no way. I remember you warning me about her vulnerability."

"Which had to do with the ruby."

Voice emphatic, he said, "She didn't have it."

"You're positive?"

He pressed his palms together. "Yes. The ruby was under my control. It was still there when she decamped. To tell you the truth, Maya, I can't imagine who might have wanted to get rid of her for any purpose whatsoever. She was, after all, a decent person. She had no enemies. The last time she stopped by to see me, she returned her wedding ring—that's the custom in her family. 'You gave it to me,' she said, 'but it's no longer mine.' I was stunned. When I offered to pay her to move to a better flat, she declined it."

In the long pause he took, Maya watched him. Voice doleful but steady, legs crossed, he said, "And no, Maya, it wasn't me. I didn't hire a hoodlum to stalk my wife or kill her. Believe me."

TWENTY

DAY 10

HOW DID ANITA ADANI FIT IN THIS PICTURE? An embezzled ruby coveted by many, and a horrible death occurring only yesterday perhaps due to it; did she have a role in either crime?

It had taken Rana days to arrange this visit with Anita and now finally Maya had wound up at her house, ready to interview her. Maya strolled in through the gate, never having met the lady before, but having gotten warnings about her temper. Remembering the late Bea and her reservations about Rana's family, Maya felt queasy. She assured herself that she might unearth a clue or two as well as discern where the ownership of the ruby lied. She might pick up a few things about the late Bea.

Now Maya tried to get an impression of Anita from her surroundings. Located in a gated community, the large, three-storied, white-washed villa had an appearance of being exclusive but did not exude a welcoming air. The exterior cried for a bit of paint. The landscaped front yard, though saturated with radiant sunlight, needed weeding and watering. Mature trees on the left formed a canopy over a pair of run-down benches that once served as a seating area, but now appeared to be desolate. A blanket of weeds covered the lily pond next to it. It became obvious to Maya that Anita had stopped paying attention to her estate as she once had. Her conditions had somehow changed.

Maya climbed the front steps and rang the doorbell. An attendant—a timid young woman swathed in a green sari—opened the door. "May I help you?" she asked in a low, edgy tone of voice.

"Maya Mallick. I'm here to see Ms. Adani. I have an appointment."

"Where are you from?"

Not the usual, *The purpose of your visit?* "The States."

The attendant stared at her, but Maya wouldn't reveal any more. She lingered in place, holding her head high, strong, and confident, the only way she'd be able to snag a few minutes of Anita's time, this despite a referral from Rana or perhaps as a consequence of it.

"Follow me, please." Led by the young woman, Maya proceeded down the hallway to a bright, airy, spacious living room. "Please make yourself at home." The woman gestured toward a club chair. "Ms. Adani is finishing a class. I'll tell her you're here."

Maya took a seat; she swallowed her feelings of discomfort. Through the French doors, she could view an enclosed patio drenched in abundant sunshine. A bevy of twelve or so women of various ages had finished a vigorous workout, as evident from their sweaty foreheads and wet clothes. Breathing heavily, they chattered, smiled, and mingled, giving the impression they'd won a prize fight. At the center stood their teacher, an attractive woman, an authority figure—Anita Adani, Maya guessed from her facial resemblance to Rana. Tall, fit, and fifty, clothed in a peacock blue tunic-and-pants set, Anita had a feisty quality about her. She bantered with her students in a loud tone, her attention shifting constantly, and projected an attitude of *You better not mess with me.*

Soon Anita, accompanied by the same attendant, bounced into the living room. Up close, Anita sported a deeply lined forehead. Her neck was adorned with an elaborate emerald-beaded silver necklace. The reddish cast in her blazing eyes indicated either anger or dissatisfaction. Maya held herself tall and extended a greeting.

Anita gave her a quick once over. "Bring us chai," she ordered the attendant in a haughty manner, who turned and departed. Then, to Maya in a screechy voice and a not-so-friendly expression, "You're from the U.S.?"

"Right, yes, I—"

"Are you a journalist? Here to do a story?"

"No, I—"

Anita cut her off again. "What brings you here then?"

"I'll be happy to explain." Although perturbed, Maya kept her voice calm. She could tell Anita would be a difficult person, perhaps also one of those people who could grow on you. "Only if you'll allow me to finish."

"If you're from the police, then you're not welcome in my house. Get the point?" The voice was rougher than before.

"Rest be assured that I'm not."

"Where did you meet Rana?"

"On the running track."

"You do look like a runner. Is that how you stay so slim?" She grabbed a chair across from Maya. "All right, then. I don't mean to be curt, but you see, I'm rattled. I've put on five extra pounds. It could even be ten."

Maya regained her seat. "It might be in your interest to listen to me." She paused for a beat when the attendant wandered in, hefting a tray. She put down two cups of chai and a plate of shiny white, diamond-shaped borfee cookies on the low table between them and eased out of the room. "Yes, it might be a matter of importance to you. You must have gotten the news of Bea's death."

"I have. Oh, my heavens. The death was unfortunate, tragic, and accidental, or so the police said." Anita's voice had a melancholic note to it. "I feel so out of it. Should have spent more time getting familiar with her, talking more, listening more. I didn't dislike Bea, although I have no idea what Rana saw in her. Our family was relieved when they separated. Bea didn't fit in, marvelous person that she was, and that disconcerted her. You might say she killed herself."

"I liked Bea," Maya said. "She was real. Why do you say that she—?"

"When people lose their desire to live, they get into 'accidents.' Do you follow? They put themselves in mix-ups, where they . . ."

Anita paused. "It was a mistake from the beginning. Bea was taken by our family's glamor. Bright lights, big Jaipur, you know. She had no inkling the price she'd have to pay to be an Adani. Always having to present yourself well, being judged by the society at every turn, never measuring up. She couldn't handle it. She was miserable. Do I weep over her death? You bet I do. It could have been me."

They stayed quiet for a few eyeblinks. Anita, taking a bite off a cookie, scrutinized her. "Are you Uma Mallick's daughter, by any chance?"

Maya's heart came up to her throat. She nodded and checked for Anita's reaction.

Anita's voice softened. "You look alike. She's one of my most dedicated students. Joining the program late in life but picking up things fast. Your mom's strong point is what's known as a 'friendly-style wrestling' that I teach."

It thrilled Maya to hear such high praise about Uma. "What is a friendly-style wrestling?"

"Haven't you heard of *kusthi*? A three-thousand years old practice, restricted to men, employed to gaining victory over oneself. I've simplified the moves of *kusthi*, making it easier for women to master them. I've also incorporated other techniques I've acquired from our masters. All that suits your mother fine, nice person that she is, dedicated that she is. She brings so much to the group. The other students love her, even though she's much older. She finished her class and left only a few minutes ago."

Once again, a wave of suspicion spread through Maya. How odd that Uma would be enrolled in a strenuous wrestling class, let alone she'd excel in it. She'd never cared for a structured workout, preferring to take long, solitary nature walks at an easygoing pace. And her teacher was no other than Anita Adani, Rana's aunt. What would prompt Uma to enroll in a program of this nature? Had personal protection been weighing heavily in her mind? Had Neel been abusing her physically or emotionally?

At the very least, Maya had news about Uma. Now perked up, she replied to Anita by saying, "Wish I could have run into my mom."

"You'll get the chance if you're willing to wait. Uma forgot her shawl, you know, the red one. She left it hanging on the patio railing. My assistant noticed and called her. Uma said she'd be here in a few minutes."

A lucky stroke, indeed. Words flew out of Maya's mouth. "Good, I'll get a chance to see her then."

"You don't hang around your mother? What kind of a daughter are you? And what are you doing in the States? Why do you live so far away from your family? This country isn't good enough for you?"

"Look, Ms. Adani. I'll explain those concerns another time."

"Did your husband come with you?"

"I'm single."

Anita's shrewd gaze appraised Maya. "Why doesn't your family arrange a marriage for you? A pretty thing, slim too, getting older day-by-day?"

"I had a partner until . . . oh . . . not too long ago, but . . ."

"The jerk didn't appreciate you, did he?"

"I wouldn't quite put it that way. There were complications beyond his control. To change the subject, I'm a private eye, recruited to locate a ruby that has vanished. I wish to discuss that matter, if I may, which I believe is of interest to you."

"You're a cop? How dare you come to my house?"

"I've already told you I'm not." Maya noted the undertone of amazement and even hope in Anita's voice. "I work privately. Please, wouldn't you like to see the ruby returned to your family?"

"You better believe it, Girl Detective." Under the ceiling light, Anita's complexion looked blotchy, despair showing in her dark eyes. "You see the condition I'm in. I must apologize for my rudeness—I seem to have lost control of myself. Nobody has ever called me a sweet person, but now I've turned into a 'mad bitch.'"

Maya shot her a sympathetic look. "Due to the loss of the gemstone?"

"You could say that." Anita paused. "Tell me—can you help us find it?"

"Before I can do that . . . I need information. First, who does it belong to?"

"I'm Anita Adani and the ruby belongs to me. Don't ever question that."

"Pardon me, but how could the ruby have been in Rana's safe box, if it belonged to you?"

"How could it, indeed?" A mocking tone surfaced in Anita's voice. "Now you're getting to the heart of the matter. The situation is this. I turned the jewel over to Rana temporarily for safekeeping when I traveled abroad. I stayed in New York for several months, visiting, sight-seeing and shopping. After I returned home, I expected to have the piece returned to me, but Rana wouldn't even consider it. I suppose his guru, Neel, advised him to appropriate it. Much as I adore Uma-di, I can't stand Neel."

"Why?"

"An arrogant S.O.B., he acts like he's an expert but doles you wrong advice. Do you have to ask me?"

"Maybe he's an expert. After all, it's his passion in life."

"Passion, yes. Like father, like son."

"You mean Neel's father—?"

"Don't you know the elder Saha is a gem-cutter and gem-setter par excellence? He mastered the trade at the tender age of fifteen from his father. Years later, a newspaper article described his jewelry as 'ethereal and enviable' I called it super-duper awesome. I could kill for his pearl necklace. It'd add more shine to my eyes than an eyeliner ever would. They say that for Kavi, who worked all day with saws, as well as grinding, and faceting tools, sitting on the jeweler's bench was meditation.

"Apparently, one of his ancestors was a gem cutter and gem-setter for, no other than, a Jaipur *Maharaja*." Great King. "Imagine that. No doubt Kavi inherited much talent. Once he became partially blind, however, he couldn't work for long stretches of time, nor could he concentrate on the intricate details of our jewelry. Things went downhill for him. Ever since, he's been having a case of blahs. Now he serves as an astrologer, one with spiritual integrity, and makes his living that way. He's the opposite of his son, you might say. Kavi Saha deserves respect. Now, should I have shared all that with you? I met you fifteen minutes ago. What has come over me?"

"Thanks for sharing," Maya said. "Here's a hypothetical question. Suppose we retrieve the stone. Both you and Rana seem to claim it. Who should it go?"

"What a question, even though it's an interesting one. You believe the stone will be found? You're projecting into the future? I'm beginning to think you're okay and you're in the right line of work, so I'll answer." Anita paused. "The gemstone should go to Rana. Yes, to him, without any doubt. Much as I complain, I love him dearly. In our family we stick together. We're Adanis. I remember him as a cute, mischievous boy. He'd come to our house and finish all the laddoos. It was okay with us. His mother died when he was young. Well, Rana is still young. He's a dish, his eyes are on the stars. After his breakup with his wife, he went through hell. And now she's dead. He loved her. Even if it wasn't love forever, he's suffering. He needs the gemstone worse than—"

A noise at the door interrupted Anita's answer. Uma swept into the room, striking in a mauve-bordered white sari and a white beaded necklace, her hair caught in a bun. She held a proud posture and a slight smile. And yet Maya noticed weariness in her expression and fatigue lines etched on her forehead. Mom—she had to deal with Neel, among other mishaps in her life. Who knew how he treated her?

"Oh, my dear, you're here." Astonishment stealing into her voice, Uma turned to Maya, who stood with open arms.

The assistant interrupted Uma and handed her a red shawl with geometric design and zigzag finishing. Uma accepted it with thanks. Then she extended her arms, gave Maya a hug. Her usual, but looser and brief.

Although Maya harbored an unsettling feeling, she managed a calm voice. "How're you, Ma?"

Her tone edged with strain, Uma replied, "I'm fine, dear."

Not everything was all right. However, this would afford Maya a rare opportunity for a long-delayed talk. "Can I walk you home?"

"Oh, it's only five minutes from here but, fine, dear, we can have a stroll." Uma made a show of studying her watch and turned to Anita. "My darling daughter is here for a short stay. Will you please excuse us?"

"By all means," Anita said. "I bet you two have a lot of catching up to do. I can tell you don't see each other often. Hard for me to fathom. Mother and daughter becoming strangers to each other? What has our society turned into? See you in class next week, Uma-di. Be sure to practice at home."

Maya noticed the respectful "di" that Anita had added as a suffix to Uma's name, indicating they had a solid relationship. She said to Anita, "We'll continue our chat at another time."

"By all means," Anita replied, her tone warmer now. "I've picked up a few things from you, such as staying calm, taking the time and trying to see the larger picture. I'm the opposite. I mouth off at every opportunity, get myself in a fix, I'm too tightly wound in my problems. Yes, come by again, Girl Investigator. You're most welcome to join my class."

Outside, Maya and her mother wandered down a tree-lined street, elbowing their way through a crowd of shoppers. Uma, her face paler than usual and subdued, stayed silent. A light breeze puffed up her short-sleeved blouse.

Finally, unable to bear it any longer, Maya said, "What's going on, Ma? Why are you avoiding me? Why are you so pissed off? You don't even make the effort to answer my phone calls."

"Please forgive me," Uma said in a brittle voice. "I'm busy."

"I don't buy that. What makes you so busy?"

"Sam, my domestic helper, hasn't returned yet."

"Good grief. I could help you with the chores if only you'd ask. I suspect there's much more that you're hiding from me. I left Kolkata and flew here in a hurry because you needed help. And now you refuse to have any contact?" Seeing Uma not speak a word, only carry an expression of guilt, she continued, "I'm sure you're aware that Neel threw me out of your house. How did that make me feel, you ever wonder?"

Uma retrieved a tissue from her purse and wiped her eyes. "Wish I could . . ."

Maya could tell how torn Uma was inside, yet she had to continue. "Try as you might to hide important facts from me, I'm aware that Neel belongs to L.L.A. Have you considered the consequences of his holding membership in a terrorist organization? I mean . . . are you able to see how serious that is? What kind of danger you're in yourself? For your own protection I'd suggest that you . . ."

Reading hurt and disbelief in Uma's face, Maya stopped speaking. Uma halted and met Maya's eyes. "My dear daughter—I love Neel. I'll stay with him, even if he were a terrorist. Which I doubt he is." Uma blinked. Voice turning thinner, she said, "He's a respectable member of our society, a professor, a gemologist, a storyteller. Not a word about this topic again, okay?"

Regardless of what Uma said, Maya could see the change in her. Her delivery lacked conviction, indicating she harbored doubts about Neel. Hope bloomed in Maya. She might be getting somewhere. She remained concerned about how to protect Uma from possible domestic abuse. "Do you have any idea what you've gotten yourself into? Will you please consider your physical safety? And the ruby—could you tell me who swiped it?"

"What are you suggesting? That I walked off with it?" Uma's pinkish face was set in a hard line. "After all I did to raise you? Alone, with little money, with only a few relatives around. Do you have any idea how many times I skipped a meal to feed you? How ungrateful, how selfish, how low."

She had hit a nerve; Maya could see that. She fought a clogged throat and misty eyes. "I love you, Ma, I love you dearly. I'm not making any accusations."

Uma turned and began walking in the opposite direction. Standing on the sidewalk, with traffic all about her, Maya felt at a loss. She watched Uma look both ways before crossing the street and land on the other side, soon lost amongst a crowd of people. She sighed, turned, and began strolling down the avenue. A big-eyed boy, seated on a cycle rickshaw carrying school children, gave her a curious glance. Her mom, a single parent, with whom she'd been close, who always had her back, now abandoned her. Churning over Uma's bizarre behavior in her mind, Maya paid scant attention to what was going on nearby. She and Uma had been so close over the years. They'd sit and share the littlest of secrets, sipping tea, voices animated, and cell phones turned off, the afternoon ripening into the evening.

What changed? Maya felt a stab in her chest. Who could blame her if she caught the next flight back to Seattle, especially after she'd received warning from Alain? But, with Uma's safety in her mind—she could no longer rely on Neel after that run-in—leaving Jaipur wouldn't be a smart move. And she wouldn't give up on Uma, either. She'd take a different tack with her. She suspected from Uma's guilty looks that she was implicated in the disappearance of the ruby.

Taking a right, Maya wondered: Why would Uma pilfer the ruby, if she had indeed done so? The very thought caused a crimp in her stomach. Monetary profit wouldn't be the motive. No, Uma lived simply and never aspired to have more funds than she needed for basic expenses. Would she steal the gem on behalf of someone else? That was possible, given the amount of kindness Uma possessed but who might be the recipient? And where would Uma hide the precious object? It couldn't be at their flat. That'd be too risky, and the police would have found it. So, where?

It sprang to Maya's mind: Uma's weekend cottage—rural, out-of-the-way, woodsy—situated in the environs of Jaipur. Uma had gushed about her retreat and sent Maya photos, but so far hadn't invited her daughter there. Then and there, Maya made a pact with herself. She'd have to see that cottage with her own eyes. She pulled out her cell phone, called Boman, and arranged for him to drive her to Anatpura the next day.

Boman, who ferried Uma on an on-call basis, replied, "I'm familiar with her 'chalet.' Mrs. Uma says she 'roughs' it there, even though it's quite cozy. I drove her back to Jaipur yesterday and did some shopping for her. Something must have gone wrong. When I delivered the package, Mrs. Uma looked terrible. Like she'd had it."

"Any idea why?"

"No. Let me drive you to the cabin tomorrow. Mrs. Uma might be there. Even if she isn't there, you can see the place for yourself. As long as you feel safe to venture so far out of the city."

TWENTY-ONE

DAY 11

IT WAS EIGHT A.M. WHEN MAYA'S CELL PHONE dinged in her
hotel room. She jumped. Could it be Uma?

No. Instead, it was a text from Sophie that said: *Slept in. Hank
gone. I'm shook.*

Maya detected an urgency. Had Hank taken off for an L.L.A
forum? If so, when was he expected back? What if he got in a tight
spot there? A shiver went down the back of Maya's neck. Concern
rising, she sent Sophie a reply: *Come up to my room.*

No reply came. Sophie, young and impulsive—where was she?

Minutes later, when someone rapped on the door, Maya
answered. Sophie stood, clad in a lehenga-choli-dupatta ensemble.
It consisted of a light green crepe ankle-length skirt, a darker green
fitted brocade blouse, and a delicate jade silk dupatta scarf in beige,
her eyes red from crying. Only Sophie could get away with being
outfitted in such an elegant party gown so early in the day.

A wave of relief washed over Maya. She welcomed Sophie in.
"Hey, what's going on?"

"You wouldn't believe it, Maya-di. Hank and I had the nastiest
fight we ever had." Sophie blinked away her tears. "About that darn
L.L.A forum he was going to attend this morning. I suggested I go
with him. I promised to be quiet. He insisted it was for men only. I
said I'd wait for him in the lobby. He told me women aren't allowed

even in the lobby. We argued. He had a hissy fit. This morning when I woke, he wasn't there."

Sophie's obvious distress disturbed Maya. She'd never seen her like that. "Don't get worked up quite yet, okay?"

"It's not me alone who's worked-up, Maya-di. Hank's mother texted me minutes ago from Seattle. She's not feeling well. She'd like Hank to call her ASAP."

"In that case, we can't sit and wait. We'll rush out there and rescue Hank from the L.L.A headquarters. That's our only option."

Sophie's eyes rounded with worry. "What if that doesn't work? What'll we do then?"

Maya smiled. "We'll make it work."

"Cool, let's have a crack at it." Sophie piped up. "I'll be ready to give you a hand if you need it."

Gutsy girl. "Hey, do you see yourself as a criminal investigator when you grow up?" Maya asked, trying to distract Sophie.

"Yes, Maya-di, I want to be like you. Be out there, collaring bad guys and putting them to jail, 'hook'em and book'em' like they say on television."

Maya, feeling a blush of pride at Sophie's assertion, said, "Let's get started, then."

"Bet," Sophie said, giving her okay.

Her laptop was resting on the coffee table. Maya clicked a few times and zoomed in on a map of Jaipur and its environs. She pointed to a spot. "Right here is Anatpura, about an hour's drive from here. That's where Hank's meeting is taking place. We can kill two birds with one stone, pardon the pun. We'll get Hank out of that meeting somehow. That's our most pressing issue right now. Afterwards, we'll drop by Mom's weekend cottage."

"Will Uma-ma be there?"

"Don't have a clue. If she's there, jolly good. You'll get to meet her. If not, then we'd at least have checked out her mysterious hideout and what she might have kept out of sight there. How does that sound?"

"*Bahut achcha.*" Very good. Sophie looked animated as she spouted out another newly acquired phrase. "Countryside. A hide-out. Who knows what kind of mischief?" She paused. "I've done some groundwork on my own on L.L.A. using the internet. I'll share with you, Maya-di. For what it's worth, those thieves underpay their employees. They don't follow the Minimum Wage Act, make their employees work extra hours, and hold their overtime paychecks. As you might expect, they have a high turnover."

Maya gave Sophie a warm look. "Well, that's good information. It opens opportunities for us to give a gratuity, 'to grease the palm,' so to speak. I don't like to indulge in it if I don't have to but will take a chunk of cash with me in case the opportunity arises. Thanks for the tip."

"*Bahut achcha.*" She paused. "How do you like my new outfit?"

"You look so lovely."

In the next few minutes, Maya dressed herself in a cropped denim jacket, worn over a red camisole, and light blue corduroy pants. She wanted to appear efficient and business-like. In less than a half hour, she and Sophie shared the backseat of a taxi driven by Boman, heading toward the outskirts of Jaipur. Boman navigated through a semi-arid basin, with views of hills, thorny scrubs and sand deposits, an occasional eagle flying. This was followed by more habitable land. After a while, a soaring roof, with the backdrop of a plush forest came to view. Up ahead a waterfall, flowed like a shower of silver, making a gentle sound.

"We're getting close," Boman said.

His taxi bumped along a road full of potholes. Soon he entered a village dominated by a series of narrow streets. Torn old posters decorated the walls of the buildings, which had stood there for at least a century. The cracks, the peeled paints, and the debris held much history, Maya could tell. Before long, a wider paved street and a spacious, two-story, glass-and-steel office building with a shaded walkway loomed before them. At first sight, this renovated part of the hamlet seemed incongruous.

Boman slowed. "You have a view of the L.L.A headquarter, the most modern building in this neighborhood. By the way, this block has an interesting history. Would you like to hear about it?"

Sophie stirred. "Yes, spill the tea."

"The story commenced long ago, during my father's time. A bamboo shack stood in that spot, a shelter of sorts, furnished only with floor mats. The shack would sway in strong wind and whenever it rained. Called a *baithak*, it was a social gathering spot for men only, for them to smoke, gossip, and play cards, off-limits to women. Not only that, after a certain hour of the day, only men were allowed to walk these streets. Women dared not leave their homes."

"They put up with that?" Sophie asked.

"Well, Madam, what choice did they have? But times have changed. The modern building standing in front of us rents out office space to clients, which include several women entrepreneurs. L.L.A, a militant, men-only movement, sublets the entire ground floor. By the way, that landmark building is named WorldView."

Sophie laughed. "What a name for an out-of-the way location."

"Is it pretty modern inside?" Maya asked.

"From what I hear they have power back-up, an escalator, an atrium, a large hall, and other amenities. On Saturday afternoons, when most businesses are closed, L.L.A takes over the site. Their members, hundreds in number, gather for their weekly conference. Even to this day, they don't allow women to be members." He pulled into an empty parking spot behind the building. "Ladies, are you sure you want to get off here?"

Maya emerged from the car and shook her legs. "Of course, we are. We must see Hank to safety."

"They better let me in." Sophie hopped out and glanced at her wristwatch. "Or I'll call my dad in Sydney. He has many important connections. He can pull some strings, although the time difference . . ."

"We can't count on your dad." For a moment Maya considered the implications of barging in a so-called terrorist headquarters. "We have to depend on our own wits."

"I'll hang out in the parking lot." Boman paused. "And oh, please holler if you need help."

Up close, the building exuded a cold vibe. As they approached the entrance, through an open ground floor window, Maya could see a digital screen in a hall on which a graphical presentation was being made. Nearby, a young man slaved away at his laptop. That must be the office where L.L.A convened. They must catch Hank before the meeting was dispersed and he disappeared. Maya reached the front door and pushed it, only to discover it was locked. She pressed the buzzer and waited, silence following, her impatience growing.

A frowning aide, attired in the uniform of a security guard, peeked out from a lobby done in shades of light blue and yellow. A burst of high voices drifted from a room. "Yes?" the aide asked.

"We're here to pick up Hank Richardson," Maya said. "He's attending a meeting. Please tell him it's urgent and we're waiting for him."

"Never heard of any Hank Richardson," the aide replied, in a perturbed manner.

"Why don't you go and ask?" Maya said.

"I mean no offense, Madam, but I'm not allowed to disturb a closed-door session."

"Don't be such a hard ass," Sophie muttered under her breath.

The aide vanished, only to return in a nanosecond and say, "There's no Hank Richardson here."

He could be lying. Maya stood, posturing confidence. "Let me have a word with your general manager."

The aide mumbled something about this being a "Damn Day," but replied, "Very well." He let them in the building lobby and departed.

Within minutes, Maya heard the squeak of shoes, looked up, and saw the manager. A frantic-looking, well-muscled man in his thirties, with a mustache, he sized up his callers and introduced himself as Yash. With a wave of his hand, he led them to a small office—tidy and efficient—on the other end of the lobby. The walls were plastered with posters depicting historic Jaipur palaces.

Yash pointed to a pair of guest chairs, saying, "Have a seat, Ladies." Stalking around a large desk in which a laptop rested, he installed himself in a chair. He asked for their names and addresses, which he keyed in the laptop. Maya held her breath for more questions to follow.

Yash said, "How may I help you?"

"My boyfriend Hank is attending a session here." Sophie leaned forward; a look of discomfort was etched on her face. The dupatta scarf flew off her throat. She caught it with a trembling hand and rearranged it around her throat. "We want to get him out of here. He's 5'8" and handsome. Can you find him and tell him to come out immediately?"

"What do you mean 'get him out of here?'" Yash's face reddened. "This is not a prison. Everyone comes here voluntarily."

A pulse of panic ran through Maya. The air felt stagnant. How vulnerable they were, two women in a building in which a men-only assembly happened, not a soul around to help them. Each passing moment meant this could go bad. To assume control, she felt the hard floor beneath her feet, rolled her shoulders back, and looked Yash straight in the eye. "What Sophie means is that an urgent call has come from Hank's mother, who lives in the States." Maya's voice rose as she tried to drive home her point. "She's ailing and desperate for Hank to get in touch."

"Are you telling me the truth?" Yash asked in a taut voice.

"I'd never disrespect you like that."

"Don't you see I'm being extra accommodating to you, Ladies? That's because my mother is in the hospital. I acknowledge what you're going through." Yash paused. "But . . . be aware that you're violating a strict rule we have in our organization. Women are not allowed in this building when we're in session."

Maya bit back a reply. A quiet tension reigned in the room.

Sophie fiddled with her cell phone. "That's a nineteenth-century rule."

"L.L.A didn't exist in the nineteenth century, Madam."

Maya got the sense of what was expected here. Her fingers trembled a bit as she clicked her purse open, reached into it, yanked out a wad of rupee notes, and made a show of it. "If Hank's mother's condition worsens, then you'll be responsible for it."

"Do you realize what you're asking? You have a lot of nerve. I'm not high enough in the rank to disturb a closed session." Yash extended his hand on the top of the desk, palm open. "This is my third day on the job. I'd be fired on the spot."

Maya hesitated for an instant, then bounced up from her chair, reaching across the desk and dropping the rupee notes, the so-called "speed money" on the open palm. "Please ask Hank to come to us immediately. Tell him it's an emergency."

"This'll help pay my mother's hospital bills." Yash stared at the notes for a second, then pocketed them. "She'll appreciate it. But the thing is, Madam, you can't wait here."

Sophie sank deeper into her chair. "I'm not leaving without my boyfriend."

Maya crossed her arms. "Once again, let me emphasize for Hank's mother's sake how urgent this is."

"As you wish." Yash walked around the desk and exited through the door, only to return in a few minutes accompanied by Hank.

Hank, wearing a T-shirt that said, *Normal is boring*, burst into the room, his forehead filmed with sweat. His eyebrows went up a notch and he breathed quicker when he saw Maya and Sophie. "God almighty. What are you two . . .?"

Maya hoisted herself up from her seat. "We're here to collect you."

"Hey, how did you even find this place? Of course, of course, Maya, as a detective, you figure things out pretty quickly."

"Detective?" Yash said to Maya. "You're the law—?

"No, I work privately."

"Taking time out from your investigation?"

"What if I said this is part of my—?"

Yash turned to Hank in an eyeball-to-eyeball exchange, his voice rising. "You're spying, aren't you? You must never come back to our premises. Follow? We'll arrest you if you do."

"Hey, chill out," Sophie said.

"Wait a minute. Who are you to arrest me, you son of a bitch?" Without any warning, Hank pivoted, his right side coming forward, hand forming a tight fist, and he delivered a punch to Yash's gut.

Maya braced herself for a move of retaliation to come from Yash. Her face on fire, she positioned herself to deliver a front kick to his groin. In an unexpected development, Yash staggered backward, then caught his balance and breath, scrunched his face, and rubbed his belly, regaining his self-control. His eyes flashed; nose flared. "You, fucking foreigners, vacate our premises right this minute, or else I'll summon our security guard."

"Let's get outa here," Maya said to her companions.

"*Chalo.*" Let it be. Sophie jumped up from her seat, adding, "Hooroo," an Aussi form of goodbye.

They rushed out the door, with Maya sensing Yash's glare on her back. Outside, they speed-walked, three abreast, through the spacious parking lot punctuated by pebbles and potholes. Aside from a few parked vehicles, the lot was empty. Maya turned often to see if they were being followed. Elated to find they weren't, she inhaled deeply, taking in the calming woody fragrance from a nearby grove of trees.

"My mother would freak out," Hank said, "if I told her I attended a terrorist meeting. Big yikes."

"Call your mom ASAP," Sophie said to Hank and related a few details regarding his mom's health.

Hank's gaze flew to his watch. "Gosh, darn it. It's late over there. I'll buzz her the first thing tomorrow morning."

"Hey, did you have to punch that guy?" Sophie, now walking at a slower pace, said to Hank. "He was only trying to do his job."

"I'm sorry for what I did." Hank matched Sophie's footsteps. "Something came over me, my college days, I suppose. I went up the wall."

"You were macho," Sophie said. "You made a fool of yourself. Did you notice he didn't retaliate?"

"That's because he was fearful of me."

"No, he was bigger than you, he had fight in him," Sophie said. "Chose not to get into a boxing match. He looked like a nonviolent, vegetarian Buddhist to me."

"You've been here less than two weeks, Soph, and you already can tell a nonviolent, vegetarian Buddhist?"

"NC," Sophie said. No Comment.

"What are your thoughts, Maya?" Hank asked. "Why didn't that guy fight back?"

"He would have been in worse trouble if he got into a confrontation with you." Maya swung her purse, the sun on her back, enjoying the brisk walk. "The L.L.A is trying to improve its public image. It'd be bad form if words got out. Their new slogan is that they're an ambassador of peace."

"Peace? No kidding. I'm thrilled that you guys came looking for me in the nick of time and rescued me."

Maya listened to the wind blowing through the trees on the periphery of the lot and making a murmuring sound. "Were things getting a little dicey?"

"Yes, it was a rattrap. The meeting leader . . . well, I was afraid he'd interrogate me after the meeting was over. Maybe even sent me to the big house. I was freaking out. Big surprise. Gordon didn't show up, even though he'd promised me he would be there. I was all alone. I wanted to get the hell out of there. Then you showed up. Pretty cool." Hank smiled. "And oh, do I have an exclusive for you, Maya? It's a bit of troubling news, which has to do with Neel, and which makes me antsy. He's left L.L.A, it seems."

"Is that a fact?" Maya asked, squinting against the blinding sunlight, rattled by what she might hear next. "Was he expelled?"

"I wouldn't be too bewildered if he'd been booted out. About a month ago they caught him looting their treasury. Big bucks were missing."

"Did they recover the treasure?" Maya asked.

"No, he said he'd pay them back. So far, he hasn't."

"Can they unload him that easily?" Maya asked. "My guess is he knows an awful lot about what goes on at L.L.A."

"Right you are, they can't. Sounded like he was in a jam with the management for throwing a tantrum, for showing them disrespect and, most importantly, for overlooking his responsibility in paying back in their coffer."

Maya passed by a beggar sitting on the edge of the lot with a bowl in front of him. She reached into her purse, drew out a few coins, and put them in his bowl. He looked up with grateful eyes. "That's Neel for you," she said to Hank. "Mostly he gets away with his outbursts. But the money issue makes him vulnerable. L.L.A could play dirty, could come after him, ruthless as they are. That partly explains his recent behavior to which I've been privy."

Hank cleared his throat. "They also mentioned his father, Kavi Saha. They'll look him up, I suppose."

"Uh-oh. That's common practice around here. Your family pays for what you do. The poor man might be in danger. He needs to be warned."

"Have you ever met Mr. Saha?" Hank asked. "I hear he's a nice man, the complete opposite of his son."

"Haven't met him so far, but I'll make a point to. My mom stays in touch with him."

"What would happen to Uma-ma?" Sophie asked. "Will she be safe?"

A cloud of dust blew from a nearby road. Maya closed her eyes for a second. "One of my big preoccupations—I must figure out what my mom needs in terms of protection. As per our original plan, we'll now go to her cottage which isn't too far away and meet her there."

They'd reached the parked taxi. There stood Boman, opening the car door for them. "Relieved to see you're back safely, Ladies. And you, too, Mr. Hank."

"I appreciate your giving us rides," Hank said to him. "I don't drive much even in Seattle, much less try to find my way around here."

They piled onto the taxi. "Let's leave this place as fast as we can," Maya said from the backseat.

Boman turned the ignition. "Where to?"

"To my mom's chalet." Maya punched keys on her cell phone and recited the address. "Can't be too far away. Same street, a higher house number."

"That's correct. Like I said, I've taken Mrs. Uma there several times. Sometimes I drive her, at other times Mr. Neel drops her off."

"I don't mean to be difficult." Sophie moistened her lips. "But I'm dizzy and nauseous from hunger. Where can we get some chow?"

"Don't be cheeky," Hank said.

A happy note appeared in Boman's voice. "Funny you should ask. There's a fabulous carry-out joint not far from here. The cook is known for a famous dish, called undhiyu. Have you ever tasted it?"

"Nope," Sophie said. "But it sounds good and spicy. I suppose it takes hours to make and requires the help of several prep cooks."

"Right you are, Madam. Undhiyu is a casserole of stuffed vegetables, made with four or more selected seasonal produce, and at least twelve spices. It's a must for certain festivals. In earlier times, it required a complex cooking process, which has now been simplified. The dish is a specialty of Gujarat, considered fit for the royalty, and done in many styles. Our cook specializes in the Surti style."

Maya liked it that Boman was distracting Hank and Sophie from the chilling experience they'd gone through. Her mind wandered into the past, to the luxurious undhiyu spread she'd tasted during her youth. "That style happens to be my fave."

"It'll be a treat for you then," Boman said. "Rice and puri bread come with it at no extra cost. We'll stop on the way and do a carry-out. You can chill with it."

"Perf," Hank and Sophie said in unison.

TWENTY-TWO

DAY 11

AS THE TAXI SLOWED, A LOW RUSTIC COTTAGE loomed before them. Maya recognized it from the photos she'd seen: A small brick bungalow, nestled in a forested area, with wooden shutters and large windows. It sported a covered patio warmed by brilliant sunlight and decorated with potted plants overflowing with showy flowers. An orange butterfly fluttered over the flowers, flapping its silky wings. A shallow stream, making a low tinkling sound, formed a border on one side. A trail leading to a dense jungle hugged the other edge.

They climbed out of the car, crunching leaves under their feet. Maya led everyone to the front door. A smell of wild vegetation was all around her. She knocked on the door, hoping Uma would be there. She wanted to speak with her mom, thereby resolving any misunderstanding between them, bringing up the topic of the ruby if she could. Listening for any sound, her heart beating fast, she allowed a long minute to pass. Silence reigned save for an insect humming. No answer came.

"Doesn't look like my mom's here," Maya said.

"Let me try opening the back entrance," Boman said. "I saw Mrs. Uma hiding a spare key after she got locked out. If it's under the same marigold planter, then we're in luck."

Within minutes, the front door opened with a creak. Boman

stood aside, saying, "Come in, please."

"Oh, what a relief," Sophie said. "My feet need a break."

In the snug living room, Hank and Sophie settled on the upholstered couch. Hank rested his head against a pillow. Sophie kicked off her high heels and plonked her purse on the coffee table. Maya stood by the window, which treated her to a view of the jungle: evergreens with entwined branches, sprawling trees with lush, shiny foliage, insects humming. A tiny bird flew across her vision in a ripple of pink and gray. Soon Boman entered, hefting a large package, which he placed on the coffee table. He tore the paper wrapper to unveil an undhiyu feast, a gingery scent infusing the air. The casserole style dish, displaying pieces of sweet potato, eggplant, plantain, and green beans, was dredged in a coconut-infused sauce. Along with it came a stack of freshly made flatbread, puris, that were a requirement of most meals.

Sophie served everyone, doing so happily, then dug her fork into the dish. "I'm not much for vegetables, but I'll vouch for this one."

Maya, not quite at ease, took a few bites of the tasteful preparation. She had a sense that she should explore this spot, a rare opportunity to find out what Uma had been up to, if she'd indeed been up to something. "Excuse me," she said, "I'll be back."

Traipsing down a small corridor, she entered a small bedroom on the left and looked around. The décor consisted of a double bed, a reading lamp, a writing desk, and a chair. To the left there stood a walk-in closet, an arm's length deep and five feet wide. It pricked Maya's curiosity, this shady closet with a shelf, a horizontal rod for hanging clothes, and a chest of drawers. She stepped closer.

Next to the chest of drawers stood a lock box which could barely be seen due to the lack of light. A compact specimen with a touch keypad on its top cover, it had a single compartment which, to Maya's amazement, was open. She located an interior light and flipped the light switch.

The box was empty. Nothing there.

Maya stood for an instant. Did Uma—if she had indeed run off with the ruby—put it in that box originally for safekeeping? That'd make sense, given how secluded this hut was. Had the stone vanished? If so, who might have swindled it this time? Or had Uma transferred the priceless object to another location or person? If so, who and where?

She heard a click of the back entrance and Uma's voice, laden with astonishment, cried out, "What's all this noise? Who's there? Why do I smell chili?"

Before Maya could answer, Uma tiptoed into the bedroom. She was draped in a peach silk sari with an embroidered border and an allover jacquard design. Despite the festive nature of the outfit, she didn't radiate her usual energy and poise. A shocked expression pervading her face, she stood inside the doorway, facing Maya. "What are you doing here? How did you even get in? You didn't even call?"

"We happened to be in the vicinity, Ma—Hank, Sophie, and I. Thought we'd drop by. Boman let us in."

"Let me get this," Uma said, eyes wide in disbelief. "You just happened to be in this rural area, huh."

"Yes, Ma, that's the—"

Uma interrupted her in a stern voice. "You're intruding, looking for the elusive gem, I suppose?"

Maya's head pulsed with remorse. She didn't wish to have this sort of a conversation with Uma, ever. But, all things considered, she might as well lay all her cards on the table. "Yes, where is it? You bought a lock box, which now sits idle."

Uma stiffened and took a step back. "You think I lifted the ruby?"

"Breaks my heart to say this and I'm sure you have your reasons, but—"

"Drop it, will you? Drop it."

"No, Ma, I won't." Standing tall, Maya remained steadfast in her resolution. She must confront Uma on this issue. Her voice clear and strong, she said, "You put me onto this case. Remember? You can't back out now. As if the loss of ruby wasn't enough, there's been a death, a murder. More than likely, Bea, an innocent person, gave her life because of the ruby. It was stolen by someone else. I must locate the darn object. I must."

"Now you're accusing me of a murder? How dare you? Have you forgotten our tradition of showing respect to our mother?"

"I haven't forgotten, Ma. I haven't. It devastates me to say this and I'm not fully sure of this, but many things point to you as being someone who might be hiding the jewel."

"That's the craziest thing I've ever heard. Ungrateful daughter. Why would I want to embezzle? Can you tell me? You can very well see I don't want more material goods than what I have. Have I ever asked you for a penny?"

Maya sighed. "You haven't, Ma, this is only a hunch."

Uma's forehead hardened into a frown. She made an eye contact. "Preposterous."

Uma—acting angry, possibly because of feelings of guilt she carried, yet showing softness around her eyes. Did she have something to hide? Afraid that it'd slip out? Maya steeled herself and made a mental calculation. At least for now, she must distract Uma from this topic. She wouldn't get too much more now.

Aware that Uma loved social gatherings, herself an awesome hostess and party thrower, she said, "Shall we go to the living room and make our acquaintance with my assistant and his girlfriend? Sophie, a darling young woman is dying to meet you."

Maya heard Sophie's voice. "Maya-di, where are you? Join us, we're missing you."

Perfect timing. Maya stepped into the living room, with Uma trailing behind her. Hank and Sophie were stretched out on either end of the sofa, with blissful expressions on their faces, several soiled dishes resting in the coffee table in front of them. Seeing Maya enter, they sat up straight. Maya made the introductions. Both Hank and Sophie stood up from their seats, smiled, and exchanged words of greeting with Uma.

Drawing closer, Sophie gave Uma a hug. "Uma-ma, where have you been?"

"My darling girl, I'm so happy to meet you. Don't you look

lovely in a lehenga?" Uma, wearing a loving expression, caressed Sophie's hair and placed a hand on top of her head in a gesture of blessing. "Please forgive me for not having you over to my flat in the city. I've been a terrible, terrible host. These crazy couple of weeks."

Classic Uma.

"Please," Hank said, "You don't have to apologize. We're here to do a job."

"A job?" Uma said curtly. "Yes, of course."

That offered Maya an excuse to blurt out, "We must be on our way. I've kept Boman waiting a long time. I'll be in touch. Love you, Ma."

For one tiny instant, Maya noticed how Uma's eyes misted, as she replied, "Love you, my dear daughter."

All three said goodbye to Uma, exited the house, and climbed into the taxi.

As the taxi plodded along a rural road, Sophie said, "Pleasant, Maya-di, but did you find what you were looking for?"

"No, not the stone, it wasn't there. But I understand my mom. She's clever. My guess is she's moved it somewhere else."

"It's been a bumpy ride so to speak," Hank said. "Your next move, boss?"

"I'll arrange to meet a gentleman I haven't run across thus far, despite several attempts on my part, one who might hold some answers."

"Neel's father, Mr. Saha, isn't that so?" Hank said.

"Right you are," Maya said.

Sophie's face lit up. "Are you aware he has a new website, Maya-di? I've checked it out. Now you can make an astrology appointment with him directly from his site. Seems to me he's getting his shit together."

"That'll make it easier to contact him. I'm grateful to you, Sophie." In a flash of inner knowing, Maya figured out the rest. She took a little delight as she said, "Gut instinct, but also the circumstance points to Kavi Saha as someone to brainstorm with. He'll have a strong motivation for wanting to see the stone back and safely tucked away. My first order of business tomorrow morning will be to call him again."

THAT AFTERNOON, WHILE STROLLING THROUGH A multitude of stalls displaying textile and handicraft items, Maya made a call to Simi. With several new developments, she decided it'd be helpful to bounce ideas and observations off her. It was not quite six p.m. and Simi, known to stay at her desk late, should be there.

Simi answered on the second ring. "Be with you in a flash."

As Maya wandered her way through the stalls, the driver of a cycle rickshaw slowed and asked, "Where you want to go, Madam? I'll take you there for only hundred rupees. Fixed price. No? Okay, seventy-five."

Maya smiled, thanked him, and waved him away. She browsed the window display of the front façade of a textile emporium, her eyes mesmerized by the colors, fabrics, and designs.

"Where are you calling from?" Simi had returned to the line. "I hear sounds of honking, haggling, and happy chatter." When Maya recited the name of the store, Simi replied, "Oh, my favorite haunt in Jaipur when I go there. Any particular piece that grabs you?"

"Several," Maya said. "A hand-block printed Jamdani cotton, a sequined georgette and a Banaras silk adored with gold brocade."

"To serve as bed linens, window curtains and sofa covers, I suppose," Simi said. "Back to the matter at hand. How did your excursion to your mom's cabin go?"

"It helped sort out a few things," Maya said. "The ruby wasn't there. She's moved it somewhere. But first, allow me to back up and explain in detail how the ruby was burgled to begin with."

"I'm all ears."

"On that fateful evening, the ruby disappeared, Neel and my mom were at Rana's." Maya took a deep breath and drew the scene, the way she had put it together in her mind. All three of them lounged in Rana's bedroom, darkness descending outside the window, friendly conversation surrounding them, music playing.

Minutes before, Neel had finished cleaning the ruby, as he did peri-
odically. He placed the dazzling stone back in the safe box, a look
of satisfaction on his face. Then Neel and Rana excused themselves
and retired to the living room to have tea or a smoke. Uma stayed
in the bedroom alone and listened to music. Rana, who loved and
trusted Uma, thought nothing of leaving her with the precious
object. "At that point," Maya continued, "with no one else around,
Uma seized the ruby, as she'd been planning to do, with a pair of
gloves she carried, and shoved it in her purse."

"Goodness gracious. How could Uma . . .?"

"My mom—she didn't do it for her own gain. She had a purer
motive, which I'm yet to fully grasp. I'm also sure that her heartbeat increased, legs became like jelly, but she put on a calm face
and joined Neel and Rana in the living room, as if nothing had
gone on."

"So, when did Rana discover the stone missing?" Simi asked.

"After Mom and Neel left for home, Rana did a look see and
found the safe box to be empty and the stone to be absent. There
was no sign of forced entry anywhere and the servants had gone
home hours ago. At first dumbfounded, Rana soon concluded it
was my mom who had stolen the ruby. He couldn't figure out her
motive. He loved and respected her so much that when he contacted the police and they questioned him, he avoided naming any
suspect. The police detained Neel because he was already under
their surveillance, which has to do with his L.L.A affiliation."

"I'm baffled by Uma's behavior, I must say."

"It gets a little tricky here. My guess is my mom wanted to get
the ruby in her possession before Neel ran off with it. She sensed
that he was plotting such an act, which he'd execute in very near
future. Yes, she could sense the threat was there."

"Why might Neel want to do that?" Simi asked. "He's not a
collector. Did he want to sell it? Did he need gigabucks on short
notice?"

"Absolutely. Neel being extravagant, money is always a motivation. Quite often, his spending gets out of hand. He's also lost

a bundle in betting on horses. Here's something more serious. He had a fallout with L.L.A. and he owed them serious money. It appears that he'd appropriated from their treasury and been found out. Instead of turning him over to the police, they've negotiated an agreement with him. He'll pay them back with interest and thereby avoid a jail term. But . . . Neel doesn't have the funds.

"So, the question is: What is he going to do? You know how ruthless L.L.A can be if you don't follow through on your promises. My guess is Neel is scared, as scared as he's ever been. So, he considers appropriating the ruby. He believes, with the connections he has, he can trade that ruby quietly in the international market and make a mint." Maya paused a brief instant. "So, this is the way it has turned out to be. Both Mom and Neel had their eyes on the ruby, each having their own motivations for wanting to possess it. My mom—she has good values. She gives more than she ever takes. My conjecture is she must have had another strong motive for robbing, which is yet to be revealed."

"And how does Rana figure in all this?" Simi asked.

"Rana is devoted to my mom, respectful to her as an elder. My guess is: He's simply waiting to hear the rest of the story, without any guarantee that the stone will ever be returned to him."

"Okay, that devotion, that respect, speaks to his moral character, doesn't it? Simi said. "As far as our society goes, however modern we are, however many space missions we launch, however great our technology hub is, we assign a high value on a person's character, beliefs, and moral codes. You know how in our matrimonial ads we ask for, 'Slim, handsome, pleasant, educated.' Then, when the time comes, we also look for integrity and genuine caring."

"Agreed. Rana is much more than what he appeared to be at first. Only after meeting him several times and observing him have I realized that he has good values. Even so, a question about him haunts my mind. How would he handle the final fate of the ruby?" Maya checked the time. "It's getting late. You probably want to get home. I'll share the rest of this puzzle piece with you in due time."

"I can hardly wait, fascinated as I am by the various angles of this case—the missing ruby with its aura, cosmic significance, and what it means to the family who owned it and lost it. How the stone is more precious in human terms than its market value. How it rocks relationships. We've never had an inquiry like this." Simi paused. "In speaking with my own mother yesterday, I came to know that in ancient times, people offered rubies, if they could at all afford them, to their favorite deity in the temple. They'd set the ruby down at the feet of the statue, along with an offering of fresh flowers. The belief was that by doing so they'd be blessed with good fortune, such that they'd be reborn under more affluent circumstances. Big incentive for the worshipper. Nice profit for the temple priests. Call me any time, Maya."

TWENTY-THREE

DAY 12

"**W**ILL YOU PLEASE COME TO OUR STATION, Maya, for an interrogation?" Inspector Dev said on the phone the next morning at about ten a.m. "We got Sam, but we can't get much out of him."

Maya suppressed her sorrow at hearing about the free-wheeling kite flyer, now under police custody. She was filled with apprehension about his part in Bea's death. "I'll be right over."

It was ten-thirty a.m. when Maya made it to the police station. A stern-faced attendant with erect bearing showed her to the interrogation room, adding that he'd wait outside. The small, sound-insulated, windowless chamber, with chalky-white walls, appeared to be non-threatening and conducive to conversation. The furnishing consisted of a table and several office-type chairs, as well as audio and video recording systems.

Sam, who sat with his head down and back rounded, raised his eyes. Maya slid into a chair on the same side as Sam, leaving a companionable distance between them. She preferred that the interview process be non-adversarial.

His tone guarded, Sam said, "Maya-di, you're here?"

Projecting warmth and openness, she replied in a cheerful voice, "How're you doing? Your finger—has it healed?"

"I'm so-so and my finger is getting better. Happy to see you. A surprise, I must say."

"I'm here to work with you, Sam. Allow me to speak about a few things."

His face brightened. "Naturally, Maya-di. I'll answer any question you ask."

"Hope you won't mind sharing a few details. You have the right not to answer any or all questions. This is being recorded, by the way. Also, everything you say or don't fully say can be set against you in the court of law. You have the right to a lawyer."

"No lawyer for me, Maya-di. I'm a simple man. Lawyers scare me. They speak gibberish." His gaze scoped out the room. "Why am I being detained here, in this hole? I didn't do anything wrong."

"What can you tell me about a recent kite crash in front of Radha Produce?"

"Oh, that one. An accident, a pure accident, kites fall from the sky all the time."

"Maybe so, but Bea Adani died in that accident." Maya took a breather, feeling heart-sick at recalling the news of the incident. "A fallen kite thread looped around her throat and cut into it, causing her to bleed a most painful death. We need to understand where the kite descended from and if she was being targeted. Which is why I'm here. Can you tell me if it was *your* kite?"

His face gloomy, Sam rubbed his eyes, then looked away.

"You, a champion kite-flyer, were kiting close by. More than likely, it was your kite that killed Bea Adani. Some might suspect it had been planned that way." Maya paused. "Remember, you have a right to remain silent. You can make mental notes of everything that's going on around you."

"Okay, okay, I won't deny it. It was my kite."

"Was this 'accident' planned? Was someone else involved in this? If so, please tell me who. Did you get paid?"

Sam said nothing. His silence made the room seem stark, formal, and forbidding.

"The police are interested in finding out who was behind this, Sam. If you cooperate with them, they may ask the judge to be lenient with you." Seeing him lower his head, she added, "Please,

Sam. What can you tell me about whoever offered you a bribe, a side-hustle to carry out a scheme such as this? I can offer explanations to prove Bea was innocent. She died because of a scheme. Whose scheme? Not my mom's, I don't think."

"No, no, Mrs. Uma never asked me for any favor."

"Who then?"

"All I ever wanted was to have all the time in the world to fly kites."

"Someone hatched a plan, then tempted you with a bundle of cash. You went along with it, so you'd be able to buy as many kites as you wished, stay in pricey hotels, and travel. Who did that?"

Silence.

"Didn't you fancy new kites and new equipment? Wish you had spare funds? When the opportunity arose, when someone made such an offer, didn't you give into temptation? If yes, who was it?"

Sam's lips trembled. "He'll kill me if . . ."

Maya dragged her chair closer. "He won't get a chance. Rest assured you'll be safe."

"If you must know . . . I hate to be the bearer of bad news and he's part of your family. It's Mr. Neel."

"Neel? My God. What did he ask you to do?"

Sam looked to the left; his voice was teary. "He tasked me with tracking down the ruby. 'Go find it, you fool,' he ordered. So, he could sell it in the gem market and make a killing. Looked as though he needed a large sum of money, several hundred times more than what he paid me, on short notice. I told him I was no good at what he was asking me to do."

"What did he say?"

"If he didn't produce the funds, the militants, the L.L.A, would come after him. They'd threatened to chop his arm off. He seemed nervous, desperate, spooked. The sick thing was despite all that he wouldn't let me off the hook. Time and again, he asked me to meet him secretly at the Lord Shiva Temple after dark. Hardly anyone would be there. He insisted no one would suspect what we were up to. It was eerie to plan a murder in front of God Shiva, I tell you.

But I quietly recorded all our conversations, assuming he'd try to screw me later. Pardon my language."

"So, he bullied you to . . .?"

"Yes." Sam's voice trembled. "'Get the job done,' he told me. 'As quickly as possible. Like in a few days.' Or else, he threatened that I'd be busted. On false charges. Then I'd be in dungeon for the rest of my life. 'What's the big deal?' he said in a tough guy voice. 'Say yes. And don't believe for an instant that you can run away. I have someone following you 24-hours.' Given that I was employed in his household as a servant, how could I not obey, antsy beyond belief like I was? He got me into this mess."

"Was there pay-off?"

Sam nodded. "At our last get-together, he handed me a suitcase. Filled with bundles of cash. It was more money than I'd ever seen in my life. I couldn't breathe. 'Get the job done,' he said. 'The cops aren't too smart. They'd believe it was an accident. I'll protect you. You'll be safe. Don't worry.'"

"Did you believe him?"

"No. How could I? At first, I declined the money. Oh, you should have seen his reaction. He fisted his hand. He forewarned me— he'd blind me. Then I'd never be able to fly a kite again. Again, he said he'd have the cops put me away in the big house. He was serious, I could tell. I'm a nobody. Who'll care about me?" He paused. "Through all this, he kept Mrs. Uma in the dark. He told me so. He instructed me not to say a word about this to her, or else—"

"Was anyone else involved in this scheme?"

"I doubt, although I was convinced Mr. Neel had contracted ruffians to shadow me, to keep tabs on my comings and goings. Remember I talked to you about that?"

"Yes. Where did Neel believe the ruby went?"

"He was convinced that Mrs. Bea had lifted the ruby and stashed it away in her apartment. Who else would have access to Mr. Rana's bedroom? Also, her family in KL was poor and she must be trying to help them. And who else but Mrs. Bea would have the knowledge that Mr. Rana often forgot to turn on the security system? Mr. Neel didn't game out other scenarios, so confident was he of his belief."

"Why did Neel want Bea to be killed? Why not steal the ruby from her apartment, if indeed she had it hidden there?

"To keep her mouth permanently shut. I have no doubt Mrs. Bea could tell she was being trailed by thugs. They were Mr. Neel's accomplices. If any of them were ever caught, then the whole story would come out, the fact that Mr. Neel had enlisted them, that he wanted the ruby for himself. Mr. Neel couldn't take a chance, or so he confided in me."

"You accepted Neel's offer. Did you realize you were violating the law?"

Sam nodded, a painful nod, his face crumpled. "I was afraid, Maya-di, so afraid I couldn't sleep at night." He wailed; tears streamed down his cheeks. "What choice did I have, me, a lowly domestic helper, with no connections?"

A few silent moments passed; Maya allowed Sam to pull himself together. "You snuck into Bea's apartment right away, didn't you, after the kiting 'accident?' What was your reaction, realizing she was no more?"

"I was sorry that I had taken someone's life. Nothing would ever be the same for me. My chest was tight, I had trouble breathing, but I had to finish the job."

"You hunted for the ruby but didn't come across it. How did you feel?"

"Terrible." Sam replied in a resigned tone of voice. "It made me miserable when it hit me that Mrs. Bea was innocent. She hadn't committed a theft. She was all packed. Like she was ready to leave town."

In the pause, Maya ruminated: If only Bea had taken off, she'd still be alive today.

"An instant later," Sam continued, "I got the creeps, being fearful of Mr. Neel, what he might do to me. He didn't have the ruby and I knew too much. We were supposed to meet that evening. I decided to pull out of the town rather than face his wrath."

"Did he try to get in touch?"

"Yes, many times, but I stopped answering his calls. I've been on the run ever since, town after town, often sleeping on a park bench, a fugitive. The police personnel found me on a bus. I sat by a window, looking at the high sky, wishing I could be out there with one of my new missiles." His voice caught; the corners of his mouth were pulled down.

"Take your time; I'm in no rush."

"Then I spotted cops rushing into the bus. They ordered me to disembark with my luggage. Standing on the sidewalk, I responded to their preliminary questions, without trying to obstruct. I also complied with their command to hop into their vehicle and be transported to this station. They raised their eyebrows when they found bundles of cash in my suitcase—called them dirty cash—although not the ruby." Sam fixed Maya with a pleading stare. "What'll happen next, Maya-di?"

"The police will cross-examine you further. In compliance with the Indian Penal code, Section 302, Punishment for Murder, a charge sheet may be filed against you. You may be fined or booked for homicide. A court case could follow."

Sam, trying to control his tears, avoided eye contact. "If I'm found guilty of committing a felony, then will they incarcerate me for the rest of my life? Or will I get a death sentence? Will they take my kites away? Or maybe I should reserve these questions for the officer?

"Yes, you may." Maya shuddered, contemplating the future that awaited Sam, hoping for a fair trial for him. She posed one last question. "Should I have asked you anything else?"

"No, Maya-di. You listened to my sad story, the hell I've been going through, and all the rest. Please, locate the ruby. That'd at least prove I didn't steal it. I won't be punished for it. There's more." Sam pulled a cell phone from his pocket and handed it to Maya. "You'll find all my conversations with Mr. Neel recorded here, proof of what I've confided in you."

Maya grabbed the phone and expressed her gratefulness for the evidence received. "Is there anything else *you* want to add?"

Sam dragged in a breath. "Sorry . . . so sorry to have disappointed you. You cared about me. You spoke to me kindly. And Mrs. Uma—she treated me like her son. I failed both of you."

Maya spent a quiet instant with Sam, glanced down at her watch, and rose to her feet.

Heart heavy, she said to Sam, "I must go now."

"Before you go," Sam said. "I must warn you. Mr. Neel would try to harm both you and Mrs. Uma. He'd said so himself. Please take this seriously. Please protect yourself and Mrs. Uma, will you please?"

Rattled but gathering up her confidence, Maya thanked Sam. Silently, his eyes brimming, Sam bent forward and folded his hand into a namaste.

The same impassive-faced attendant opened the door and stood facing Maya. "The inspector-saab would like to see you now, Madam."

Perfect timing. Now that she'd gathered enough case history, it was time to speak with Inspector Dev and verify the information. She'd ask him to bring Neel, the architect of this crime, back into the picture. It was only a matter of time, a day or two. Police officers would nab Neel from his apartment and bring him to the station, following which both she and Inspector Dev would cross-examine him.

Maya waved to Sam, gave him a last look, and turned, feeling a push behind her eyes.

TWENTY-FOUR

DAY 13

THE RUBY MUST BE FOUND. SOON. If only to prove Sam didn't swipe it. Which would only add to the trouble he had courted already. Maya's taxi halted in front of a multistory apartment complex: Kavi Saha's abode. A stunning view of the cloud-shrouded Aravalli Mountain range greeted her. Her watch read nine-forty a.m.

"What a lovely sight," she said to Boman. "Those are some of the most ancient mountains, aren't they?"

"Yes, we consider our hills most sacred." Boman pulled his cab to the curbside. "Many medicinal herbs grow there. Unfortunately, much mining is going on, although we do try to conserve the range through a 'Save Aravalli' project. And oh, we also maintain a biodiversity hotspot in the wooded areas. Even our school children will not break a tree branch, while doing a trek. They fear an evil spirit will come after them."

Maya climbed out of the taxi. In front of the apartment complex rested a garden patch dominated by a dense evergreen hibiscus shrub. Next to it stood a grouping of pink-shaded butterfly flower plants, orchid look-alikes. In the background, a lily pool blooming with blue lotus invited the viewer to linger and savor the peaceful ambience. As far as Maya's eyes could see, the neighborhood was dotted with parks, paved roads, shopping malls, and modern buildings, as well as shrines and temples.

"Everything is 'nearest to this location.'" Boman smiled. "That's our local way of saying this area is convenient."

Maya appreciated his colorful phrase and arranged for a time to be picked up. Apprehension zipped through her mind; Kavi Saha, Neel's father, was known to be shy and quiet. She must create a climate of goodwill and offer him every opportunity to share his viewpoint. Stepping to the front door, she located the bell, and rang it.

The door swung open. "Come in, Maya." It was Kavi Saha himself. He ushered her into the apartment, speaking in a voice that had a touch of chill to it. His face was lined with wrinkles, each of which hinted at a story. A distinguished man with unremarkable features, he showed flair in the way he was dressed: a well-fitted camel vest over a formal cream shirt. His smoothly shaven head attested to a sense of quiet self-confidence.

Feeling awkward but maintaining a pleasant expression, Maya surveyed the apartment. It was airy, spotless, and tastefully decorated, with a few carefully positioned furniture pieces to convey an ambience of elegant austerity. On the coffee table stood a water bowl of white floating jasmine blossoms, so white they were said to compete with moon light. All of which astounded Maya. She'd heard that Kavi, once renowned as a stone cutter and stone setter, had succumbed to a series of misfortunes. He was rumored to suffer from clinical depression. These lively decorations indicated otherwise.

"So, what brings you to see me?" Kavi asked sharply.

"What would be your guess?"

A look of alarm passed over Kavi's face; his hands clenched. "You're wondering if the ruby is to be found in this house? Are you going to call the cops and have me apprehended?"

His reply and facial expression had given something away. Maya chuckled to herself. "Rest assured that the authorities have no idea I'm here."

"Why should I trust you?"

"It's frustrating," Maya said. "It seems like almost everyplace I go in this town, I run into a mistrust of the police and a mistrust of me as a P.I."

"Do you know why?" Kavi said, wariness in his eyes. "It goes back to the colonial era when the police force put down all dissension and oppressed the common folks at every chance they got. They tried to instill fear of the authorities. What else? Times are different—we're an independent nation. Now their motto is: We're the 'Protector of the People.' But if truth be revealed, they intimidate and harass us like before and provide zero protection."

"Allow me to explain my position," Maya said. "What I do and how I do it is different. The police enforce the law and make arrests, but they can't afford to spend too many hours investigating a case unless it's a major crime. As a P.I., I'm retained by a client, and I devote as much time as is necessary on their behalf to break a case." She made a gesture to rise. "If my presence makes you uncomfortable, then I should leave."

His face cleared. "No, no, please sit down, and please forgive me. I'm an old man, I have my phobias. I understand your duties and responsibilities better now. Shall we start over?"

Was he testing her? "I'll try not to take up too much of your time."

"What's the hurry? I have all day. A lady detective? I can't begin to tell you how honored I am that you've come to my place."

"Yet, for days, I couldn't make an appointment with you."

"My apologies. You try to simplify your life as you get older. You don't always succeed."

Maya noticed Kavi's vigor, perfect posture, and voluble nature. How he eased toward her in his chair, eager to engage, displaying a change of attitude. Perhaps it had helped that she'd explained herself and tried to build trust. She inquired as to his well-being.

"We have a saying in India," Kavi said. "The three uncertainties in life are women, wind, and wealth. I've suffered through all three. Lost my wife, the love of my life, to a long illness. Had to sell my gem business to pay off a debt. My only child, Neel, will not speak with me. But . . . but that's how the cookie crumbles. I couldn't leave my flat for weeks. I had no appetite. But you learn to stand up. You try to squeeze out whatever joy you can get from your life. What about you?"

"I'll share my list," Maya said. "The missing ruby—I haven't been able to recover it, not quite yet, although I might be getting closer. Tragically, Bea has passed. On top of that, my mom has severed all connections with me. So, like you, I'm surviving, continuing to do my investigative work, and trying to make sense of it all."

"I'm sorry, Maya, for what you're going through. I've heard much about you from Uma."

"When did you last see her?"

"Oh, very recently."

Maya's mind began to churn: What might have been the nature of the connection between Kavi and Uma? Astrological chart reading? Gemstone-related debates? Some other matter?

"Any help you need . . ." Kavi said. "I consider you part of my family."

"May I ask a few questions?"

"You certainly may."

"You seem to have come to terms with your losses—if you don't mind my saying so. You're following an upward trajectory, so to speak."

"How did I manage that? Passion, hard work, luck, whatever you might want to call it, Maya, not to overlook the astrology facet. My horoscope practice, which originated as a mere hobby, then a part-time job, has progressed beyond my belief. We Indian folks call astrology the 'Language of the Cosmos,' and the 'Science of Fate.' Lately, it has gained momentum with the public. I can't keep up with the flow of clients. They're all eager to have a 'cosmic chat' with me. They want to hear when they'll get a raise, when the person of their choice will propose to them, or how they should name their newborn. In other words, they seek answers from the heavenly bodies through me. I benefit from those explorations, as well."

Maya had never invested much belief in the stars. At the same time, she must show her attentiveness so that Kavi would share more. "Happy to hear that. On another topic, are you aware of what's going on with Neel?"

"That he's gotten in a bind? With L.L.A? My son—he's at once a good boy and a challenge. It was right here in Jaipur, as a matter of fact. I sent Neel, then a troubled kid, to L.L.A. At the time, they were only a school for boys—not a militant organization—that enforced strict discipline. 'Tough Love,' as Americans say." Kavi sighed. "They straightened out Neel, although not entirely. His temper—when he wants something, he must have it at all costs—hasn't subsided. Uma is the best thing that has ever happened to him. He should hold onto her with his dear life."

Somewhere a temple bell sounded, signifying the arrival of beneficial forces. Maya studied Kavi's face. "This matter between Neel and L.L.A—"

"I've heard that he's been accused of stealing a substantial sum from their treasury. Who knows what the true story is? He's also lost a fortune in gambling at horse racing. Since I'm making plenty of money, it'd be no hassle for me to pay L.L.A off and free Neel from his obligations. If only he would ask me. I'd arrange for a money transfer. That'd be the easy part."

"The difficult part is . . ."

"My son despises me. It breaks my heart to say this, and it can't get much darker, but he's written me off. He'll not take a paise from me. We can't have a civil discussion, on the phone or in person."

"That can make for an untenable situation—"

Maya left her sentence unfinished as a white-clad servant, bearing glasses of chilled pink guava juice, appeared. Along with that came a platter of rajbhog, literally royal dessert: soft, spongy, syrupy white rounds, flavored with saffron and cardamom, whose aroma infused the air. He served them both with care and strutted out.

"Please help yourself," Kavi said in an affectionate manner. "Guava is refreshing, you know. Not only is its juice sweet and tangy, but it also gives you instant pep. And rajbhog. As close to heaven as you can get. I'm exaggerating, of course. Have you had rajbhog?"

"Oh, yes, I grew up on them." Maya savored a piece that melted in her mouth. It brought back childhood memories of excursions to sweet shops in her native Kolkata. How Uma would cut corners and save a few rupees, so Maya could have a treat on a holiday. "Haven't had them in a while."

Kavi's lips parted in a smile. "Old as I am, I appreciate the finer things of life, such as this delicacy freshly flown in from Kolkata, made the same day. Rajbhog originated there before you were born. Initially offered in the temples as 'the food for the gods,' it's now reserved for special family occasions." He paused. "Where were we?"

"We were talking about Neel."

"What a pity," Kavi said. "Besides his problems with L.L.A, Neel has issues with Uma. Did you know that? That relationship is hanging by a very thin thread. From what Uma shared with me, a lack of trust has grown between them. They're fighting all the time, blaming each other for the loss of the ruby and all that has resulted from it."

Maya, in shock from hearing the latest, closed her eyes for a second. "My mom—she'll suffer. She loves Neel. They haven't been getting along for a while. My guess is their disagreements intensified with the ruby."

"Which neither of them has," Kavi said.

Maya smiled. "Of course; it's in your possession."

Kavi appeared to be startled. "Why do you suppose so?"

"This is what I believe happened. My mom took the ruby from Rana's safe box—which required a lot of nerve, I must say—so she could return it to you. That was her sole motive. It's true to her character."

Kavi straightened, alarm in his eyes. "Are you now going to …?"

"Look, Mr. Saha, The answer is again no. I will not involve the cops. As I mentioned I'd like to see the stone returned to its rightful owner."

"Who do you think the stone belongs to?"

"This is a story of two families, each owning the ruby at different points in time. You're the original owner. You loaned it to another family for a cash payment. That's all we know at this juncture. Your side of the story hasn't been told."

Kavi smiled thinly, relief spreading across his face. "You really are a detective, Maya. Could you share with me how you came to such a conclusion?"

"I'll do that in due time. First, will you please show me the ruby? I must see it with my own eyes, the object that has ripped apart so many lives. Caused a death—a possible murder. It devastates me to contemplate what happened to an innocent person like Bea. Not to forget the misunderstanding that has resulted between various parties."

"Fair enough." Kavi pushed himself up from his chair. "Come, let's have a look at our precious little trouble-maker."

Maya followed Kavi, who shuffled down a well-illuminated corridor to a tiny study and switched on the light. Against the opposite wall stood a steel cabinet that looked brand new and had a metallic smell about it.

Kavi stepped closer to it. "This cabinet is fire-safe and water-proof and has a steel cable to make it stationary." A buzz of excitement in the air, he pulled a drawer open and waved a hand like a sorcerer, urging Maya to draw closer. "Please."

Maya's eyes opened wider. The huge scarlet ruby, deep and vivid, with a bluish tinge, rested in a velvety box. Complex in shape, the stone sparkled like a cluster of stars, a symbol of wealth, mystique, and royalty, as well as a source of strength. Translucent and velvet-toned, it radiated mystical powers with its shimmering brilliance. It was as though it held a fire within. In the ruby's heart, in what might be an optical effect, she could detect a six-rayed star with beams that were equidistant. Her cheeks burned and hands trembled. Then, in seconds, she felt calm, alert, and hopeful, her heart warming. It was as though the gemstone had connected with her, hypnotized her. She could stand there forever and contemplate it.

Kavi glanced at her. "What do you think?"

That broke the spell. Maya observed a moment of silence. "It's the real thing. The color and the glow tell me so. As does the six-rayed star."

With another wave of his hand, Kavi led Maya back into the living room. "Now you understand what the fuss is about."

After her eyes had adjusted to natural light, she'd taken a deep breath, and they both were seated, Maya replied, "I do, although I wonder—"

"Why did Uma give it back to me? She didn't say much, only overwhelmed me with her magnanimity. Here was someone who cared. In the end, Maya, that's all we have. People who are close to us, who stand by us, who want the best for us, who take our tears seriously. What I've gathered is people are to be cherished more than a pricy gem. It might throw you off to hear such a statement from a gem-cutter, but that's the reality I now dwell in." He paused. "You, Detective-ji, do you care to explain your mom's motive?"

"This is what I suspect happened. My mom lifted the ruby from Rana's safe box, with an objective. She would transfer it to you, the first possessor, to whom the gem belonged. She wouldn't have it any other way. Also, and this was crucial, she wanted to get hold of the ruby before Neel did. She assumed the risk for your sake, the risk of being labelled a thief, courting the possibility of being locked up by the police and/or being ill-treated by Neel."

"I know my son's nature," Kavi said. "He'd have sold the ruby secretly to the highest bidder, which would quite likely have been an overseas collector. If that happened, then the gem, our national treasure, would have left India for good. Can you imagine what a loss that would have been? Uma, dear Uma, endangered her own life so that the ruby stayed in the country, self-sacrifice of the highest order. My respect for her has gone up."

Maya seized an instant to silently thank Uma. Despite the misunderstanding between them, she loved and cherished her mother. Pride swelled her heart. Helping herself to another rajbhog, she appreciated how this discussion had summoned the memory of her childhood, the warm cocoon of her mother.

"A question has been bugging me," Kavi said. "Why didn't Uma share the fact with you that she plundered the ruby? You two are close, aren't you?"

"Yes, we are and, under normal circumstances, such as if I lived here in Jaipur, she'd have had no hesitancy in revealing her thoughts with me. She'd have informed me what she planned to do with the ruby and why, and how she'd do it." Maya sighed. "Since my arrival in Jaipur couple of weeks ago, I've concluded that my bond with Mom has frayed, unfortunately so, little at a time, without me realizing it. Long distance phone conversations aren't enough. A yearly visit isn't enough. I must come down to Jaipur more often to visit her, to get closer to her." She paused. "Yet another reason and this is also important. My mom wanted to shield me from Neel's wrath. He'd have gone after me the worst way if he suspected I knew the whereabouts of the ruby or was in any way connected with my mom's plan. So, my mom kept me out of it. Oh, I shiver when I contemplate what could have happened, if the ballgame was different. But such was my mom's love for me. She sheltered me at all costs."

"Allow me to quiz you again," Kavi said. "How did Uma manage to hide her action from Rana Adani? When he discovered the stone missing, he must have had an inkling that . . ."

"Why, yes, Rana had figured it all out, or so I believe. Yet, when reporting to the police, wishing to protect my mom, he didn't name her as a suspect. He didn't name Neel, either. Rana was waiting to see what my mom would do with the object, where it would land. He'd told me he wouldn't have any hesitation if the true owner reclaimed it. He'd even tried to find that person, without any success." She paused. "It was you who bought the gem after it was mined, isn't that so?"

"Right, yes. So where did I procure it from?" Kavi said. "Allow me to recount the story. Years ago, as a gemologist, I went on a shopping trip, an arduous one. Buying gems was considered

auspicious in our culture. My destination was Burma—the country was then called Burma, not Myanmar—and known for its gem
deposits. After I landed, I spent a day traveling by bus, then walked
for an hour to reach the Mogôk Valley. The roads weren't safe, and
I was exhausted by the time I arrived. It was an isolated district
situated in the north, surrounded by mountains and forests, where
mining, selling, and buying of rubies happened. The gem I fell in
love with and bought at a marketplace, originated in a mine there.
How did they discover a ruby mine in that forsaken valley? Based
on a legend, a hunter, stalking birds in that area, shot one down
and found a ruby in its claw. A ruby? My heavens. Then he noticed
rubies and sapphires scattered all over the ground, like pebbles. The
news traveled. Fortune-seekers rushed there. Mogôk, abundant
with gem deposits, became an exploration site for highest quality
rubies. They called it the 'Valley of the Rubies' and Myanmar the
'Ruby Land.' My Mogôk gem radiated a shade of red not to be seen
anywhere else. It'd become the priciest ruby in the world."

A brief silence followed. With a glance at Kavi, the legitimate
owner of the ruby, Maya finished off the last of her guava juice.
With the pleasant aftertaste in her mouth, she said, "You cherished
your gem but had to sell it, or rather you loaned it?"

"Correct. I was down to my last paise and needed the funds,
so I lend my stone for a price. Done in secrecy via a dealer who
died shortly thereafter, the agreement turned out to be a loss in
many ways. I'd be plagued with one difficulty after another, physical, mental, and financial. I attributed that to the actions of heavenly bodies, who were behaving in an angry manner. Years passed
by. How much I wished to get 'my precious' back. Although the
'loan' was transacted decades ago, I was aware of the identity of
the buyer."

At Kavi's silence, Maya said, "Rana Adani's father, wasn't it? I
believe he kept the arrangement veiled. His business soon flour-
ished and so he wouldn't consider returning it to you for any price.
Rana, who inherited it after his father's death, was never appraised
of this deal."

"And I kept quiet myself. I didn't have the means to reclaim it, nor did I have any bargaining power, a simple man like myself. The Adani family has clout."

"My mom, familiar with the story, which she'd heard in bits and pieces from Neel, figured it all out," Maya said. "She wanted to right a wrong. The gemstone belonged to you. Devastated by observing your losses, hoping that the planets would turn their favor on you if the gem was back in your possession, she devised a plan. I shudder as I visualize it. She'd steal the stone from Rana's safe box and hide it in her weekend cottage. Then, at a convenient moment, she'd pay a call on you and hand it to you."

Kavi sighed. "From what I've gathered about Uma, that fits. A Good Samaritan, a rare individual, she thinks more about others and less about herself."

"Credit goes to Rana also," Maya said. "He was aware that my mom had taken the ruby. He kept the secret to himself, didn't turn her over to the police. My guess is he'd figured out what Mom was likely do—give the ruby back to the original owner. That was okay with him. He wouldn't mind the transfer of ownership. He would conclude that was justified. He'd accept such a deal."

"Never met Rana, but I think he's a fine young man," Kavi said. "And I must say he's set a fine example here. The burning question I have for you is this: Why did Uma retain you, why did she encourage you to fly to Jaipur to crack the 'Case of the Missing Ruby?' Wasn't she nervous about being caught by you?"

"She was, no doubt, apprehensive," Maya said. "At the same time, she had major concerns about Neel, who was in jail at the time. Mom needed my help in getting him out. That was all she wanted me to do. I blew in here the next day, without realizing my mom's true intentions, only to find Neel had been released from jail. At that point, neither of them wanted me around. Why would they? They each had secrets of their own, as far as it had to do with the ruby, which they would rather not share with me. Each also had devised a confidential plan, which they'd soon carry out on their own."

"So, that's where we're at now." Kavi munched on a rajbhog, the corners of his eyes crinkling in satisfaction. "Do you now understand what power the planets exert over us?"

"To be honest, I don't, not fully yet, and I may never, but I'll take your word for it. It pleases me to see that your life has changed for the better."

"You can say that." Kavi's voice was tinged with delight. "Thanks to Uma, once I got my Ratna-Raj back, bam, it was like a merciful deity had descended on me. These days I see better, think more clearly, and conduct my business with ease. I feel happier than I've been in recent times. For an old man, that's enough." He paused. "And you, Maya, what has it been like for you?"

"If not happier," Maya said. "I now feel wiser. Working on this case, I've picked up a few things. Your family and your loved ones are your most important assets. I can say that after breaking up with a partner and losing contact with my mom, missing her terribly. I'm sorry to see that the relationship between my mom and Neel has been ruined by the ruby."

"In my profession," Kavi said, "we speak about a 'gemstone's curse.' Over the years, I've seen countless family rifts, how a gemstone draws out the worst in people, brings toxicity to relationships, all that over its ownership. Throughout the centuries, battles have been fought over rubies, diamonds, and sapphire. We have a saying in India: 'He who owns a rare precious stone might own the world but will suffer misfortune.' Yes, I, too, am sorry that the ruby got between you and Uma, as well as Neel and Uma. It got Bea assassinated." He paused. "You've seen the stone with your eyes—it's safe in my possession—but my guess is your work isn't done."

"You're correct," Maya said. "I must find the key to the mystery of who killed Bea and why, and what connection it had, if mistakenly, to the ruby. Finally, Rana must be told the whole story. With the ruby's disappearance, his wife's death, and issues with his relatives, he's walked through much. My gut feel is he'll relinquish his claim to the stone—he has that kind of generosity in him if I'm not mistaken. In any case, he ought to be informed that the ruby is in a safe site, and you possess it."

"The ruby, the powerful ruby. Will you leave it up to me to speak with Rana?"

"By all means."

"As for the rest of the case," Kavi said. "Will you give me the real skinny when we meet the next time?"

Maya stood up. Nodding, she expressed her appreciation for his hospitality.

Kavi's eyes twinkled as he rose and folded his hands to a namaste. "Until the next time. I'll have a plate of rajbhog ready for the Kolkata girl."

TWENTY-FIVE

DAY 13

FOLLOWING THE MEETING WITH KAVI SAHA, Maya did a long fast walk to unwind. She'd seen the ruby tucked away in Kavi's safe box—the lustrous red gemstone—which had uplifted her and given her a momentary sense of relief.

She halted in a busy shopping area and checked her cell phone. A text from Hank said: *Urgent. Call.*

Face tightening, she phoned him, with shoppers swirling around her.

"Guess what?" Hank sounded excited, nervous, panicky. "Gordon—well, he has gone AWOL."

Maya stood rooted to the ground, felt her cheeks warming. "Are you serious?"

"You better believe it. We were supposed to have met for coffee this morning to go over the proceedings of the L.L.A meeting. He didn't show. Nor did he text me. I called his hotel room. Looks like he's checked out. His cell phone doesn't work, neither does his email."

"Who'd have thought?" Maya could hear her own voice straining.

"My blunder, my misadventure," Hank said, "I'd been set up. It blows me out of my mind that Gordon is a spy. He was planted by someone, but who and why?"

"Neel—that'd be my guess. He wanted you to be recruited by L.L.A. That didn't pan out. Just the same, you're vulnerable."

"Not only that," Hank said, regret surfacing in his tone. "I've made all of us vulnerable. I should not have . . . How seriously foolish of me. I'm beside myself." He paused. "As if that's not enough, I talked to my mom. She's checked into the intensive care unit of the Harborview Hospital in Seattle. I'm worried sick. No matter how much we fight, I love her."

"Well, in that case, you and Sophie might consider flying back to Seattle."

"But to leave you here all by yourself, no, no, that wouldn't be fair."

"Not to worry, it's part of my job," Maya said, "I can take care of myself. Guys, book your flight. And don't venture out of the hotel. It might not be safe for either one of you. Let's touch base this evening."

As soon as Maya disengaged, she received a text from Inspector Dev, requesting her to stop by the police station. Promptly at two p.m. He hinted it was about Neel. This would be an interrogation, Maya sighed, given that they now had ample proof of Neel having master-minded Bea's murder.

She happened to be standing in front of the palatial Moti Mahal restaurant. Feeling a stab of hunger in her belly, she sailed inside through a hand-carved, rosewood door into a dining room where the walls were done in crimson. A candle lantern highlighted the wall art, murals of nature paintings. Revived by the ambience, the sitar music playing in the background, and a serving of lentil kebab and millet bread, she showed up at the police station a few minutes before two p.m., equipped for the grueling task ahead.

An aide accompanied her to the same window-less, sound-proof room, where she'd interviewed Sam. The room was empty. The video-recording equipment stood in a corner, although no telephone or clocks could be seen anywhere. Several chairs were jammed against the wall. She seated herself, her mind whirling with conjectures of all sorts. Would this end up being an austere verbal jousting match with Neel?

Inspector Dev walked in, grabbed a chair next to Maya, and said a warm hello. "Appreciate your taking part in this at such a short notice. Mustn't be easy."

Maya pushed down the downheartedness welling up inside her. "It isn't. To extract the information we need from Neel, without being outwitted by him is going to be . . . let's say tough."

"Here's some good news," Inspector Dev said. "We got the guy who mugged the late Bea Adani when she was still alive. You were there. A petty criminal, a loafer, he says he was recruited by Neel."

"As expected," Maya said. "Who knows how many more people Neel had enlisted for various other schemes of his?"

She was about to say more when accompanied by a khaki-uniformed constable, Neel entered the room. Eyes intense, a scowl on his face, he seated himself, greeted Inspector Dev in a routine manner, and said to Maya, "You're still here? Didn't your mom ask you to . . .?"

"I'll be here until this investigation is completed." She stared at him until he averted his eyes, thinking to herself: *Get used to it.*

Neel turned to Inspector Dev. "Why on earth was I brought in here and ordered not to leave the premises without permission?"

Inspector Dev cleared his throat. "We'd like to ask you a few questions about the Bea Adani murder case. This is your chance to clear yourself as a potential suspect."

"Potential suspect?" Neel sat back, with pursed lips, sounding as though this was a matter of disrespect. "You must be kidding."

Even though he said so in a dismissal manner, Maya noted a flash of uncertainty, even terror in his gaze. "Do you wish to exercise your right to remain silent?" she asked.

"Since when have I been silent, Maya? Have you forgotten that I'm a college professor?"

"Would you like to speak with a lawyer?"

"Cut the crap, Maya. Fire away."

"Bea Adani was murdered last Wednesday at ten a.m.," Maya said. "Where were you then?"

Neel held a steady gaze at Maya. "Where was I?"

"You heard me right."

"If you ask the concierge of my building, she'll tell you I was in my apartment. Isn't that enough proof that I had nothing to do with that murder, if in fact it was a murder?"

"By itself, no, that's not enough," Maya replied. "We'll get to that in due time. Let's talk about the subsequent robbery of Bea Adani's flat. It didn't produce the ruby that you so badly wanted. How did you feel about that?"

Neel thought for a long moment. "Who knows where that wretched woman hid the thing in that dismal place of hers?"

"If only the ruby could have been found," the inspector jumped in. "You could have sold it and . . ."

Chin jutted, Neel said in a raised voice, "What are you getting at? I . . . I'm an appraiser. An excellent one at that. I don't own very many gems. Nor do I sell them, as a matter of fact. Couldn't even imagine having that kind of wealth."

"Consider a different circumstance in which you might need that kind of wealth," Inspector Dev said. "Such as when you're under threat to refund L.L.A. What if L.L.A put a huge pressure on you to reimburse them for the owed money—the sum they'd spent on your behalf over the years in raising you and sending you to school, and the sum you've diverted from their treasury to your own bank account when working for them as a treasurer? Where would the repayment come from, except perhaps by trading a high-priced ruby?"

"L.L.A.?" Neel rolled his eyes. "Why do you bring L.L.A into this? Enough of these wild, absurd accusations. I must go now. I have business to take care of. We're done here." He stood up, clearly intent on leaving.

"You can't leave until we've cleared you," Maya said. "And until we're satisfied with the answers you've given us. If you try to walk out that door—"

Neel interrupted Maya, sat down, and turned to Inspector Dev. "You're talking to the wrong party. Have you forgotten that I passed the polygraphy test before I was released from the jail less than two weeks ago? Doesn't that prove I had nothing to do with the ruby?"

"No, it doesn't," Maya said in a firm voice. "New facts have emerged since then. Going back to Bea's murder: Would there be any rationale behind Sam's confession that you were involved in that scheme? He insists you persuaded him to—"

"Sam . . . he's a servant—don't forget that—Maya. These servants will say anything to clear themselves when questioned by the police. Has he accused me? If so, he'll be in big trouble."

"Do you have any evidence to support that Sam is lying?" At Neel's silence, Maya held Sam's cellphone before him. "On the contrary. We have proof. He recorded his conversations with you, each time you two met."

"What?" Neel's jaw dropped. He pointed to the cell phone in Maya's hand. "I have no memory of ever meeting with him outside our apartment, none whatsoever. Maybe someone who looks like me."

"Are you sure?" Maya asked.

Eyes anxious, Neel said, "I'm certain,"

"Suppose we have further evidence?" Maya said.

"How can there be, since I'm innocent?"

Hardness dominated Inspector Dev's face. "Evidence such as: You two met in the Lord Shiva Temple several times."

"I sometimes drop by that temple. I mean . . . I have in the past, but always alone."

"What do you go there for?" Maya asked.

"To pray. To show my devotion. What else? Like I said I don't go there too often."

"Their video surveillance tapes show you coming in and leaving with Sam on certain dates/times," Inspector Dev said. "Those dates/times match up with Sam's recordings."

Neel slumped in his chair. An expression of horror surfacing on his face, he parted his lips. At first no words came out, then he spat out, "Excuse me? You're calling me a liar?"

"We have grounds to believe," the inspector said, "that you've committed a cognizable offense by bribing Sam. You've aided and abetted a murder by asking Sam to assassinate Bea Adani. As a result, she died a horrible death."

"Again, Sam is a liar." Neel's hand tugged at his shirt collar. He closed his eyes for a brief instant, then cried out, "No, no, no, I did not . . . I did not . . ."

"Our preliminary investigation suggests that Sam's statement is genuine and bona fide," the inspector said.

Neel jumped up from his chair and approached the inspector, palms nearly touching his throat, stiff fingers tightening, as though about to choke him. "Enough, enough, enough. I don't have to take any more of this, you know."

A pair of constables strode into the room and positioned themselves behind Neel, each grabbing an arm and restraining him. Eyebrows raised, mouth loose, face turning pale, Neel shook, unsteady on his feet, saying, "Let go of me, bastards."

"We're arresting you," the inspector said firmly. "You'll be detained in our lawful custody for aiding in the murder of Bea Adani."

TWENTY-SIX

AFTER HER INTERROGATION OF NEEL at the police station, Maya returned to her hotel at about three-fifty p.m., feeling distressed, her anxiety about Uma heightened. She blinked back her confusion and cheered when she saw Uma waiting in the lobby, well turned out in a lime yellow sari and a long, gold-and-pearl necklace. A soft expression of unease suffused Uma's face.

Voice bright, Maya said, "Ma! How long have you been waiting?"

"Oh, not too long, my dear child. I'd love to speak with you."

Together they walked to Maya's room. Uma surveyed her living space. "What a lovely suite, with big windows bringing in natural light and a nice décor in rose gold color. I like this velvety carpet and this glass occasional table. But next time, no argument allowed, you'll stay with me."

Feeling a little unsure, Maya said, "Hope things will be different—"

Uma broke in. "I must apologize. What I did was wrong, wrong, wrong. After you cut your vacation short and rushed out here, I . . . I . . ."

"You ignored me, acted like . . . There was an intention behind it, wasn't there?"

Face contorted with sadness, Uma said, "You figured it out, didn't you?"

"Yes, Ma, you wanted me to take on this case for Neel's sake. He, in jail at the time, and you wanted him out. That's all you wanted me to do."

"Good so far."

Maya was about to say more when a hotel attendant knocked at the door. He entered, bearing a tray filled with cups of iced tea and servings of sweet boondi balls, the afternoon refreshment hour. Maya expressed her appreciation. She needed the break.

Uma lifted a spoonful of boondi to her mouth. "You know, my appetite has made a comeback. These are tasty." She paused. "Now back to you."

Maya reached for the clove-scented, tiny round balls, made with chickpea flour and sugar syrup, simple but exotic. "Let me recount what happened after I arrived here . . . from my perspective." She talked about her checking into a hotel, Neel's release from the jail, and what became clear to her—the fact that neither Uma nor Neel wanted her around. "As for you, Ma, you didn't want me to figure out it was you who had taken the ruby from Rana's safe box, did you? You avoided me so you wouldn't be found out. Am I correct?"

Uma dabbed her eyes with a handkerchief. "I'll never be able to forgive myself for . . ."

Maya could feel Uma's breaking heart through her heavy voice. "Don't be so hard on yourself. You didn't tell Neel, either, about your wish to return the ruby to Mr. Saha, did you?"

"No, you know why? Kavi Saha is a fine man, who deserves better. I couldn't bear to see him down in the dumps any longer, I couldn't. I had to do something." Uma paused. "Neel would have wanted me dead, yes, he would have killed me. That is if he found out that his father had gotten the ruby back and it was I who had taken the initiative to do so."

"Are you aware Neel had a different plan?" Maya said. "He wanted the ruby for his own benefit. He mistakenly thought Bea had stolen it. So, why not have Bea killed by an accomplice, get her out of the picture, and have the ruby swiped from her apartment?

Then he'd be free to sell the ruby quietly to a collector, make a huge sum, and pay L.L.A off, thereby preventing any further harassment from them."

"What are you saying? L.L.A? Neel?"

"Did you have no inkling?" Maya asked.

Uma cast her gaze down to the floor. "Maybe I saw signs, over-heard phone conversations, noticed the guilty look on his face. But I discounted them. 'Can't be true,' I told myself. 'Not my Neel.' You see, love makes you lie to yourself. Yes, it does, but not for long." She closed her eyes for a second to wipe her dried tears. "Which might explain why Neel and I have not been getting along. I could tell he was up to something. He wouldn't share much. As you know, silence speaks volumes. He'd flare up, if asked a question, he would belittle me, tell me I was old, ugly, and a pain-in-the butt. It's been unpleasant to have him around, to say the least. There were times when I even feared for my life."

Maya saw things with more clarity. "Is that why you were study-ing wrestling?"

"Well, yes, I started taking the lessons a month before the ruby issue came about. Happened to hear about Anita's classes from a neighbor. My reasoning for joining was that I wanted to feel strong—mentally, physically, and spiritually. All women should. We hold the society together; that's our responsibility. Surprise, surprise. The practice came in handy within a few weeks when Neel and I had a huge disagreement. Oh, what a frightening scene that was." Rage distorted Uma's serene face. Her bottom lip trem-bled. "He slapped me, slapped me so hard that I couldn't see or hear anything for a few minutes. I still feel that slap on my skin."

"He did what?"

"It was then that I knee-ed him in the groin and fled. He screamed. He spewed invective you don't want to hear. Since then, in my class, I've been given instructions on how to do a few more nasty moves. Such as how to flick my wrist in a quick motion and land a blow to someone's stomach, which I haven't had a chance to apply so far."

It was as though someone had pushed Maya's panic button, pushed it hard. Always a defender of her mom, she said, "You need immediate protection, Ma."

"No need to worry, I can take care of myself."

Maya, unconvinced, glanced at Uma's left hand. "Where's your sapphire?"

In a quavering voice, Uma said, "Oh, that's another little tragedy. You might remember I liked to look at the velvety blue of my ring when I woke in the morning. It centered me, gave me serenity, helped me welcome the day. More than two weeks ago, after we'd had a disagreement, without any warning, Neel came closer, snatched the ring from my finger and dashed out of the room. 'What are you doing?' I asked, dumbfounded. 'It's mine, bitch,' he said and stormed out of the flat. He was gone for hours. My guess is he sold it for a chunk of cash. He was always short of money. Never stopped spending or betting on horses, never fiscally responsible. When I asked him again about the ring that evening, he threatened to chop my finger off."

A flick of anger surged through Maya; words stuck in her throat like little pebbles. "I had no idea that . . . I always believed . . ."

"I've never told you the full story. When I first met Neel a few years ago, I was lonely. Lonely like Kanyakumari, the southern tip of India, with nothing but three ocean bodies flowing around. Neel, such a charmer, with so many tales to tell, swept me off my sandaled feet. He'd take me to top restaurants, buy me flowers and furniture, whatever I wanted. I let him into my life. You know what? He needed me, saw me as a steadying influence and so, for a while, it worked. We were so much in love. Then things changed—he would be out for hours—and my feelings of loneliness circled back. Soon enough, I found out that Neel had another existence—the L.L.A—which he'd kept hidden from me, and which had stopped us from getting closer. I found out more. He bet on horses and usually lost. He had piled on more debts than he could keep track of. And I'd gotten involved with a man like him? To suppress the pain, having been raised the old-fashioned manner, I found myself looking the other way."

Maya reached out, squeezed Uma's hand, and allowed a few seconds to pass. "Getting back to the ruby—how did you . . .?

"You mean how did we each manage to keep our intentions hidden from the other? Let me back up a bit. The ruby has always been a sore subject for Neel. He resented Rana for owning it. Needless to say, he never showed his true feelings to Rana—he was being paid for offering advice to Rana's family. As far as Neel and I were concerned, we could never talk about the ruby gem, never, ever, without getting into a violent argument. That's the 'curse of the great ruby,' you might say. After a while, both of us were reluctant to broach the subject. It hung between us like a heavy curtain.

"Did I betray Neel by taking the ruby before he could get hold of it?" Uma sighed deeply. "In a sense, I did. It was a difficult decision for me to make. What I had in mind might be described as 'answering the call for greater good.' I was compelled to help Kavi, to get him out of doldrums. Quietly, I took the ruby from Rana's safe, went to visit Kavi, and handed it to him. He was astonished beyond words. I was super pleased. I left his place quickly."

"Did you ever have an inkling that Neel had a monetary obligation to L.L.A?"

"Much as I didn't want to admit it, I'd overheard phone conversations, seen a pattern in his behavior, caught small lies." Uma took a deep breath. "My God. L.L.A, the formidable L.L.A. He's in trouble with them? I've done enough reading about them to know . . . When I brought up the topic with him, he told me in no uncertain terms to stay out of his affairs, or . . ."

"Or?"

"You don't want to know." Uma hesitated for a long moment. "Perhaps you'd be well pleased to hear that Neel and I are separating. I must say this, however. Regardless of all that has happened, my insides split apart when I think about it."

"You're a strong person, Ma. Don't you realize you're better off without—?"

"Yes, well, in most ways I do, and I've come upon a few lessons. Our Prime Minister Nehru said ages ago, in a different context that when we step out from the old to the new, when an age ends, then we can hope to become free agents." Uma sighed. "It's time for me to step out, forgive myself, land on my own two feet and live my life the way I'd like, a free agent. But first, I must ask for your forgiveness."

"I forgive you, Ma. Always know that I hold nothing but love for you."

"My precious daughter, I have you and a few close friends, people who bring me joy. I also have books, nature, and a weekend cottage. What more do I need?" Uma's voice cracked. "Neel announced this morning he's relocating to a residence of his own. No apology, nothing. I couldn't speak, I was so overwhelmed. I left the flat for a while.

"So, that's the end of our relationship. He's already finished packing. He's ready to move."

"He'll be moving alright," Maya replied grimly, "but not to a residence of his own."

"Why do you say that?"

Maya's heart sank, cognizant of the fact that Uma would now be appraised of the gravity of the criminal act Neel had undertaken. "The police have already taken Neel in for questioning. It's painful for me to reveal the details behind all this to you. If you can bear it . . . Neel brought in Sam, your absentee servant, to do a hit job on Bea for him, and steal the ruby from her apartment. Problem was, Bea didn't have the ruby. So, Neel had her killed for nothing. Can you imagine? Taking the life of an innocent woman? We have credible information supporting this."

Her face crumpled; Uma covered her eyes with both hands for a few seconds. "Dear me, I'm shaken to the core. Bea, so young."

"I don't want to add to your distress, Ma, but—"

"Are you saying a criminal complaint will be lodged against both Neel and Sam?" Seeing Maya nod, Uma added, "And you, my dear, it's been tough for you, to say the least, hasn't it?"

"The investigation isn't closed yet, but my part is finished," Maya replied. "There's a saying in my field: 'It'll get to you sooner or later.' This one did. As soon as I can arrange for an air ticket, I'll fly back to Seattle. A case is waiting for me. Hank and Sophie are also leaving. Hank's mom is ill. They'll soon be on their way to Seattle."

"Too bad, I didn't get to know your young friends. Sweet kids. I regret that." Uma turned to Maya. "Will you forgive your mother? Will you fly back to see me again?"

Maya could hear the pain in Uma's voice. "With pleasure, Ma. As often as I can manage. At least every six months."

"The next time it'll be different. I promise you that." Uma paused. "Being with you fills my heart."

Maya wanted to hear Uma out, validate and support her, reconnect with her, and feel some peace at her own center. "Before I leave, I'd like to hang around you for a few days. How does that sound?"

"I'd like nothing better." Uma cast a warm look at her daughter, a happy smile playing on her lips. "We'll talk, eat, and do Jaipur. How'd that be?"

"Marvelous." Maya rose from her chair and gave Uma a hug. Although she wouldn't show it, a sense of concern shuddered through her. It had to do with Uma's role in the missing ruby affair and how it might be interpreted by the authorities. Her knees shook picturing Uma being questioned by the police. How tough that'd be for her. For now, they sat together in each other's loving presence, smiling, and catching up, eyes misted, warm afternoon light bathing the window.

TWENTY-SEVEN

DAY 14

At ten a.m., Maya arrived at the Central Park and took a seat on a bench under the silvery cloud. Tingling with anticipation, she awaited Rana's arrival. She'd phoned him earlier today and asked him to meet her here, giving no indication that it was her last day in Jaipur.

Birds chirped, a motorcycle rumbled, leaves rustled in the gentle breeze, and a creature scurried through a nearby bush. She'd miss this park, this green sanctuary, how it had helped her unwind. A runner strode past, reminding her that soon she'd be back in Seattle, doing her morning runs around the periphery of Green Lake. A familiar pattern of life would once again reestablish itself. Yet it saddened her to let go of all that she'd experienced in this town.

She sighed, even as Rana turned up and took a seat next to her. Eyes a grief-stricken red, he had on a well-pressed, pale yellow cotton shirt worn over a pair of jeans. A current passed through her as they said hello and looked into each other's eyes.

"I've been feeling so down in the dumps," he said. "Your call . . . well, it lifted my mood. You saw the ruby?"

"Indeed. I met with Kavi Saha, who now has the stone, and he treated me to a view of it. Finally, I could see what the fuss was about."

Rana's face brightened. "Would it startle you if I told you Mr. Saha dropped by my house this morning?"

An inner sense prompted her to reply, "To return the ruby, I suppose?"

"You guessed it right. A move that surprised me. I told him I'm at peace with myself, with or without the ruby. He insisted I keep the heirloom. That it should belong to my family. That my children, if I ever have any, will own it. At first, I was speechless."

"Then you accepted it?"

"Correct, he won't hear of it otherwise. We had a long discussion. To him, the ruby is the best gift one can make to a loved one. It showers the owner with the finest life can offer. Listening to his reasoning, I was overwhelmed by his largesse. The best I could do was to squeak out an offer to reimburse him. But he refused. Instead, he gave me his blessings and said I could call on him for consultation whenever I wished to do so."

"What an exceptional man. I'm overwhelmed by his generosity."

"Beyond doubt. He reminded me why we cherish our gems. He put it so well. 'It is to pass on our love and legacy to the next generation, to preserve memories, to strengthen our bonds, and to build a family heritage.' I'm in a state of shock even as I speak."

Maya smiled. "I think these qualities of the heart win out over the highest price gem in the market."

"Well said."

"I suppose Mr. Saha would also like to see that you get your life back."

"Undoubtedly. He insists he sees a fine future for me, astrologically speaking." Rana laughed, a mischievous light glinting in his eyes. "I'll take his word for it. Guess what else he suggested?"

Maya gave him a questioning look.

"We should be together as a couple."

Maya felt a blush surge into her cheeks. She glanced at him, the man she'd been attracted to from the instant they'd collided on the running track. "But . . . this is my last day here."

"You're leaving already?"

"I'm closing the case as my involvement is ending. All I have left to do is go back to my hotel, finish packing and catch a flight to Seattle."

A shadow descended on Rana's face. "You couldn't be persuaded to stay longer?"

Maya shook her head, downhearted.

"I understand you have professional obligations in Seattle. Will you miss our little town?"

"Certainly. Jaipur has grown on me, even though I've spent only about two weeks here. Always after finishing a case, I find that I'm leaving a part of myself behind. People I've met, places I've frequented, relationships I've begun forming."

Voice husky, Rana said, "Wish I could have gotten to know you better."

Watching sunshine slipping in through the curved, caramel branches of a tree, she felt heartened. "I'll be back to visit my mom at least twice a year."

He turned toward her, gaze direct and intense. "Has to be sooner than that, Maya. I won't be able to stand it otherwise. My company has an office in Portland, Oregon, which is not that far from Seattle. Can I come up and . . .?"

Maya cheered. "Nice idea. I'd like that."

He closed his eyes for a second and whispered, "I've never said this to you, Maya, and I don't know how to express myself, it might sound crazy, and please don't be offended, but . . . I have deep feelings for you. I mean . . . I think about you, I dream about you. I want you to be mine. Do you . . . do you feel . . .?"

Her cheeks flushed; her forehead burned with a deep, hot desire. Voice husky, she replied, "Yes, from the first day we met . . . when we collided . . . right here, as a matter of fact."

Lips flickering into a smile, he placed a hand over hers. "It's like . . . through all that has happened, through this disastrous period, I've found you, what I really have been looking for . . . my real ruby . . . " Overcome by emotion, voice faltering, he couldn't speak.

For her, the moment stretched, not a sound anywhere, the two of them sitting close to each other under a brilliant sky. "I'm out of words . . ."

"Words are not necessary." With that, Rana drew her to him and kissed her gently on the lips.

EPILOGUE

THE FIRST TEXT MAYA RECEIVED upon returning to Seattle cheered her. It was from Rana confirming the date of his upcoming visit. "Only nine more days."

Then Inspector Dev called, saying he wanted to bring her up to date. As expected, the police would press charges against both Sam and Neel in connection with the murder of Bea.

"There's more. Let me tell you about my briefing with Rana." The inspector elaborated: With the rare gem back in his possession, Rana wished to revise the statement he'd originally made to the police regarding its disappearance. The amended information included the fact that it was a family misunderstanding that led to the loss, nothing more. No one would be held accountable for the theft of the priceless object, which had gone missing for two or so weeks and was now back in place in its original location.

"Including my mom?" Maya asked.

"Oh, yes, Uma is well loved by the Adani family and she's a relative, isn't that so? We look up to that family, one of our most distinguished clans. So, this saga ends happily." The inspector sighed. "As for me, Maya, I just returned from the scene of a heinous crime. You wouldn't believe this one. A triple murder case. I'll be responsible for the investigation. Wish you were here."

AN AWARD-WINNING AUTHOR, BHARTI KIRCHNER HAS published eight previous critically acclaimed novels (in various genres, such as historical, literary, and mystery) and four cookbooks, including the best-selling *The Bold Vegetarian*. Her historical novel, *Goddess of Fire*, was shortlisted for the Nancy Pearl Award. Her first novel, *Shiva Dancing*, was cited by *Seattle Weekly* as one of the top novels in the last twenty-five years.

Bharti also excels in magazine writing and short stories. She's written for *Food & Wine*, *Vegetarian Times*, *Writer's Digest*, *The Writer*, *San Francisco Chronicle*, and eleven anthologies. She has been a book reviewer for *The Seattle Times*. Her short fiction has appeared in *Khabar* and other magazines. "Promised Tulips," first published in the anthology, *Seattle Noir*, was recognized as a top noir story by *Publisher's Weekly* and it reappeared in *USA Noir*.

Bharti's many awards include a 2020 SALA Award in Creative Writing, several Seattle Arts Commission literature Awards, a City Artist Project Award, several GAP grants and a Virginia Center for the Creative Arts Fellowship. A popular teacher she has taught widely at writer's conferences. She has been honored as a Living Pioneer Asian American Author. Visit www.bhartikirchner.com.

CPSIA information can be obtained
at www.ICGtesting.com
Printed in the USA
BVHW031911170523
664364BV00012B/136